CRAVE

CRAVE

○ ○ ○ ○ ○ ○ ○ ○ ○ ○ ○ ○ ○ ○ ○

LAURA J. BURNS &
MELINDA METZ

NEW YORK LONDON TORONTO SYDNEY

SIMON & SCHUSTER BFYR

An imprint of Simon & Schuster Children's Publishing Division
1230 Avenue of the Americas, New York, New York 10020
This book is a work of fiction. Any references to historical events, real people, or real
locales are used fictitiously. Other names, characters, places, and incidents are products
of the author's imagination, and any resemblance to actual events
or locales or persons, living or dead, is entirely coincidental.
First SIMON & SCHUSTER BFYR paperback edition September 2010
Copyright © 2010 by Laura J. Burns and Melinda Metz
All rights reserved, including the right of reproduction in whole or in part in any form.
SIMON & SCHUSTER BFYR is a trademark of Simon & Schuster, Inc.
For information about special discounts for bulk purchases,
please contact Simon & Schuster Special Sales at 1-866-506-1949
or business@simonandschuster.com.
The Simon & Schuster Speakers Bureau can bring authors to your live event.
For more information or to book an event, contact the Simon & Schuster Speakers
Bureau at 1-866-248-3049 or visit our website at www.simonspeakers.com.
Book design by Chloë Foglia
The text for this book is set in Jenson.
Manufactured in the United States of America
2 4 6 8 10 9 7 5 3 1
CIP data for this book is available from the Library of Congress.
ISBN 978-1-4424-0816-6
ISBN 1-4424-0817-0 (eBook)

FIRST
EDITION

"... *your soul holds on to them.*"

To the memory of our fathers,
Thomas F. Burns and Richard J. Metz

CRAVE

ONE

○ ○ ○ ○ ○ ○ ○ ○ ○ ○ ○ ○ ○ ○ ○ ○

DREAMS

CHAPTER

ONE

○○○○○○○○○○○○○○○○

SPECIAL [SPEH-SHUL]: *distinguished by some unusual quality; being in some way superior.*

Here's what it really means: It means you're the kid that nobody wanted to play jump rope with at recess because if you fell and scraped your knee, you'd have to miss three days of school. It means you're the girl nobody wanted in the sixth-grade fashion show because your arms and legs were always covered with bruises. It means you're that kid that the teachers gave a lecture about at the start of every school year, a boring and annoying lecture saying that you had to be treated like some kind of fragile glass figurine.

It means you're the freak.

But nobody is allowed to say so. Nobody is allowed to make fun of you, or bully you, or write nasty notes about you. Because you're special.

So instead they treat you like a pet or a mascot or something. You get invited to all the birthday parties. You get elected president of all the clubs. You always have a seat in the cafeteria. People like to be seen with you—it makes them feel all saintly and generous. Plus it gets them noticed by teachers and parents and potential make-out buddies. They must be good people if they're nice to the Sick Girl, right?

"Shay! What is up, girlfriend?"

Shay McGuire slammed her journal closed. *Case in point,* she thought as she turned to Olivia. Olivia Willett was Shay's best friend. In Shay's head, the phrase always had quote marks around it. "Best friend." The one you hung out with the most. The one who shared all your secrets and your dreams. The one who was there for you no matter what.

Shay gave a mental eye roll. Olivia didn't really care about her. Olivia hadn't listened to a word Shay had said since seventh grade. Sure, she thought she knew everything about Shay—and she did know all about the rare blood disorder Shay had been born with, the disease with a diagnosis that changed every time Shay saw a new specialist. As far as Olivia was concerned, that was what Shay was. Sick. Not creative or strong-willed or addicted to bad reality television. Just sick. As if the disease had robbed Shay of the kind of interior life that everybody else had. That Olivia had.

"I think the phrase *what is up, girlfriend* was officially retired fifteen years ago," Shay told her, leaning back in the cafeteria chair. Around her, the place was emptying. The second bell would ring in two minutes, signaling the start of next period.

"I know." Olivia shrugged, her perfect strawberry blond hair sliding along her perfect almost-too-skinny shoulder. "I'm being retro."

Shay inched her arm over the journal, hoping Olivia wouldn't think to ask what she'd been writing.

"You're coming with me. I booked the big study room in the library for you and me and Kaz," Olivia informed her.

Shay almost laughed at her own worry. As if Olivia would ask about the journal. As if it would even occur to her that Shay might have secrets of her own. "Sounds like a party," she said dryly.

"Bonetto said we could skip class and spend the time helping you prep for the test on Friday," Olivia explained. "Since you missed so many days this month."

Translation: I want to spend the next hour with my boyfriend's tongue down my throat, so I conned Mr. Bonetto into letting me and Kaz out of class under the pretense that we're helping poor little you. Oh, and am I not the best person?

"Cool," Shay answered. It's not like she particularly wanted to listen to Mr. Bonetto ramble for an hour anyway. Bio was a joke, even AP Bio. She'd learned more about biology by the time she was ten than Bonetto knew even now. That's what growing up in hospitals did for you.

Shay pushed a loose strand of her long dark hair out of her eyes, took a deep breath, and slowly stood up. She picked up her stack of books, wincing at the weight.

"You okay?" Olivia asked automatically.

"Yeah." She wasn't okay. She was as weak as an infant. But she didn't want help. As soon as it got to the point when she needed help, it was only another few hours before the total collapse. Before the extended bed rest. Before the next transfusion. And it was only Wednesday. Usually she could make it through a week at school at least. When she was younger, it had been even longer, sometimes three weeks at a stretch.

But now . . .

I'm getting worse, a voice inside her whispered. She knew it was true. Nobody ever said it out loud. Her mother and her stepfather still acted as if the cure was only a few days from being found. But there was no cure. And she was getting worse.

Olivia led the way down the hall toward the library, running one perfectly manicured fingernail across the long mural showing the dark waters of the river that their town, Black River, Massachusetts, was named for. "Did you hear about Jacey?" Olivia asked.

Shay shook her head, sending a snowstorm of cold dizziness through her body.

"You won't believe this. She let Brian use Saran Wrap for protection. And the girl is in the honor society. How stupid is that?" Olivia snorted.

"Pretty stupid," Shay said. She had to concentrate to get the words out. Her brain felt like it had started to ice over.

"I know. So of course it came off. And now she's in the bathroom between every class peeing on a stick," Olivia yammered on. Her voice sounded far away, distorted by the rushing sound in Shay's head. She stared down at the tile of the hallway, willing herself to put one foot forward. Then the other. No point in thinking about how far it was to the library.

"There's my woman." Kaz's voice startled her. Shay jerked her head up, and the hall swam around her. Kaz and Olivia were kissing. It was a good excuse to stop walking.

By the time she caught her breath, they were done. Kaz was grinning at her. "Shay Stadium!" he crowed, holding up his hand for a high five.

"Moron, that nickname doesn't even make any sense," Olivia grumbled.

"I don't mind." Shay summoned all her strength and high-fived him. Her other arm buckled from bearing the entire weight of her books.

Kaz grabbed her Bio text before she dropped it, his dark eyes immediately serious. "You all right?"

Shay nodded.

"She needs to sit down," Olivia said. "Let's just get to the library."

Without a word, Kaz took the other books from Shay. Olivia looped her arm through Shay's and they kept walking. She couldn't manage to keep up a conversation, but they didn't seem to care. They were busy talking about Kaz's birthday party that weekend. He was the first one of Shay's friends to turn eighteen. She wanted to be there.

She *would* be there, she decided. The blood transfusion would wait. She didn't need bed rest; she needed a party . . . and a beer . . . and a boy who wasn't too afraid of her to kiss her. Maybe she could ask Kaz to invite some guys who didn't go to Black River High.

I have to be strong. Shay shook off Olivia's arm and stood on her own, letting the rush of students push past her in the hallway. She willed the dizziness to subside. Her stepfather, Martin, was always telling her that a positive attitude was the best medicine. And he should know, he had about six different medical degrees.

"Shay, what are you doing?" Olivia sounded annoyed.

"Sorry . . . I thought I heard my cell," Shay lied. "I guess not. Let's go." She pasted a smile on her face and started toward the library. The door was only twenty feet away. She could make it, and she could make it without Olivia helping her.

One foot forward. Then the other.

"I need to . . ." Shay couldn't finish the thought. It was too late. She'd waited too long. She should know better. She should know by now.

The floor lurched under her feet. Her knees buckled. And the whole world went white around her.

Shay rested her head against the cool glass of the Range Rover's passenger-side window, pretending that the row of average suburban houses going by was the most interesting thing she'd ever seen. *Don't try to talk to me,* she silently willed her stepdad. *I'm very busy here. Looking at the identical houses.*

But Dr. Martin Kuffner was not easy to fool. He'd been dealing with sick kids since before Shay was born, and he knew how to manage them, as her mother said.

"How were you feeling this morning before school?" Martin asked casually.

I was feeling psyched to see Chris Briglia because he winked at me yesterday and his new haircut looks incredibly hot, Shay thought. But her stepdad didn't want to hear that. He wanted her vital statistics. He wanted facts, numbers, data—was her heart rate a little fast, or had one of those headaches started behind her eyes, or was her temperature up a fraction of a degree?

"I was okay, I think," she mumbled.

"You *think*? You need to know, Shay. You always have to be on top of it. Every two hours, you need to do a self-check," Martin told her.

God, she hated this. She hated having to analyze the workings of her body every single second. Shay let out a sigh that felt like it started at the tips of her toes. Martin reached over and squeezed her shoulder. She forced herself to look at him.

"It's not always going to be this way, sweetheart," he said.

No, pretty soon I'm going to be dead. Shay couldn't stop the thought from worming its way through her brain. *And does it really matter? I'm only half-alive now. I go to school; I go home; I rest; I do my homework; I watch some TV; I go to bed. And that's on a good day, when I'm feeling basically okay. Okay for Shay.*

"Trust me," Martin continued. "I'm going to tweak your next transfusion a little. I'm trying something new. It could be the thing that does it for you."

"Mmm-hmm," Shay murmured. She was afraid if she actually talked, she might start bawling. And nobody needed that. Sick girls were supposed to be strong, an inspiration to everybody.

And mostly Shay was. Or at least she managed to put on a pretty good act. She didn't have much choice. Her so-called bravery was the glue that held her entire family together. Her mother's life was almost as much about Shay's illness as Shay's was—being a single mother with a sick baby hadn't left her time to do anything else with her life. And Martin's career was all about Shay now too. He had stopped writing papers about his specialty, leukemia. He'd stopped researching anything but Shay's disease. He'd staked his entire professional reputation on her. If he didn't manage to find a cure, he'd look like a failure. And failure was something that Martin did not allow.

"Do you ever miss it?" she asked suddenly.

He shot her a confused look. "Miss what?"

"Your life. Your superstar-doctor status. All that." It had never occurred to her to ask before. "I mean, you were on *Oprah* and everything. You were Mr. Leukemia Crusader."

Martin was quiet for a while. Had she offended him? "I'm sorry—" Shay started.

"Don't be. It's a fair question." Martin's voice was even and calm, the way it always was. His bedside-manner voice, that's how Shay had always thought of it. "Are you thinking you need a different doctor?"

"No." *Definitely, no.* She'd seen other doctors. Too many of them. Her mom had dragged her all over the country until they'd finally found Martin, the only one who actually seemed to listen. The only one who didn't try to force her blood disorder into some easy, popular diagnosis, regardless of whether her symptoms actually matched. Martin was the only one who was willing to admit that he had no clue what was wrong with Shay, that her disease was unique, one of a kind. *Maybe I am special, after all,* she thought.

"I don't miss it," Martin told her. "I'll be back there soon enough."

Shay raised her eyebrows, and Martin smiled.

"After I've isolated a treatment for your disorder, I mean," he said. "There are plenty of people working on leukemia. There's no one helping you."

"You help me," she replied. "You always have." And not just as her doctor. Martin had been like a Disney fairy godmother—a six-foot-four, 230-pound male one who used money instead of a magic wand. As soon as he and her mother got married—poof!—a little apartment became a McMansion. Poof!—a beat-up Toyota Corolla with a broken CD player became a fully loaded Mercedes S-Class sedan.

Shay wondered if that's what had made her mother fall in love with him. Not the money, her mom didn't care about stuff like that. But Mom definitely loved what the money bought for Shay—absolutely anything that could help fight her disease, from organic produce to a lap pool. And she really loved that Shay now had a brilliant doctor as her personal physician.

Martin was a great guy and all. He was just sort of serious, all work all the time. Every once in a while he attempted a stupid pun. But nobody—no-body—but him thought they were at all humorous. Would her mother have ended up with somebody completely different if Shay hadn't been so sick? Would she have found somebody closer to her own age? Or somebody a little more . . . fun? Shay had no idea if her stepfather was at all like her real father. She'd never even met the guy. Mom didn't talk about him, and whenever Shay had tried to force it, her mother's obvious pain had always made her back off.

"Are you strong enough to hit the smoothie place?" Martin asked. "You could use some glucose and calories before your transfusion."

"We're doing one today?" Shay had known it the instant she hit the floor at school. Hell, she'd known it half an hour before that. But she'd still been hoping it was all just a fluke. Her last transfusion had been only a week ago.

"I think we'd better, don't you?" Martin replied.

Like that was an actual question. "I guess. Yeah."

"So . . . smoothie?"

"No, thanks. I'll just grab juice or something from the fridge," Shay answered. She knew the Jamba Juice on the way home would be jammed with kids from school. She hated the idea of sitting in the Range Rover while her stepdad went in, everyone watching her from inside and pretending not to. Or, even worse, going in there with Martin's arm around her, propping her up.

Martin nodded, and a few minutes later they were turning into the cul-de-sac where they lived. He hit the garage door opener at just the right moment for him to pull in without a beat of hesitation. Shay's mother was at the car door a second later, studying her face with frightened eyes. "I knew I shouldn't have let you go to school today," she said in a rush. "You looked off."

"I'm fine, Mom." Shay tried not to let any of the impatience she felt sneak into her voice. Sometimes the overwhelming mother concern made Shay feel like all the air was being sucked from her lungs. It had gotten worse in the three years since Mom and Martin had gotten married. Her mother's worry level hadn't gone up. That was impossible. But before she had married Martin, her mom had had to work like a dog to pay even the minimums on Shay's medical expenses—not to mention stuff like rent and food. She'd been exhausted most of the time. Now she didn't have to work. She could devote all her energy to taking care of Shay.

It was like having a personal assistant and a nurse and a babysitter all at the same time. At first Shay had been psyched to have Mom around so much. But these days it felt like a burden. Practically the only time she could have a private thought was when she was writing in her journal.

"Why don't you get Shay some juice while I take her upstairs," Martin suggested. "Do we have any pomegranate?"

It was Shay's favorite. She knew they were out of it, but she kept her mouth shut.

"No . . ." Her mother looked slightly panicked. "I'll go get some from the market."

"Mom, you don't have to—" Shay began.

"Nonsense. It's a five-minute drive. And all those anti-oxidants will fix you right up." Her mom pulled the Mercedes keys out of her pocket and opened the door. She was gone in seconds.

Martin climbed out of the car and made it over to Shay's side before she had her door all the way open. He stepped back as Shay swung her feet onto the ground, letting her get out by herself. The good thing about Martin was that he always knew when she didn't want to be hovered over. Mom was a hoverer—no matter what.

She led the way to her room. Martin followed a few steps behind, giving her some space. She sat down on her bed. A hospital bed. The same pink flamingo Pottery Barn quilt might be on the beds of half the teenage girls in America, but it didn't hide the metal bars.

"Stretch out, and we'll get you started in a minute," Martin instructed.

Shay obediently lay down and stared up at the ceiling. There were new pictures taped up there. Her mom's handiwork. She was always doing little things like that for Shay. She'd even put up one of the new Calvin Klein underwear ads. *Mom's really my best friend,* she thought. *She's the one who knows absolutely everything about me.*

She knew way too much, actually. Shay spent so much time at home that sometimes it felt like her mother knew her better than she herself did. It was nice, kind of. But it definitely contributed to the sucking-the-air-out-of-her-lungs phenomenon.

Think about the guy in the picture, she told herself. It was the ritual she'd had since she was fourteen, although back then she'd been looking at posters of her celeb crush of the moment. It didn't work so well anymore. She felt a little pathetic fantasizing about an imaginary guy.

Maybe I should just think about Chris Briglia instead, she thought.

"Ready?" Martin asked.

Shay hadn't even heard him come back in, wheeling the IV pole over to the side of her bed.

"Yeah, ready." Shay turned her head aside. Even after all these years, she didn't like to watch the needle pierce her skin.

Shay looked over at the thin tube snaking from the bag on the IV pole to the needle in her arm. The blood looked the same as it usually did—a rich, deep red. But the sensation of the blood entering her, it was like nothing Shay had ever experienced. Her heart thudded hard, as if to urge the new blood through her body. She wanted to feel it everywhere. Her cheeks flushed as the warm liquid hit the capillaries of her face.

The room swirled around her, and Shay tasted the blood on her tongue. Slightly salty, almost sweet. She wanted more. She bit deeper with her fangs, sucking on the nectar.

Fangs. Wait. What? Shay's thoughts felt strange, strange and wrong, as if someone were shouting them at her from far away.

Under her hands, the Giver twitched, wanting to escape, but without the strength. Shay was much too powerful for him. And she wasn't done drinking, not nearly done. The blood, warm and silky, slid down her throat, and with it, all the emotion the Giver had experienced in his life. Shay pulled him closer.

No . . . That's not me. Not . . .

The fear and love and jealousy and hate and anger and passion bolting through her blotted out her own, already faint, thoughts. Every neuron in her body was lighting up. She could actually feel the individual molecules of blood popping through her veins. And the emotion—she wanted to laugh, and cry, and scream all at once.

She slid her hands along the Giver's body. She needed to feel skin. She needed to touch. Her fingers were alive with sensation—the soft skin of the Giver's neck, contrasting with the calloused skin of his elbow.

The smells were distinct and almost intoxicating in their intensity—pungent sweat mixed with the odor of the sandy dirt under the Giver's nails, lamb fat from the meal the youth had eaten several hours ago, and the fruity odor of the wine that had accompanied the meal. Nearby grew a patch of thyme and farther away a cedar grove, and their tangy scents floated by on the breeze.

Still, everything Shay experienced was secondary to the warmth and taste of the blood. The food and wine from the Giver's meal were reflected in the taste. She tasted salt, too, as well as iron and other minerals she couldn't identify.

"Enough, Gabriel! Enough!" someone ordered.

Automatically, Shay glanced in the direction from which the voice had come. She saw a silver-haired man at the top of the hill, holding aloft a torch. Even without the fire, she could have seen him clearly. The stars were so bright she could see every leaf on the oak tree to her left, every pebble on the ground, every line in Ernst's face.

Ernst? Shay's thought was fleeting, confused. *But I've never seen that man before.* Yet at the same time, he was as familiar to her as Olivia, or Martin, or her mother.

"Let him go. You've near drained him," Ernst called. Shay obediently, but reluctantly, released the Giver. The youth crumpled to the earth, his red hair forming slashes across his pale, pale face.

What did I do? What was . . .

Shay stared at the unconscious boy, hyper-aware of his blood dripping from the corners of her mouth. She slid out her tongue and licked it away. More. She wanted more.

"Gabriel, come. Now."

Again, Shay obeyed. She ran down the street after Ernst, the muscles in her legs contracting and releasing with each long stride. She was fast. God, she was fast, her heart and lungs engines that could beat and pump away forever.

This was incredible. She could feel the wind slapping against her cheeks, blowing through her collar-length hair.

But her hair was long. And it was pulled back in a French braid.

Shay ignored the thought. It was easy. It had nothing to do with her. All she cared about was the strong, steady thudding of her heart, the impact of her feet on the dirt, the glistening stars over her head, and the blood . . . all that fresh blood ripping through her.

Except I'm inside; there are no stars. And I can't run like that. My body couldn't take it.

"All done," Martin announced.

Shay blinked as he slid the needle out of her vein, then taped a cotton ball over the tiny wound.

"Shay? You okay?" Martin's eyes narrowed as he studied her.

"Yeah. I'm good, actually. I feel good," Shay replied slowly. When was the last time she had felt *good*? Had she ever? Her body still felt the way it had in the vision. If that's what it had been . . . a vision. Or had she fallen asleep? Was it a dream? Whatever it was had affected her entire body, every one of her senses.

Martin placed two fingers on her wrist, then looked down at his watch as he checked her pulse. Shay raised her eyebrows, asking a silent question. "Excellent," Martin said. "This afternoon you have the pulse of a marathon runner." So his results matched what she was feeling. She felt like a marathon runner right this moment, except for the lying in a hospital bed part.

He released her, then started to push the IV pole out of the room. They kept it in the hall closet. Keeping it in Shay's room was way too big a reminder—for them all—of what her life was like. "Your mom will be in with your juice."

The way Shay felt, fetching the juice from the kitchen herself would be no problem. *Don't let some freaky dream make you think you're Supergirl instead of Sickgirl,* Shay cautioned herself. But she eased herself out of bed and onto her feet, just to see how she did.

And she did fine. No head rush. No heart flutter. No cold extremities. She headed down the hall, ready to lean against the wall if she had to. But she didn't. Her legs didn't tremble as she walked. Her knees didn't go Jell-O.

No transfusion had ever made her feel like this. Martin said he was tweaking it, but still . . . It was more like the strength and power she'd felt in that strange, amazing vision had stayed with her when she'd woken up. Woken up. Is that what had happened? Because then what she'd seen would have been a dream, not a vision. But a dream couldn't have tastes and smells that were so, so real. At least no dream Shay had ever had.

Maybe some new component in the transfusion had given her a hallucination. Maybe she'd been on some kind of drug trip. Or—

"Shay, get back in bed," her mother exclaimed from the kitchen, practically dropping the juice bottle when she spotted Shay.

"I'm fine. I'll get the juice myself." Shay pulled open the cabinet and stood on tiptoe to reach a glass.

"I don't think that's such a good—" her mother began.

"Mom, please!" Shay snapped. "You know I like doing things myself when I can," she added more gently.

Her mother nodded. She put the juice bottle on the counter and headed for the living room.

Shay wished she had something more exciting to use her strength on, wherever it had come from. Something way better than—whoa, hold on there, tiger—getting herself a glass of juice.

Something like . . . Kaz's party.

She poured her juice and pulled open the refrigerator door. The cool air fanned across her flushed face. She shoved the bottle onto the top shelf, but her eyes went straight to the bottom. Should she? Could she?

Yeah. There was no party she could go to right now. No boy to kiss. But she could have a beer. Her first beer ever. How insane was that? She was seventeen years old, for God's sake.

Shay wrapped her fingers around a bottle of Duvel, the Amsterdam brew Martin went for. He was a best-of-everything guy—even though sometimes Shay thought it was more about status than about what he truly enjoyed. She got the bottle opener and took off the top. Then she hesitated.

Self-check, she thought. *I need to do it. Just to be sure.*

She took her pulse. Normal. No, make that slow and low. No sweaty upper lip. She pressed her hand against her forehead. No fever. No nausea. Inside her chest, her heart beat calm and steady.

She had no idea how long this amazing feeling would last. She had to hurry.

Shay grinned. Then took a swig of the beer. A long swig. It tasted fine.

It tasted a million times better than pomegranate juice.

CHAPTER

Two

○ ○ ○ ○ ○ ○ ○ ○ ○ ○ ○ ○ ○ ○ ○ ○

"Weekend!" Kaz yelled, practically throwing himself into the cafeteria seat across from Shay.

"Not for another three hours," she said.

"Yeah, I have to endure P.E. before I'm officially happy it's Friday," Olivia grumbled. "I hate getting sweaty for no good reason."

"It is a good reason. Healthy for Life!" Shay said, before Kaz could make the obvious filthy joke. The cartoon apple that appeared on every classroom poster about eating right and exercise always said, "Healthy for Life!" That apple had been with them since first grade, and Shay had always felt it was mocking her.

"Easy for you to say, you never have to go to gym," Olivia said.

"Liv. Jesus." Kaz shook his head, and Olivia looked stricken.

"I don't mean it's fun for you or anything," she added in a rush.

"Chill," Shay told her. "You're allowed to be bitchy to me. I won't be scarred for life." She took a bite of the turkey sandwich her mother still sent her to school with every day. "In fact, maybe I'll come with you today." So far, the energy from her transfusion hadn't faded.

"To gym?" Olivia frowned. "Why?"

"I feel strong." Shay grabbed one of Kaz's fries and popped it in her mouth. She never ate anything fried. Never ate anything that tasted good, was more like it. Martin's self-checks included food checks, too. Iron, protein, iron, protein, it was like his mantra.

"The gym teacher won't even know who you are," Olivia said.

"So? They can't stop me from going."

"Yeah, but why would you? Hanging out in study hall can't be that bad." There was an edge to Olivia's voice that was starting to grate on Shay. As if hanging out in study hall was a vacation, not a punishment. As if Shay's life was somehow better than everyone else's just because she didn't have to go to stupid gym class.

"Do you have some sweats I can borrow?" she asked.

"Shay, you are not serious." Olivia sounded disgusted. "Just 'cause you feel strong doesn't mean you should act like an idiot. Two days ago you collapsed walking down the hall. You wouldn't last a minute in P.E."

Fine. Someone else will have clothes to lend me, Shay thought. Nobody ever said no when she asked for a favor. And now that Olivia was acting all momlike about it, Shay was determined to go to P.E.

"You ready for the party?" she asked, turning to Kaz.

"Mostly. I'm still trying to figure out how to smuggle in booze.

My mom promised to stay upstairs, but I know she's gonna do beer checks." Kaz pushed his tray closer so she could grab another fry.

"We'll just have to spike the OJ or something," Shay said. "Or, wait, what about a watermelon filled with vodka? I read about that once."

"Nice! I didn't even think of that." Kaz grinned. "I love vodka fruit!"

Shay smiled back, but she felt stupid. She'd read about vodka fruit, but of course Kaz—and Olivia, and probably everyone else in school—had actually had vodka fruit before.

"Martin has a bottle of bacon-infused vodka in the freezer. I can snag it," she offered.

"Bacon infused?" Olivia wrinkled her nose.

"He got it as a birthday present from one of the researchers he used to work with. Scientists get up to some weirdness in the lab, apparently," Shay explained.

"I don't think bacon and watermelon will taste very good together," Kaz joked. "But are you really coming to my party?"

"Of course. I'm not going to miss your eighteenth," she said.

"Shay, the party doesn't even start until nine. You'll be in bed," Olivia pointed out.

"You know what, Liv? I don't actually have a bedtime," Shay snapped. She didn't usually use her friend's nickname. It was too ironic—the terminal girl with the friend called Liv. "I'll be there," she added firmly.

Olivia's face was already changing, her brow furrowing in concern, her eyes wide, her mouth opening to apologize. Shay jumped up so fast that her lunch bag toppled over from the movement.

"Shay—"

"I don't want to hear it," she mumbled. She grabbed her insulated bag, with her uneaten healthy lunch, and dumped it in the trash can on her way out of the cafeteria. *I don't want to hear it* again, she mentally corrected herself. The worry, the embarrassment, the I'm-so-sorry-I-didn't-mean-to-offend-you words that were never really anything more than Olivia covering her ass after she'd slipped and actually treated Shay like a human being.

It was quiet in the hallway; the period wouldn't end for another ten minutes. Shay turned toward the library, not knowing where else to go. She'd never walked out on anyone before and she was kind of surprised that Olivia hadn't come running after her.

"Hi, Shay!" the hall monitor, Mr. Roque, called.

"Hi." She didn't need to give him an excuse for wandering around during class time. He wouldn't dare question the sickie. *It's weird,* Shay thought. *Why do they all assume that being sick means being good?* For all Roque knew, she was heading off to start a fire or pop some oxy in the bathroom.

Instead, she went to the library just like she'd planned. It was pathetic, but true: She had no idea what kind of trouble there was to get into or how to get into it.

"Feeling okay, Shay?" Mrs. Boutry, the librarian, asked.

"I feel terrific, actually," she said. "My new treatment is unbelievable."

"Oh." Mrs. Boutry didn't seem to know what to do with that information. "Well . . . fantastic!"

Shay matched her big smile. "I know!"

She dumped her bag on one of the study tables and headed

down the nonfiction aisle, past all the old copies of books on ancient Egypt—an obsession of hers from two years ago—past the random selection of biographies . . . to the science shelves.

Was it science, to have strange visions during a transfusion? Or was it science fiction? Shay had never gotten a vision before that transfusion on Wednesday, so maybe it was just a fluke. She pulled out a book on near-death experiences—those people always seemed to have visions, right?

"Shay?" Mrs. Boutry's voice was high-pitched now, frightened. Shay turned to find the librarian behind her in the aisle.

"Yeah?" she asked, confused. And then she got it: Mrs. Boutry was staring at the book in her hands. "Oh! I'm actually looking for something about visions, um, psychosomatic visions, I think," she said quickly.

"I'm sorry?" Mrs. Boutry blinked in confusion.

"Medically induced visions, heightened imagination, that kind of thing . . ." Shay's words trailed off. She was never going to convince this woman that she wasn't looking at death books because she was going to be dead soon. Shay sighed. Clearly, a visit to the school psychologist would be in her future. "I had a weird reaction to my last treatment," she said.

Mercifully, the bell rang before Mrs. Boutry could ask if it had led to a near-death experience. Shay shoved the book back onto the shelf and edged past the librarian. "Gotta go. Can't be late for gym," she muttered.

Shay didn't bother going to study hall to tell the teacher. It was officially her PE period, so what if she'd never once set foot in a gym class? She was going.

But the hall was unfamiliar. She'd never been to the girls' locker room, and the only times she'd been in the gym itself were for pep rallies, which, given how lame Black River's football team was, didn't happen too often. Shay's heart began to pound as she turned down the small corridor that led to the athletic rooms, and she had to read the signs on each door—weight room, exercise studio, pool—before she found the locker room. Shay took a deep breath and pushed open the door.

She wasn't sure what she'd expected, but Olivia had been complaining about the locker room ever since middle school. Back then, it had sounded like girls spent the whole time comparing their breast sizes and making fun of fat kids. Now Olivia usually whined about the lack of good lighting and the fact that the lockers were too small and your clothes always ended up getting wrinkled. What she had never mentioned was the smell.

Shay caught her breath in surprise. The whole big room was warm and smelled sickly sweet, some combination of sweat, product, and perfume. She laughed. For some reason, she'd thought only boys' locker rooms would be stinky.

"Shay? What are you doing here?" Mindy Ryman asked, not even seeming to care that she was standing there in her underwear.

"I'm in this class," Shay told her, forcing herself not to look at Mindy's bra. It wasn't normal to be talking to your friends when they were half-naked. Or maybe it was? In the hospital, people always walked around with the gowns falling off, but that was different. Those bodies were old, or sick, or superskinny. In here, everyone was normal, and they didn't seem bothered by letting everything show.

"Since when?" Mindy grabbed an old T-shirt out of her locker and started pulling it on. "I mean, I thought you had a permanent doctor's note for P.E."

"I do, usually," Shay admitted. "But I feel good this week. Like, really good."

From the corner of her eye, she noticed Olivia in one of the other banks of lockers. Shay turned so that her back was to her best friend. "Listen, Mindy, do you have any sweats I can borrow? I don't have gym clothes."

"Oh. Sure." Mindy peered into her locker—which *was* pretty damn tiny, Shay saw—and frowned. "All I have is an extra pair of shorts."

"That's okay, I can wear shorts. It's better than jeans, right?" Shay said.

Mindy bit her lip. "No, you take my sweats. I'll wear the shorts. It's chilly out."

"Well, won't you be cold in shorts?" Shay said. "I'm the one mooching. You shouldn't have to suffer."

"Yeah, but . . ." Mindy didn't finish the sentence. She didn't have to. Shay got it. Mindy was worried about her.

"Thanks, Min." Shay took the sweats, then looked around, baffled.

"The locker on the end is always empty," Mindy told her. "There's no combination lock, though. You can stick your wallet in my locker."

"Thanks." Shay went over to the empty locker and shoved her books inside, trying to ignore the growing feeling of embarrassment. She didn't know how to do the first thing in this class. Who knew you had to bring your own lock? Shay reached for the button on her jeans, and stopped. It just felt bizarre to be stripping down in front of everyone. She glanced at Mindy, and Mindy was looking back at her.

It's because I'm freakishly thin from being sick, not because it's weird to change clothes, Shay told herself. She pulled off her jeans and yanked on Mindy's sweats. Thank God she'd happened to wear Chucks today. They weren't exactly running shoes, but they were better than a pair of boots or something. She didn't have a gym shirt, but so what if her regular clothes got sweaty? There was only one more class after P.E.

It took less than a minute for Olivia to notice her. "Shay, are you serious? Just because I said not to?" The tone of voice was an exact replica of Shay's mom's.

"No, Olivia, because I feel good and I want to do something normal for a change," Shay snapped, turning to face her friend. "Sorry if that rocks your world." She handed her wallet to Mindy, and Mindy took it with raised eyebrows.

Olivia stood there with her hands on her hips just like a disapproving Sunday school teacher. Shay wished—desperately wished—that she could storm off into the gym and leave Olivia behind. But she had no idea where the door from the locker room to the gym was.

"This way, Shay." Mindy snapped her combination lock closed and gestured toward the right.

"Thanks." Shay went with her, pretending that she didn't notice Olivia's eye roll.

"I think it's cool. Take charge of your life," Mindy said as they walked.

"Yeah, I'm seizing the day," Shay replied. "Going to P.E. Watch out!"

Mindy laughed. Olivia, following them, didn't.

Inside the gym, a bunch of guys were hanging out, some of them shooting hoops. Was P.E. co-ed? Shay didn't even know.

"Ms. McGuire, can I help you?" the gym teacher asked as soon as she spotted them. Shay knew for a fact that they had never met before, but obviously all the teachers must know who she was.

"Shay's coming to class today. She feels good!" Mindy chirped, assuming the role of ambassador to the sick girl since Olivia was clearly out of favor.

The teacher looked skeptical.

"My stepfather has me do about fifty self-checks a day. I can tell you my current heart rate if you want," Shay said, resisting the urge to mention Martin's famous/brilliant doctor credentials. "Or you can just take my word for it that I feel fantastic."

"Fine. You just take it easy," the teacher said. "Everybody outside. I want a mile around the track, and if you're over twenty minutes, you're doing it again."

The other girls shuffled toward the double doors that led out to the playing fields, so Shay went with them. "That was easy," she said, surprised. She'd expected a lecture about the school's legal responsibility to keep her healthy.

"Ms. Mead couldn't give a shit," Mindy told her. "She's been phoning it in for years."

"That's why we spend half the time jogging," Lai-wan Huang put in, joining them. "So she can sit on her butt and read the paper."

"You don't need to jog," Olivia said. "Just walk fast and you can do a mile in twenty minutes."

Shay didn't answer her or even look at her. Mindy and Lai-wan were being totally cool, and Shay noticed a few of the other girls shooting glances her way and smiling. Why couldn't her own best friend be like that, instead of constantly telling her what not to do?

The track ran around the football field, which was at the top of a slight hill. It was colder up there, and the early October breeze had a bite to it. Mindy shivered.

"I wish you'd let me wear the shorts," Shay told her.

"It's fine. I just have to run," Mindy said. "Believe me, I'll be warm in no time." She took off at a jog, kicking up little clods of dirt under her sneakers.

"It's four times around. That's a mile," Lai-wan said. "I'll walk with you guys if you want."

Shay glanced over at Olivia, who was still right next to her. Did everybody see them as a package deal? "I'm going to run," Shay said.

"You have never run in your life," Olivia pointed out.

I ran in my dream just the other day, Shay thought. She felt as strong now as she had then. Without waiting for an answer, she took off down the track, the muscles in her legs pumping hard, working just like they were supposed to. Just like they had in her vision.

I'm doing it! I'm really running! The locket she always wore—the only thing she had from her father—bounced up and down against Shay's chest. Her long ponytail whipped in the wind, slapping against her cheek, and she laughed out loud. Who needed a vision when there was this? Her own feet pounding on the dirt, her own heart and lungs working perfectly.

"Shay!" Olivia's voice was frightened, but it was also far behind her. Shay picked up speed, pushing her legs faster, pumping her arms. She'd never felt so powerful. The thudding of her heart was loud in her ears. . . .

Loud everywhere in her body.

"No," Shay whispered, her pace slowing. The thudding sensation didn't stop. Her heart was beating too fast, too hard. She could feel it in every pulse point, pounding in her neck, her wrists, her temples. "No."

"Oh my God, what are you thinking?" Olivia came running up to her and grabbed her arm. "Are you okay?"

"Shay? You all right?" Mindy was breathless as she hurried back to them.

"I'm fine," Shay lied. She wasn't fine. She was sick, like she'd always been sick, like she always would be sick. "Just a little tired."

"Let's go back to the gym." Olivia sounded exasperated.

Shay went along, letting herself lean on Olivia a little.

"You could've killed yourself," Olivia said.

"But I didn't," Shay replied. *A week ago, I would've. But after that transfusion, I ran—ran!—and I'm still here.* "I didn't."

"You overdid it," Shay's mother said, frowning across the green beans.

"I'm fine; I'm just tired," Shay protested. "I didn't even have to leave school early."

Her mother shook her head. It was clear she thought she understood Shay's body better than Shay did.

"What made you think you could run?" Martin asked. "Were you feeling that good, or was it some kind of peer pressure situation?" The questions were in Martin's detached, thoughtful doctor voice. Not the disappointed, lecturing parental voice Mom was using.

I guess there are some good things about not having two real parents, Shay thought. She didn't really consider Martin her parent.

Maybe no one did who acquired a stepfather when they were four-teen. Martin had been an awesome doctor. He'd paid attention to everything Shay said, and he'd never rushed out of the room because his beeper went off. And mostly, Shay's feelings for Martin were the same as when she'd been his patient. She suspected he still saw her more as a patient than a daughter too. Mom never wanted to hear that, but Shay didn't see it as a bad thing.

"Please. The peer pressure was to sit in study hall like always," Shay said. Her mother shook her head again.

Martin took a second helping of salad, half of it landing on the tablecloth instead of his plate. His big hands were surprisingly clumsy when he wasn't performing some kind of medical procedure. "Just the tip of the iceburg," he joked as he swept the spilled lettuce into his napkin.

He never seemed to run out of the puns. Shay gave him her usual fake smile, but her mother was still busy studying Shay through nar-rowed eyes.

"What do you want me to say, Mom?" she asked. "Nobody told me to go to gym, and nobody told me to run. I just wanted to."

"So you felt that strong?" Martin said before her mother could answer. "That you thought you could do something you've never done before?"

"Yeah." Shay met his eyes, and a smile spread across her face. "Yeah, I did."

"Was it just a sudden surge, sort of a rally? Or have you been feeling this way since the new treatment on Wednesday?" Martin asked, shooting a quick glance at her mother, who still hadn't taken her eyes off Shay.

"I've felt great ever since the treatment," Shay said. "What did you do to that blood anyway?"

"You have not felt great ever since. You're exhausted now," her mother pointed out. Again with the I-know-how-you-feel-you-don't.

"Emma, you're overstating things. She's sitting at the table, she's eating and drinking," Martin said.

"And she's got bags under her eyes."

"I always have bags," Shay said. "But I am tired, Martin. Maybe I should have another transfusion? The new kind."

"You just had one!" her mom protested.

"Usually you make it a few more days." Martin chewed on his lip, thinking. "It may mean this new version is faster-acting. You felt much better, but the effect was short-lived."

"Because she overdid it." Shay's mom sent her a guilt-inducing look. "We can't tell how long the effect would've lasted if Shay had just behaved herself."

"Behaved?" Shay repeated incredulously. "I'm sorry, am I a bad girl because I decided to go for a jog?"

"You know what I mean," her mother said. She glanced at Martin. "She doesn't need another transfusion yet. She just needs to rest a lot this weekend to make up for the running."

"I'm sitting right here," Shay said. Regular seventeen-year-olds got to talk to their doctors by themselves. Why did Mom insist on translating for Shay?

"You don't seem superexhausted to me. You didn't faint. You've got more energy than you did before the last transfusion," Martin said thoughtfully, actually talking *to* Shay. "I'm not sure it's time for another one yet. Do you really feel like you need it?"

Need? No, Shay thought. But she wanted it. They were right that she didn't feel as awful as she sometimes did. But she felt sick, and weak, and normal—her own lame version of normal. She wanted to feel strong again, like she had for the past two days. She wanted to feel normal by everyone else's standards.

"It's just that I don't want to be too tired to go to Kaz's party tomorrow night," she said.

Her mother laughed—a harsh, sharp sound like a bark. "You are not going to a party."

"It's his eighteenth birthday. It's a big deal," Shay said.

"I don't care, you're too tired to go." Her mother took a sip of wine. "You can't risk your health for some silly party."

"Did you not hear me? He's turning eighteen. It's not some silly party," Shay snapped.

Her mother sighed. "You can send him a gift."

"Oh my God." Shay pushed her chair back from the table. "It's not a second-grade birthday party, Mom. I don't care about getting him a present. I care about having a good time at a place where every single person from school will also be having a good time."

"Sweetheart, believe me, passing out in the middle of a party is not a good time."

"That's why I want another transfusion," Shay cried.

"Emma, you know how important socializing is when you're a teenager . . ." Martin began, sounding as if he were giving an anthropology lecture.

"I know how important staying alive is for Shay!" her mother cut him off. Her eyes went wide, and her hand flew to her mouth. She never said things like that, never implied that Shay's disease was fatal. Shay realized that she should be freaked out by her mom's slip-up, but instead she felt relieved. It was refreshing to hear the truth for a change.

"Mom, if I can't even run around the track at school and I can't go to a party with my friends, I'm not really alive now," she said. "Why can't I just have another transfusion and live the way I want?"

"No," her mother said, her gaze flitting between Martin and Shay. "It's just too soon."

Shay's hands tightened around her napkin. Her mother really needed to realize that Shay was old enough to understand her own body and make her own decisions about what she could and couldn't do.

Because she was going to make her own decisions, whether Mom liked it or not.

Martin shook her awake at eight in the morning. "Your mom went for bagels," he said.

Shay rubbed her eyes and tried to process that. Bagels were fine and all, but it wasn't really their thing. Saturdays were for scrambled eggs with cheese. "Why?"

"She felt like something different." Martin took Shay's pulse as he spoke. "Weaker than last night."

"It always is." Shay sat up, shivering in the cool autumn air. "Can't we turn the heat on?"

Martin looked surprised. "It hasn't been cold enough yet. But sure, I'll put it on. I, um, I thought you might want to do another transfusion first."

Shay stared at him. "Mom said no."

"She's worried because the effects of the last one wore off so quickly." Martin shrugged. "I'm more interested in how much better you felt during that time."

"Mothering versus doctoring," Shay said. *Smothering* was more like it.

He smiled. "The eternal battle."

"Mr. Bonetto says you can't tell anything from an experiment run one time," Shay said. "You have to do it over and over before you get any meaningful results."

"Exactly. So this time, we'll try this new type of transfusion and we'll take more notes." Martin looked her straight in the eye. "And you won't skew the outcome by exhibiting any behavior beyond the mundane."

"No running," Shay translated his science talk. "Got it."

"I can only tell how well it's working if you keep your activities at the same basic level they're always at," Martin said. "Promise?"

"I promise no running," Shay told him.

Martin went out into the hallway to get the IV stand, and Shay leaned back against her pillows. Mostly naked Calvin Klein man stared down at her from the ceiling, but he just seemed bland. She didn't need him to take her mind off the transfusion. She wanted her mind *on* it now. She couldn't wait for the strength.

"Please let it work again," she whispered, to Underwear God or actual God or anyone else who might be listening. "I don't care if it only lasts a day, please just let it work."

"Ready?" Martin came back in, excitement in his eyes. He was as hopeful as Shay was; she could see it. Well, if he found a way to treat her, it would make all his research worthwhile. It would mean he was right to have left his position at the Anderson Cancer Center in Houston. It would mean he really had saved her life.

"This is a big deal, huh?" she asked him. "It's the first thing that's ever made me feel good."

"It's only a small step. I want you off transfusions entirely and still feeling good," he said, but he shot her a smile. "I'd say if it keeps working, it will mean we're finally going in the right direction."

He examined her for a moment, looking for an unbruised spot on her rail-thin arm. There weren't many left—every transfusion left a bruise, and she'd been having them more and more often. The ugly splotches took forever to heal. She knew soon they'd have to move to other places on her body, but for now Martin seemed satisfied. He swabbed her skin with alcohol, then slid the needle into her arm.

This time Shay watched it.

The blood, thick and red, slid down the tube . . . too slowly. Shay willed it to move faster, to get into her system.

And finally, there it was.

Shay's heart seemed to jump, as if she'd just been shocked with a defibrillator . . . and then warmth spread through her as her heart sent the new blood speeding through every artery, to every inch of her body.

I don't need the heat on after all, Shay thought as her eyelids fluttered closed. The sun was so hot, beating on her face, warming every inch of skin as she stretched out on the bluff above the ocean. So hot. She could see it even through her eyelids, a bright orange color that made her think of the persimmon tree near the orphanage.

What orphanage? Shay wondered, but it was an idle thought. She could picture the tree, right near the path that led up into the hills.

She didn't know the name of the hills, but it hardly mattered, not when the sun was so warm.

"Are you falling asleep?" Sam called from the cave in the bluff face.

Who's Sam? Shay's thought asked, drifting in from some faraway place.

"I might be." It was hard to stay awake in the heat of the late afternoon, with the sun on her body like a blanket. "Will I always feel cold now?"

"No," Sam said.

"It's hard to imagine life without the sun." She opened her eyes, blinking in the dazzling light, and slowly sat up.

"We still have fire. And wraps." Sam's voice sounded amused, even across this distance. "And it never turns too cold here, as you know."

"Very unlike Germany. Ernst spent nearly a century there, shivering the entire time." Shay laughed, the sound deep and strong. She got to her feet and sprang across the five feet of grass that separated the edge of the cliff from the cave.

"He might've come south sooner, if it was that cold," Sam agreed with a chuckle.

Inside the cave, it was nearly black. Lichen overhung the entrance from above; tall grass hid it from below. It was a deep cleft in the ancient bluff, and the dazzling sun of Greece didn't reach inside. Even so, Sam sat huddled as far back as was possible, bathed in darkness so complete that Shay had to squint to see him at all.

"Fire isn't sunlight." Shay moved back toward the entrance of the cave. She could see the ocean far below, the sun's reflection dancing on the aquamarine surface. "It will be different."

"*You* will be different, Gabriel. Your senses will be intensified. You, more than anyone, will appreciate that." Sam's tone was serious now.

"But the sun . . ."

"We pay a price for our strength," Sam said. "It is not to be taken lightly, Gabriel. You know what would happen if you sought the sun after undergoing the ritual."

"I would turn to ash." Shay said the words, but she didn't quite believe them.

"I saw it happen. Ernst's original partner, Gret, had tired of her long life." Sam's voice was thick with sadness now. "She was gone when we awoke from the death sleep of daytime, and when we looked for her outside there was nothing left. Just a pile of ash like black sand."

Shay—*Gabriel*—was silent, trying to picture it. It was as unimaginable as life without the sun.

"Gabriel. Are you certain you're ready?" Sam asked gently. "The ritual need not be tonight."

"Ernst has been patient. I'm nearly twenty years old."

"You speak of Lysander," Sam guessed. "He turned at seventeen."

"I feel I've let Ernst down." Shay felt the weight of worry in her own chest, the love and respect for Ernst, the powerful sense of doubt.

"You have not let him down. He loves you. We all love you." Sam's voice was calm, comforting. "No one joins the family until it is right in their heart. You and Lysander are very different. Sander has always been rushing forward, wanting to get to the next thing, whatever it was. But you—you experience things very deeply, Gabriel. It's been that way since you were a little boy. I can still picture you on the beach, holding a seashell in your hand, tracing all the curves, smelling it, holding it to your ear, even giving it a little lick."

Gabriel and Sam laughed together at the memory. "You and Sander both want to experience everything, but you've always gone deeper," Sam said. "I'm not surprised you haven't undergone the transformation yet. I wouldn't expect you to, until you felt you'd fully understood and enjoyed the parts of the world you'll have to give up."

"The sun," Gabriel said. He tilted his head back, letting the sun's warmth stroke his face. "It's hard to imagine ever having enough of it."

"There's no rush," Sam told him.

Shay turned and peered through the darkness, studying Sam's face. He was tired, she could see. Beyond tired. The death sleep must be pulling at him, but he was forcing himself to remain awake against every instinct, just to be there for Gabriel. It was hard to even imagine what this effort was costing Sam. He should be asleep during the day, not playing nursemaid to an ambivalent youth.

"It's time. I am ready." Shay drew in a deep breath, filling her powerful lungs with the sea-salt air. "Tonight I join my family."

"Then I will leave you to bid the sun farewell." Sam gestured toward the entrance to the cave. "Go back out into the light while you can. I will wait."

"You should sleep."

"I've wakened for this long; I can make it through the day." Sam smiled, weakly. "I will wait."

The warmth of the sun felt like a magnet, drawing Shay forward.

From the cave's entrance, out onto the bluff. And then down, down the winding path from the top of the cliff to the beach. As soon as her feet—*his feet*—hit the sand, he began to run. Straight toward the horizon, right into the surf. He swam, arms lithe and powerful, slicing through the sea as he followed the golden-red trail the sun left on the surface of the water. It hardly took any effort. His pulse remained slow, his heartbeat regular.

So strong, and he doesn't even know it, Shay's own thought whispered in her head. Gabriel turned over—floating—cool, silky water against sun-heated skin, a fish occasionally flicking against him.

From now on, he would swim only in darkness. For a lifetime—or ten lifetimes—he would never see the sun on the water again.

The sadness of that realization almost crushed him. Slowly, reluctantly, he swam back to shore, not wanting to know if the salt on his lips was from the water or from his own tears. Crawling onto the beach, the sand felt hot and soft under his feet . . . but the sun was sinking now, its heat beginning to fade. The change was almost imperceptible, but Gabriel felt it. Shay felt it.

This is the last time I will ever see the sunset.

Shay lifted her hand—his hand—and felt tears on the smooth skin of his cheek. The sun dropped quickly toward the horizon, growing larger every second, until it was a tremendous ball of fire, deep red in color.

"Like blood," Shay whispered.

Would blood be enough to replace the sun? The way the family spoke of it—warm, life-giving—sounded wonderful. But Gabriel had grown up on the sun-drenched islands of Greece. Could anything ever take the place of that beauty in front of him? The entire sky seemed lit from below, streaks of shocking pink and hazy purple breaking through clouds that glowed orange.

Faster now, the sun dropped, dipping below the ocean it seemed. Sending its ruby reflection into a million lights that danced crazily on the darkened water . . . and then it was gone.

Gabriel blinked. The pink and purple streaks still filled the sky, but they were fading. Twilight had come. It felt like a spear piercing his heart.

Shay gasped, her hand moving to her heart. Somewhere, Martin took her hand, felt for the pulse at her wrist. But it wasn't real, not compared to the grief overwhelming her—overwhelming Gabriel.

He crumpled onto the sand, crying. Never to see the morning glories in bloom again, never to hear birdsong when he awoke, or see the early morning dew on the grass. How could anything take the place of day?

"It is not the end, Gabriel." Sam's arms were around him now, Sam's voice strong in his ear. "The ritual is not an end, but a beginning. You have lived with the family almost all your life, and yet you have not known all that we know or felt all that we feel. But now you will. You say good-bye to the light, but you begin anew in the darkness." Sam ran his finger over the stylized tattoo of the phoenix on the side of his neck. Soon, Gabriel would have a matching tattoo, a symbol of his rebirth into a new life. But the phoenix had lost its old life too.

"You are not tired anymore," Gabriel said, surprised by the power of Sam's voice.

"It is the sun that saps my strength. But the sun has set."

It was true. The beach was dark now, the water a deeper black even than the sky. Sam must have climbed down from the cave while Gabriel cried. And suddenly he understood why Sam had forced himself to stay awake—to be here for Gabriel's last sunset. "You knew I would need you," Shay said with Gabriel's mouth. "You knew I would be weak."

"I knew you would need a brother to help you," Sam said. "And after the ritual, that is what we will be. Brothers."

"That's what I've wanted since I was a child." Shay pushed herself to her feet, ready to follow Sam. Eager for her new beginning.

"Shay! Lie back!" Martin's voice broke into her thoughts, harsh and grating. He slid the needle from her arm, and Shay cried out.

"But the ritual," she moaned. "I want to see it."

"You were standing up in the middle of a transfusion." Martin gently eased her shoulders back against the pillows, his big arms holding her there without effort, even though strength and energy was pulsing through her body. "What were you thinking?"

"I was . . . I was dreaming," she said, still in shock at the sight of her bedroom and her stepfather. The beach, the bluffs . . . they had felt so real.

"Do you still feel tired?" Martin's brow furrowed as he studied her. "You fell asleep last time too."

"No. I feel great," she said, stretching her arms up. The vision was gone, but the health and vitality she'd felt in it were still there.

"Well, do me a favor and stay in bed for a while. Your mother wanted you to rest today, and if the transfusion is making you sleepy, it couldn't hurt to take it easy." Martin collected his supplies and headed for the door, wheeling her IV pole.

"Tell Mom to bring me up some bagels," Shay called after him.

But when he was gone, she reached over to her bedside table and grabbed her journal. Martin might want her to sleep, but that was not going to happen. The blood in her veins felt like some kind of energy drink or at least what she imagined those felt like. She could run around the entire track at school right now without breaking a sweat; she was sure of it.

Did Martin put steroids in this new blood or what? It's like blood and a drug all at the same time. I wonder what it would do to normal, nonsick people. Turn them into superheros? ☺ If this keeps working, maybe it'll turn out to be Martin's artificial heart or polio vaccine—his chance for immortality, as he calls it. He wants to be one of those doctors who have made such a contribution that they're never forgotten. And I, personally, am never going to forget this!

I don't even care what he's done to the blood. I just love it. And I love the dreams it gives me. Or visions. Whatever. There was another one while I had the transfusion just now. It felt as if I was actually there, in the body of this guy. I knew everything he knew—like that we were in Greece and that he really loved his friend Sam. When I moved my arm, it was his arm. And my thoughts were his thoughts. Wait, that's not right. His thoughts were my thoughts; his emotions were my emotions. It was incredible—even the sadness. I don't think I've ever felt anything that powerfully in my whole life.

And now I'm sitting here in my pathetic hospital bed, all by myself, and what is there to feel? It's not like I can get all worked up about doing my homework. Just in that one dream, I did more than I've ever done in my real life. I climbed, and ran, and swam in the ocean.

Well, I guess I ran in gym. So I can check that off.

But I've been alive for seventeen years, and all I've done is just survive. It's not really living. It's not experiencing life the way that the people in my dream talked about—I haven't fully understood and enjoyed the parts of the world I'll have to give up when I finally get too sick.

I want to run again, for more than twenty feet. I want to try things I haven't—and not just Martin's beer. I don't even know what, just . . . everything. I want to feel everything as deeply as I did in that dream.

I am going to Kaz's party tonight! I don't care what Mom says; I'll climb down the tree near my room if I have to. God, I feel so good! Like I could do anything, without even needing to take a rest. Is this what it's like to be normal? I can't remember. I always say I can't remember, but the truth is I never even knew. Just because I didn't need transfusions all the time when I was little doesn't mean I was healthy then. I still couldn't even climb the swing set in Olivia's backyard without passing out. But still, is this what it's like? Does everybody feel this way, so strong?

I never knew it would be this good.

It just seems stupid now to worry about the things people worry about—like grades, or boyfriends, or getting grounded, or whatever. I couldn't care less about any of that crap, not when I'm so healthy! If this is normal, people take it WAY too much for granted. So what if Mom is mad at me for going to Kaz's? So what if idiot Mr. Bonetto was insulted that I corrected his mispronunciation of **deoxyribonucleic** *yesterday? (Not that he could do anything about it. When the Sick Girl calls you out on being stupid, you know two things: 1. You are stupid, because the Sick Girl knows everything about DNA. And 2. You can't reprimand her, because only unforgivable meanies yell at sick girls.) I'm healthy enough to sneak out, and I'm healthy enough to talk back to a teacher, and I'm healthy enough to take the punishment!*

That's it. I promise myself that I'm going to experience everything I can before I'm forced to say good-bye. I don't want to use all this wonderful health just to stay alive. I want to use it to live, to take in everything the way he did in my dream.

Honestly, I don't think I was dreaming. I've never had a dream like that, where it felt so completely true and real. And where I remembered every single detail afterward. And besides, I don't think I ever really fell asleep.

But mostly I don't think it was a dream because I was with the same person as during the last transfusion. Gabriel. His name is Gabriel.

And I think he's a vampire.

THREE

o o o o o o o o o o o o o o o o o

"YOU'LL CALL ME THE SECOND you feel tired." Shay's mother anxiously kneaded the steering wheel with her fingernails, one of the habits that Shay hated the most.

"I won't feel tired. I'm doing great," Shay said for the hundredth time.

"And make sure Olivia keeps tabs on you. Tell her she can call me if you're too sick."

"Mom, God," Shay burst out. "Olivia is not my doctor. I'm perfectly capable of dialing a phone. But I won't need to, because I feel great. Which part of that do you not understand?"

"What I don't understand is why you insist on pushing yourself too hard," her mother replied. "Honey, I know it seems important right now—"

"Do not even give me that speech." Shay grabbed the door handle. They'd been parked outside Kaz's house for five minutes now, having this same conversation, while music blared from inside and people walked by them on their way in.

"I know friends and parties seem like a huge deal, but in the big picture, high school really doesn't even matter that much," her mom went on, undeterred. "Once Martin finds the right treatment for you and we get the disease under control, you'll have your entire life to socialize."

"The reason parties are a big deal to me is that I've never managed to go to one. And, no, sitting on the couch for twenty minutes and then leaving does not count as actually going to a party, and that's all I've ever done." Shay shook her head. "Don't you get it? Maybe this *is* my entire life. I don't know if there is a future. You always want me to be patient, wait until I'm better before I do *anything*. Well, I'm sick of waiting." She wanted to be like Gabriel, squeezing every drop out of every experience. Even if Gabriel didn't exist, even if he was the product of some random neurons firing in her brain, she wanted his passion for the world.

"Honey, if you're feeling depressed about the sickness—"

"I'm going." Shay opened the door. "I'll get a ride home. Don't spend the whole night staring at the phone."

"But you'll call me—"

"No. Mom, I'm going to stay as late as I want, and then someone will take me home. That's what high school seniors do. Everyone drives, and everyone has a car, except me." Shay climbed out of the

Mercedes and smoothed her shirt over the skinny jeans she'd finally decided on.

"Please, Shay . . ." her mother's voice trailed off. Shay leaned down and looked in the car door. Her mother's expression was confused and frightened, and Shay's stomach did a little roll. Mom wasn't trying to be a pain in the butt, she was just terrified of letting her sick baby out of her sight.

"Mom, trust me. I am fine." She smiled. "Go have a date night with Martin or something." Although that was kind of hard to picture. Her mom and Martin had never really done the traditional dating thing. They couldn't have—Mom would never leave Shay's bedside for long enough. They'd maybe gone out to dinner a few times, but mostly they'd been with Shay. They'd only had a honeymoon weekend. Her mother hadn't wanted to stay away from Shay any more than that, even though Martin had hired the best round-the-clock nursing care available.

Shay closed the car door and turned away before there was any more pleading. She couldn't handle the parental anxiety. It was too much a part of the disease, and Shay wasn't going to think about the disease tonight. Walking up Kaz's driveway, Shay thought she could probably fly if she wanted to. Her body was strong, her heart beat like a machine, and all her senses were sharp. That kind of feeling had to be used.

Tonight was for enjoying this rush of energy that had filled her ever since the transfusion.

Tonight was the first night of her life on her own, without her mother, and without her disease. She didn't care if morning never came.

"Oh my God, it's Shay!" Lai-wan squealed as soon as she stepped in the door. She threw her arms around Shay as if they were besties, and Shay almost recoiled from the smell of alcohol on her breath.

"Hey, Lai-wan," she said, peeling the girl off her.

"I can't believe you made it. Do you have to leave early?" Lai-wan asked. "You really looked sick in gym yesterday."

"No, I feel better," Shay said. "Where's Kaz?"

"In the kitchen." Lai-wan suddenly froze, cocking her head as if she were deep in thought. "Oh my God, I love this song!" she cried, her voice about two octaves higher than usual. She let out a shrill "whoo," flung her arms in the air, and headed into the living room, dancing all the way.

About ten other people replied with "whoo"s of their own, and everyone began grinding right in the middle of Kaz's tasteful beige carpet.

Shay watched with a sinking heart.

"What's with the sad face?" Chris Briglia asked, appearing at Shay's side.

Her stomach immediately exploded into butterflies, but she managed not to stammer when she spoke. "I thought parties were supposed to be fun, but somehow Lai-wan's IQ seems to have dropped fifty points. And I can't dance. Maybe I shouldn't have come after all." So much for her resolve to live like Gabriel.

Chris burst out laughing. "You just haven't had enough to drink. Nobody can dance when they're sober."

"Most of them can't dance even when they're drunk," she said, peering at the crowd in the living room.

He laughed again, and Shay felt her cheeks heat up. She'd never really flirted before—why bother, when she'd probably end up fainting from the stress of it? But Chris seemed happy to see her, and his eyes were now wandering up and down her legs and checking out her butt. Shay felt a burst of giddiness. Since the new transfusions, her skin had looked better, less sallow. Her lips and cheeks had more color, and her blue eyes actually looked clear instead of tired and bloodshot. She'd wondered if it was just her imagination, but maybe not.

"You look different," Chris said.

"Is that good?"

"Definitely." He nodded toward the kitchen. "You want to get drunk and dance?"

"I do," she said. "I really do."

"Wait . . . can you?" he asked, his smile faltering. "I mean . . ."

"You know what? I've never been drunk before. I have no idea what will happen," Shay told him.

She could see by his expression that he was back in *Shay-is-a-delicate-flower-who-must-not-be-touched* mode. Damn it. She wanted more flirting. "So then you shouldn't drink," he said.

"Probably not." She winked as she started toward the kitchen, trying to remind him that she was the girl whose ass he liked. "But I'm going to."

She didn't look over her shoulder to see if he was following her, even though she wanted to. Olivia always said you never check on what a guy is doing because it makes them feel too important. And Olivia had been dating since eighth grade, so she must know.

Still, when she got to the kitchen and Chris wasn't with her, Shay felt a pang of disappointment. But the small crowd of people gathered around the center island all smiled. Jacey Hadel moved to make room for Shay near the birthday boy.

"You made it!" Kaz cried, his face lighting up when he saw her. "Olivia went out for more chips and stuff."

"That's okay, I can survive without her. Happy birthday," Shay said, standing on tiptoe to hug him. "Sorry I didn't bring any vodka; there was a full maternal taxi service."

"No worries, I took your watermelon idea. They had to sit overnight anyway." Kaz gestured to a huge bowl of melon chunks. "That's the second one. People started early."

"I know, I smelled them," Shay joked. She picked up a hunk of watermelon and popped it into her mouth. It tasted like cold medicine.

"Are you allowed to do that?" Jacey asked.

"Sure. Fruit is good for me," Shay said.

"But it's eighty proof," Anthony Ativa put in, frowning. "The vodka transfers to the watermelon—"

"Shay's not an idiot, Ativa," Kaz cut him off. "She was kidding."

Anthony's mouth opened and closed, like a fish. Shay laughed. "I have a disease, not an impaired sense of humor. I do know how to make a joke."

"Just don't let Olivia see you," Kaz told her. "She'd take the watermelon away to punish us all for letting you drink."

Shay rolled her eyes. "She's as bad as my mother."

"Worse than my mother," Kaz said. "My mom has retreated upstairs and locked her door. Says she's not coming down unless someone calls the cops."

Shay grabbed another piece of watermelon. "I can't even imagine that. My mom comes from the Bizarro World of yours. I wouldn't be surprised to find her hiding in the bushes outside."

Kaz laughed. "It's just 'cause you're sick."

"Doesn't make it any less annoying." Shay never talked this honestly with Olivia. Liv came from the Mom-and-Martin school of pretending that Shay's illness didn't define her, but still assuming that she had no personality beyond her illness. Kaz totally knew that Shay's illness *did* define her—and he never pretended that it didn't suck. "You know, you're my favorite one of all Olivia's boyfriends," she told him.

Kaz choked on the Coke he was downing.

"Sorry, guess I shouldn't be so blunt." Shay giggled. The vodka was kicking in, she could tell. Her skin felt warm, and even the amazing healthy blood pumping through her veins seemed heated.

"I'm the only boyfriend who matters," Kaz said.

"Well, you've been around longer than the others," Shay said. "Maybe she'll keep you."

"At least until college. All bets are off then." Kaz looked a little sad as he said it.

"Don't think about that; it's almost a year away," Shay told him. "You'll be happier if you live for today."

"Deep." Kaz grabbed a watermelon chunk and tossed it through the air to Anthony, who managed to catch it in his mouth, knocking over a bowl of pretzels in the process.

"It's not deep," Shay said. "I just never think that far in the future."

Kaz looked at her, his dark eyes sad. "But you seem better now. I mean, look at you!"

"I know, I look so hot," Shay said, giggling again.

"Yeah, you do." Kaz held up his hand for a high five, and she slapped it without even noticing the effort.

"Last two pieces." Shay nodded toward the bowl.

Kaz grabbed them both in his big hand, then handed one to Shay. "Drinking with Shay on my birthday—the start of a good year," he said, holding his dripping piece of melon up in a toast.

"Technically it's eating, but cheers," Shay said, touching her piece to his. They both shoved the watermelon into their mouths and laughed.

"Okay, now it's up to everyone else," Kaz said. "Lai-wan has a bottle of rum to spike the Cokes."

"And Briglia has a flask of vodka in his jacket," Jacey put in.

"I'm getting some of that," Shay said. "I heard you should never mix alcohols." She also wanted another excuse to talk to Chris, but she didn't mention that part.

There was more *whoo*-ing in the living room when she went back in—apparently dancing was no fun without it. Everybody was laughing, though, and the dancing looked better than it had before. Shay spotted Chris Briglia near the bay window, moving his shoulders but not his feet.

"What's that move?" she asked, walking right up to him.

His cheeks reddened.

"Or are you just not committed to dancing?" Shay guessed.

"I told you, nobody sober can dance. I guess I'm not drunk enough yet."

"I heard you had vodka in your pocket," Shay said. "So you have no excuse."

Chris shrugged. He pulled out a silver flask and took a swig. Shay grabbed it before he could stick it back in his jacket.

"Whoa," Chris said as she put it to her lips.

Shay gulped down as much vodka as she could fit in her mouth and tried desperately not to cough. It burned like fire going down her throat. Chris grabbed the flask back and stared at her, his brow furrowed.

"Oh, don't worry," she sputtered as soon as she could talk.

"If you pass out, I'll get blamed," he said. "So, yeah, I'm worried."

"Wow. You are not the badass I thought you were," Shay teased, and then she clapped her hand over her mouth. She'd expected the vague dizzy feeling of being drunk, but she hadn't really expected it to make her say whatever came into her head.

"I'm badass," Chris muttered, insulted. "I'm just not the jerk who gets the Sick Girl wasted."

The Sick Girl. The words echoed through Shay's mind. *The Sick Girl.* Not the hot girl, or the fun girl, or the interesting girl. Just the sick one, even with these tight jeans, even with this incredible strength pulsing through her veins.

Were all boys like this? Shay had about as much experience in the romance arena as your average six-year-old. And it had always been just her and Mom, not even a brother to maybe tell her how the male brain worked.

If her real dad had stuck around, would he have been able to give her advice on how to deal with guys—stupid, chickenshit guys? Martin certainly couldn't give advice on social situations, and her mother didn't even believe Shay should have a social life.

Not worth thinking about Mr. Hit-and-Run, Shay told herself. Every time she mentioned her father, her mom either looked like she was about to cry or about to explode. So he probably wouldn't have been too great with the advice anyway. Maybe she could just do what he did, and get the hell out of the situation.

Shay shrugged, going for casual. She refused to let Chris see that his words had stung. "Okay. The Sick Girl will find someone else to get wasted with," Shay said. "Shouldn't be too hard. Like you said, I'm looking different tonight—in a good kind of way."

"Shay . . ." he began, but she didn't stay to listen. She turned her back on him and waded into the knot of dancers in the middle of the room.

Shay threw her arms in the air and let out a "whoo" because why not? Lai-wan and two of the other girls responded enthusiastically, and everyone kicked their dancing up a notch. Shay shook her hips as fast as she could, mimicking the others. She'd never danced before. She never had the energy. For a fleeting second, she wondered if she looked stupid, but the warm happiness of the alcohol overpowered any doubt. Moving her hips felt sexy, not dumb. The music seeped through her body, and her shoulders seemed to sway on their own. Shay closed her eyes and let herself go.

Her locket slipped free of her shirt, and for once she didn't immediately tuck it back in. Her mom wasn't around to be freaked at the reminder of Shay's dad, and the locket was really pretty—silver, with tiny diamonds circling it, and a pair of birds etched in the middle, both a sun and a moon behind them.

"I'm so psyched you're here," Jacey's voice broke into her reverie. "You never get to have any fun."

"Thank you!" Shay opened her eyes and impulsively threw her arm around Jacey. "Everyone else is so down on me."

"Well, Kaz is glad you're here." Jacey grabbed Shay's hands and they danced together for a few seconds.

"Kaz is always cool," Shay agreed. "But I guarantee the instant Olivia gets back, she's gonna throw a fit."

Jacey giggled.

"Olivia was more worried about you yesterday than Ms. Mead," Lai-wan put in. "But I thought you guys were best friends. Didn't you tell her you were coming?"

"Like a hundred times," Shay said. "She didn't believe me."

"Chris Briglia is fixated on your butt," Jacey murmured, moving closer to Shay. She nodded toward Chris, still pseudo-dancing by the window. "He's, like, mesmerized."

"He can *kiss* my butt," Shay said. "I'm over him."

Lai-wan and Jacey dissolved into laughter, and Shay shook her ass a little harder just for Chris's benefit.

"Seriously, he was like a pruny old schoolmarm when I said I was going to drink," Shay went on. "As if I shouldn't even be allowed to do what I want."

"Lame," Lai-wan commented. "It's your life."

"It is now." Shay put her arms in the air and closed her eyes again, letting the music and the good blood and the vodka mingle into a delicious hot vibration that buzzed through her with every beat of her heart.

"Shay Stadium!" Kaz was nearby now, dancing. She wasn't sure when he'd gotten there. Shay glanced around the room, and it seemed as if someone had turned down the lights. More people crowded the floor, everyone swaying together like a single organism.

"Are parties always like this?" she asked Kaz.

"No, mine are better than everyone else's," he said.

Shay rolled her eyes. "Of course."

"Makeout music," somebody yelled, and "What About Now" started playing, getting a mix of cheers and groans from the crowd.

Lai-wan and Jacey kept dancing as if the music hadn't even changed. Some people went to get food, some did exaggerated jokey slow dances, and others came rushing over to stand there clutching each other and swaying. Shay frowned.

"Slow dance," Kaz told her. "Just like the regular dance, only . . . slower. . . ." He spoke in a distorted voice, like he was in slow motion, and Shay laughed. Kaz grabbed her around the waist and positioned her arms around his neck. "Like this," he said.

"That is completely uncomfortable," Shay told him. Kaz was so tall that even with high heels, she couldn't reach his shoulders without stretching.

"Sorry." He took her hands and moved them down until she was sort of clutching his biceps. "You can do it this way too."

"And this is supposed to be sexy?" Shay laughed. "It feels more like I'm hanging on in case I'm about to fall down drunk."

"That's one reason," Kaz agreed. "Although if I'm the one who falls, I'm taking you down with me."

Shay giggled. "Well, that sucks," she said. "All this time I thought slow dancing was romantic. I was hoping I'd get to experience that, but instead you've taken the magic out of it."

"Oh, sorry, let me fix that." Kaz tightened his arms around her waist, pressing Shay's breasts against his broad chest. He looked down at her, the teasing smile gone from his face. "It's all about the attitude," he murmured.

Shay nodded, surprised. He was right, the whole mood had changed instantly. Suddenly she was aware of the muscles beneath his T-shirt and the movement of his hips against hers. Suddenly her breath was coming faster even though her body was moving slower. She glanced up at Kaz, and his face was closer than she'd ever seen it. He was gorgeous. Shay had always known that on some level, but somehow she had never really registered it before.

"Thank you," she whispered.

Kaz shrugged. "Glad to help. I want you to have fun."

"I am." Shay relaxed and let him guide her body to the music. "I don't know how long I'll feel good. I need to do as much as I can before I crash again."

"So . . . drinking and dancing?" he asked.

"It's not as exciting as knocking over a bank, I guess," Shay joked. "But even the most boring things are new to me."

"I've never knocked over a bank either," he commented.

Shay smiled, resting her cheek on his chest. "After my next transfusion we can try that."

"Deal," Kaz said. "Anything else on the agenda for tonight? You're pretty drunk."

"I am." The room was spinning slowly, along with her and Kaz. It felt fantastic. "And I'm an excellent dancer."

"Well, there's not much more to a party than that," Kaz said.

"I was hoping to get hit on," Shay murmured absently. "I thought guys always hit on drunk girls."

"They're afraid of you," Kaz said.

"No kidding. I've been crushing on Chris Briglia for a year, and he basically told me to get lost," Shay said. "I was actually dumb enough to think he might be my first kiss."

"You've never been kissed?" Kaz sounded appalled.

"Nope." Shay felt a blush creeping up her neck to her ears. Had she really just admitted to liking Chris, out loud?

But Kaz was focused on the kiss thing. "Never? How is that possible?"

"Boys think they'll hurt me," Shay said. "They don't see a girl; they see a frail little alien."

"I see a girl." Kaz's hands drifted down below her waist. "A girl with the most amazing blue eyes—summer-sky eyes. You're beautiful, especially tonight. I'd kiss you."

He was almost touching her butt. Shay's breath caught in her throat, and she couldn't concentrate on anything other than his hands. "I'd kiss you, too," she said.

Kaz bent down, his breath hot on her face. The room was still spinning slowly around them. Shay leaned into him, parting her lips, slipping her arms around his back. Kaz's mouth was an inch from hers, and his hands were solidly on her butt. Shay stood on tiptoe and pressed her lips to his.

His mouth was warm, his lips soft. She felt a jolt of surprise— somehow she hadn't expected soft lips. Kaz's body was tense beneath her fingers, and Shay vaguely knew that she was tense too, waiting for something.

Then Kaz's tongue pushed her lips apart, and her heart gave a giant *thump*. His tongue entwined with hers, and Shay found herself pressing close to him, holding him tight, moving her mouth against his.

The song ended, and it was like a spell had been broken. Shay and Kaz pulled away from each other. "Uh," Kaz said, looking a little horrified.

"Yeah." Shay felt as horrified as he looked.

"What the *hell?*" Olivia's voice was shrill, more like a screech than a voice.

She stood five feet away, holding a grocery bag, staring back and forth between them with fury in her eyes. She'd seen the whole thing.

o o o o o o o o o o o o o o o o

WISHING I COULD SKIP BIO. *I've avoided Olivia and Kaz all morning. If I could just skip Bonetto's class, I wouldn't have to face them until tomorrow. (Yeah, because they'll both be totally over it in one more day.) It's bad enough the way everyone else keeps looking at me today—half of them seem horrified and half of them act like I'm some kind of rock star.*

Maybe if I keep writing until the bell rings, they won't disturb me. Olivia doesn't even know about this journal—they'll think I'm doing homework or something. Or I could tell Mr. Bonetto that I don't feel well and go to the nurse.

But she'll just send me home and then I'll have to play sick even though I still feel okay. Not perfect like I did on Saturday, but better than I used to. And the vodka didn't even make the effects of the transfusion wear off faster. It's like my body can do anything when I have that blood!

What am I even supposed to say to Olivia? Kaz and I told her we were both wasted and we were just kidding around. But that's not totally true. Mostly, but not totally, and anyway it didn't make Liv feel any better.

It's not like I want to steal her boyfriend—Kaz is a big goofball and we were drunk. If Olivia hadn't seen us, I bet he and I would have been laughing about it in a couple minutes. It was no threat to Olivia, really. But she's mad at me. Madder at me than at him.

I mean, she completely ditched me afterward! She knew I'd been drinking and she still didn't even lecture me about my health or yell at me for being irresponsible—or even drive me home! It was amazing. She got mad and stormed off, and everyone else was all scandalized and some of the girls gave me the cold shoulder. Mindy Ryman told me I was out of control. Jacey and Lai-wan couldn't stop laughing. And Chris Briglia ended up giving me a ride! Like he wanted to not be the one to get me drunk, but he's happy to be the one taking my side after I act like a drunken idiot. This morning he even waited by my locker to make sure I was okay. He says everyone acts weird at parties, so I fit right in. My theory: He doesn't know what to think of me anymore, and he seems to like that. Hee! Weirdo.

But the point is, I didn't need Olivia. I managed fine without her, and I didn't need her being all mother hen to me. She acted *like I was a normal girl kissing her boyfriend—and everyone else acted like I was normal, too. Not, Sick Girl kisses boy. Just, OMG, Shay made out with Olivia's boyfriend.*

Slutty? I guess. But normal!

So do I have to go grovel to Olivia now? She deserves it. She deserves the best apology I can come up with. But if she gives me the silent treatment for the rest of the year, that might be a nice break.

"I thought you'd still be hiding," Olivia snapped, dropping her books onto the lab table with a thud.

Shay sighed and closed her journal. "I thought you'd still be not talking to me."

"I'm waiting for an explanation," Olivia said, tapping her perfect fingernails on the table. Shay glanced around the room. The bell was only a minute away, so most people were there, and most people were watching the two of them.

"Where's Kaz?" Shay asked.

"None of your business," Olivia said.

"Well, why aren't you mad at him?"

"I am! But he's not my best friend," Olivia said. "You are. Or you're supposed to be. Just what the hell were you thinking?"

"I wasn't. I felt really good and I wanted to have fun," Shay said. "I was drunk and so was Kaz. That's all there is to it. Drunken party moment." That definitely wasn't the best apology she could come up with. It wasn't an apology at all. But Olivia had so much attitude that Shay couldn't bring herself to say, "sorry." Even though she was.

"You shouldn't even be drinking at all. It could kill you, for all you know," Olivia cried.

Shay rolled her eyes. "Yeah, how dare I try to do something normal?"

"Macking on your best friend's boyfriend isn't normal," Olivia said. "You've been acting like a freak, Shay."

"I'm acting like myself for once," Shay argued. *Was* that herself— when she finally felt strong enough? Was she a girl who kissed her best friend's boy?

Drunken party moment, she thought. And, yes, that was herself. A girl who'd enjoyed—and then regretted—a drunken kiss.

"You are not! Pushing yourself to run, getting drunk? That's practically suicidal behavior for you. You're being an idiot." Olivia crossed her arms and frowned. "I should tell your mother what you did."

"Fine. Go tattle on me like a five-year-old," Shay yelled.

"You're not worth it," Olivia yelled back. "If you're going to act like a bitch, maybe I shouldn't even bother worrying about you."

"Thank God. Nobody asked you to worry about me," Shay snapped. "And guess what? Maybe I am a bitch, or a freak, or whatever you want to call me. You wouldn't even know."

"What is that supposed to mean?" Olivia gasped.

"You don't know anything about me. All you know about is blood counts and heart rates and whether I look pale. It's never even occurred to you that I might have actual opinions or feelings," Shay said. "Or that I might want to do things like jog around the track—"

"—or kiss someone else's boyfriend," Olivia cut in.

"Yeah," Shay cried. "You've never even asked me what boys I like. It's never entered your mind that I'm a girl with normal girl thoughts."

"Going after Kaz is not normal! God."

"Fine, so stop being my friend then," Shay said. "You just want the sick friend who's no competition for you. The second I start acting like myself, you call me a bitch."

"That is enough!" Mr. Bonetto's voice boomed through the classroom.

Shay jumped in surprise. She hadn't heard the bell ring, but the room was full and the teacher was glaring at them. Olivia immediately turned bright red, and Shay waited for her own cheeks to heat up.

But then she spotted Kaz, who had taken a seat at the lab table farthest away from them and wouldn't even meet her eye. *What a coward,* she thought. *He's the only one in the room not riveted to this performance of* Friend v. Friend.

And suddenly it all seemed funny. The way Brian Kiley was leering at her, the way Rupa Magge's eyes had widened to three sizes bigger than normal . . . even the way Bonetto's forehead vein was popping. It was just a big farce. Shay burst out laughing.

Olivia's eyes flew back to Shay's face, and Shay covered her mouth. But she couldn't stop.

"How dare you?" Olivia whispered, her voice shaking.

It just made Shay laugh harder. *"How dare you?" Who actually says that?*

"This is not funny, Ms. McGuire," Bonetto said in his stern-professor voice.

"It kind of is," Shay said. "I mean, it's not. But I've only been healthy for a week and look at all the chaos."

Mr. Bonetto stared at her, baffled.

"I'm just saying, it's kind of fun," Shay went on. Maybe it shouldn't be, but it just was.

"Disrupting your fellow students is not fun," he said. "Move to another lab table, both of you girls."

"She should move," Olivia muttered.

"I was here first," Shay told her. "Plus, I'm too weak and sick to move. I shouldn't *push* myself."

"Both of you move—now!" Bonetto yelled.

"Fine." Shay stood up and grabbed her books. "I'll go work by myself. I knew I should've just skipped this stupid class."

"Excuse me?" Mr. Bonetto said.

"This lab is a waste of time," Shay told him. "I could do it in my sleep."

"Watch your attitude, Shay," he warned her.

"Or what?" Shay asked. "You can't do anything to me. I'm too frail."

"I can send you to the principal," Bonetto snapped.

Shay just stared at him in shock. So did everyone else.

"Go!" he yelled.

Her brain numb, Shay gathered up her books and headed for the door. Brian was still leering at her and Rupa looked ready to pass out from shock. But Kaz didn't lift his eyes from the lab table. And neither did Olivia.

Shay walked as slowly as possible through the echoing hallways. By the time she got to the principal's office, she felt more like crying than laughing. Her hands shook as she opened the door, and the sympathetic looks from the secretaries made her cringe.

"Come right in, Shay," Principal Brewer said. Bonetto had obviously called him to say she was coming.

Shay sank down on his scratchy couch and took a deep breath.

That scene in Bio had sucked all the strength from her limbs, she realized, even though she hadn't noticed it at the time.

"Your mother is on her way," the principal told her.

"Oh, God." Shay buried her face in her hands. "You called her?"

"You've never had as much as one detention before. Obviously something's wrong," he said. "What happened?"

"I'm not even sure," she said. "I got into a fight with my friend, and I didn't know class had started. And then Mr. Bonetto yelled at me . . . and I just lost it."

Principal Brewer perched on the edge of his desk, chewing thoughtfully on his lip.

"I was acting like a bitch," Shay told him. "That's what Olivia said, and she's right. But I never get to do stuff like that, and it was sort of fun in a weird way. So I kept doing it."

He didn't get it, Shay could tell by his expression. She wasn't even sure that she understood it herself.

"Your mother mentioned a new treatment for your disease," he said. "I've heard some medications can cause emotional swings as a side effect."

"It's not a medication," Shay said. "It's just blood, but my stepfather did something to it. . . ." She didn't even know what Martin had done, she realized. For all she knew, he'd put uppers in the blood. "Anyway, it doesn't feel like a side effect. It feels like me being awake for the first time."

"Oh. Well . . ." he cleared his throat. "If this behavior is the result of your treatment, of course that's something we can all work around."

"I just said it *wasn't* a result," Shay said. "Not the way you mean.

Or if it is, it's a good result. I'm thinking for myself and taking risks and experiencing things."

"Shay, what happened just now isn't good. I think maybe this medicine . . . or specialized blood . . . I think it's making you confused."

"Why does everybody have to make it about my disease?" she exploded. "Isn't it possible that I'm just a brat?"

Principal Brewer got up and walked around the desk to sit down in his big chair. He clearly didn't know what to do with her. Shay didn't blame him. She slumped back against the couch. Of course he was going to make it about her being sick. That's all he saw. That's all anyone saw. How awful would she have to be before anybody started blaming her instead of her bad blood?

"Acting out is a fairly common reaction among chronically ill children," the principal said after a moment. "You've always been so even-tempered before, but I suppose you're due."

Tired. I've been tired before, not even-tempered, Shay thought. *And I'm not acting out, I'm just acting. Just doing things. Just trying out life.*

"I'm sorry I yelled at Mr. Bonetto," she mumbled.

"I'm sure he'll forgive you. Everybody understands how difficult it is to be ill."

"But why would you shout at your teacher?" Shay's mother demanded. She'd arrived at school all out of breath, as if she'd sprinted the whole way there. But then she hadn't wanted to do anything on the ride home except make Shay take her pulse and hysterically call Martin's office to report on the "out of character" behavior.

Now that they were settled at the kitchen table—with a giant glass of juice in front of Shay—the inquisition had started.

"Bonetto yelled at me, so I yelled back." Shay shrugged. "I didn't think he'd do anything about it."

Usually Shay liked being home with only her mother, at least when she could refrain from smother mode. That's how it had always been before Martin—just Shay and Mom. Shay hadn't missed having a father around, because he'd never been there. She'd been happy when Mom got married, and Martin was great. But it still didn't feel exactly like *home* when he was there. It felt more like home plus one.

Today, home plus one would feel good. Martin could diffuse a little of the tension with his science-guy objectivity.

"Well, why did he yell at you?" Her mother frowned, and Shay knew what was coming—Mom demanding that Mr. Bonetto be reprimanded for being mean to sick kids.

"Mom, I deserved it. Olivia and I were screaming at each other and I didn't stop when he said."

Her mother's eyebrows shot up. "What? But you girls have been friends forever!"

"I thought you were mad at me about school, not about Olivia." Shay reached for the juice, but the glass felt too heavy to lift. Better to just sit still for a moment.

"What has gotten into you lately? Fighting with your best friend, mouthing off to a teacher." Her mother was so busy pacing that she didn't seem to notice how tired Shay was. "This isn't like you."

"You sound like Olivia," Shay mumbled.

"It's the new treatment," her mother said. "It's making you act crazy."

"It makes me feel better. It lets me be *me*. I can do stuff I couldn't do before."

"Like get sent to the principal?"

Shay sighed, trying to ignore the way the room had shrunk down to just the table in front of her. Tunnel vision always came before the collapse. "I don't know how to be normal," she said. "I'm never strong enough to do what I want or say what I think. So when I felt better, I tried to do that. I didn't expect it to be such a disaster."

"Shay, you *are* normal," her mother began, but Shay shook her head. Dizziness swept through her at the movement.

"I'm not normal, I'm sick. That's what you all expect, sick Shay. Nobody knows what to do with me when I don't act all weak and victim-y," she murmured.

Mom's mouth was moving again, but the words were lost in the rushing of blood in Shay's ears. She tried to stay sitting up, but it didn't work.

Her mother caught her before she hit the floor.

"I don't like what these new transfusions are doing to you," her mother whispered, her eyes filled with fear.

"I do," Shay whispered back.

"Let's get you upstairs, then I'll call Martin again." Her mom hoisted Shay to her feet, and they headed for the staircase. "Maybe just a regular transfusion today."

Shay didn't answer. She was too tired to argue. And besides, Martin would give her the new treatment. He wanted information. And Shay wanted to feel normal again.

It was a win-win.

"Your mom thinks the new treatment is making you act aggressively," Martin said as he studied Shay's arm half an hour later. "Do you feel aggressive?"

"No. I just feel strong." Shay winced as he pushed on a likely vein. "That one's too bruised. Strong and aggressive aren't the same, are they?"

"I don't think so. But it's possible that your behavior is being caused by the treatments." Martin moved on to a spot lower on her arm. "We have to keep track of any side effects."

"Did you dose the blood? Am I getting roid rage?" Shay asked. Martin laughed right out loud, which she had never heard him do before. It was so unexpected that Shay joined in.

"I'm no psychologist, but I've dealt with sick kids all through my career. Want to hear my theory?" Martin said. "I think that hormones are unpredictable, and that even the best kids act out eventually. If you'd never been sick, arguing with friends and getting sent home from school wouldn't ring any alarm bells."

"So I'm hormonal?" Shay asked.

Martin shrugged. "It just doesn't seem like a big deal to me. Roid rage . . . well, you let me know if you start throwing desks at your friends during Social Studies."

Shay nodded, though the effort exhausted her. "Will do." She lay back, her hand wandering up to the locket around her neck, the way it always did when she was tired. If Martin had ever noticed, he hadn't said anything.

"For all I know, my father was aggressive," she murmured. "Maybe that's why Mom is all freaked about it. She thinks I'm turning into him."

Martin's eyes flew up to her face. He hesitated for the briefest of seconds, and then he went back to looking at her arm. "I think she's upset about you and only you."

"So you don't know?" Shay asked. "Did she ever tell you about him? Because she won't tell me."

"She said he abandoned her." Martin sat back and sighed. "To be honest, Shay, I forced your mother to tell me everything she knew about him. It must've occurred to you that your blood disorder could be hereditary."

"Well, yeah." Shay let go of the locket. "But I always figured if it was, we would've heard about it before. No one's ever seen my particular disease, not even you."

"Nevertheless, your father's medical history could be important. Your mom knew that. If she could have, she'd have tracked him down the instant she found out you were sick. She'd have done anything for you, even go through the pain of seeing him again. But he made sure he disappeared completely."

"Would've been nice of him to leave a medical file behind," Shay said.

"I hired a private detective, but he didn't find anything," Martin told her. "I'm sorry."

Shay closed her eyes. She shouldn't have brought up her dad. Was he some kind of con man? Had he just given her mother a fake name?

"You don't have to be sorry. It's not like I miss him—you don't miss someone you never even met." *Really*, a little voice inside Shay replied. *Then why do you wear the locket every day?*

She ignored the little voice. The locket wasn't even hers. Her father had given it to her mom when they were dating. Before he took off. And then one day when Shay was eleven, she'd been having a total fit about how she didn't have a father, and her mom had handed over the locket to get her to calm down. Shay had been in the hospital for two weeks, and the next day they let her go home. So she'd started wearing the locket all the time. She just had. End of story.

"We're making progress, even without his information. My research leads me more toward a mutation, anyhow," Martin said, patting her arm as if that was a comforting thing to say. "You ready for the transfusion?"

Shay nodded. She felt talked out. She felt everythinged out.

"Here seems good." Martin pressed lightly on a spot an inch above Shay's wrist. It hurt, but not too much. When she got this tired, everything hurt.

She closed her eyes as he swabbed her with alcohol, and the fatigue engulfed her immediately.

When the blood reaches me, I'll wake up, she thought. Even without looking, she'd be able to tell when it hit her veins. She'd feel the warmth, the strength . . .

"Five more flowers for the chain," Elena said. "So it will be long enough to go around both of us."

Shay opened her eyes in surprise at the childlike voice. Elena sat in the dust under the deep shade of the persimmon tree, a smile on her face and a pile of anemones on her lap. Their blue-purple petals echoed the blue of her eyes, the thing Gabriel liked most about her. He'd never seen anyone with blue eyes but Elena.

"I don't twist them as well as you," Shay said with Gabriel's voice. But it was different than before, higher and younger.

"Mistress says boys have hands for hunting and girls for flowers," Elena said. She bent over her chain of anemones, her chubby fingers working hard to braid the stems together in the gathering dusk. It would be dark soon, and they would have to go to bed.

Shay looked down at her own hands—Gabriel's hands. They were tiny, still a bit plump with baby fat, like Elena's. Was he four years old? Five?

"When fall comes, we have to move from the nursery," Gabriel said, reaching for a flower. "I'll be with only boys."

"Older boys." Elena smiled, and Gabriel smiled with her. He always did. She was his best friend. "I want to be with the older girls."

It meant they were big now, that they were too old for the nursery with the babies, Gabriel knew. Not that there were any babies. Only Gabriel and Elena, Lysander, and Philo. Philo was the youngest, and he was three. Mistress was happy when no new babies came. She said it was a blessing.

"I will miss you," Shay said, tears filling her eyes. His eyes.

Elena noticed and flung her arms around him. "We will still play every day," she promised. "And we will collect the berries together as we always do."

"Children! To bed!" Mistress's voice was strong and commanding, as usual. Elena made a face—they couldn't finish the flower chain. But there was no point in disobeying. Mistress would find them and carry them to bed if she had to.

It was dark in the nursery, and Philo was already asleep. Gabriel lay down on his cot next to Elena's, and they both giggled as Lysander began to sing. He sang every night, nonsense songs to make himself sleepy.

The screams sounded far away.

Lysander's singing faltered for a moment, then went on.

"I heard something," Elena whispered.

"It was the wind," Gabriel told her.

But the next scream was louder. Hoarse voices shouting. A woman begging for mercy, sobbing. Could that be Mistress? Gabriel's blood ran cold. Mistress never cried.

"I'm afraid." Elena was crying now too. Lysander had stopped singing. Outside, the dogs were barking and footsteps sounded in the older children's rooms.

Gabriel stood on his cot and peered over the window ledge. The fire in the central courtyard blazed, and there were people . . . grown men and women, people who shouldn't be here.

"Not the children! For God's sake, not the children," Mistress's voice sobbed. Gabriel saw her now, at the edge of the firelight. A tall man had her held against him, pinning her arms down as she struggled and cried. He bent to Mistress's throat . . . and bit her.

Gabriel dropped down onto his cot, his breath coming fast. Elena threw herself into his arms, shaking with fear.

"Your age, girl? Your age!" a harsh voice shouted from the next room.

"Nine." It was Melina, Gabriel realized. She slept in the girls' dormitory.

"Too old," another grown voice said. "Find the young ones."

Melina screamed, but only for a brief second. Gabriel pictured the man biting Mistress. Had someone bitten Melina, too?

"Run." He grabbed Elena's hand and dragged her off the cot, toward the door that led to Mistress's room. They were coming from the girls' dormitory, on the other side of the nursery. "Run!" he yelled to Lysander and Philo.

Elena was sobbing as they fled through the door. Mistress's room seemed empty without her loving presence. It had always been a place of safety before, but Gabriel knew they couldn't stay there.

He pulled Elena behind him, out the door into the garden, past the persimmon tree, up the path toward the top of the hill.

"Where is Lysander?" Elena cried. "Philo?"

Gabriel looked behind them. The other two weren't there.

"We have to take care of the babies." Elena was pulling away, heading back toward the orphanage.

"No!" Gabriel couldn't bear the thought of Elena being hurt, like Mistress and Melina. "I'll go. You hide." He pushed her down behind a bush. "They won't find you."

Elena's blue eyes were wide with fear. Gabriel turned and ran back down the path—until strong arms grabbed him, lifted him off the ground.

"Let go!" He squirmed against the man's chest, twisted about until he found purchase, then sank his teeth into the wiry forearm, breaking the skin, tasting blood.

With a cry, the man dropped him. Gabriel hit the dusty ground running . . . but he only got two steps before the man had him again.

Elena screamed, and Gabriel whipped his head toward the sound. The bush where he'd left her was rustling. She mustn't come out of hiding. She mustn't let this man see her. "No!" he yelled as loudly as he could. "Don't!"

The bush stopped moving, but Gabriel couldn't be sure Elena knew he was talking to her. He went limp in the man's arms. Maybe if he let himself be taken, the man wouldn't notice the rustling bushes, wouldn't remember the girl's scream.

"Good," the man said, holding Gabriel away from himself so they could see each other's faces. Gabriel met his eyes, determined to show no fear. The man held him tightly, but gently. "No more fighting?"

Gabriel shook his head, wishing they could just go, just leave here so Elena would be safe.

He couldn't help himself; his gaze flicked over to where he'd left her. She was still hiding, but he could see her through the branches, her eyes locked with his. She was crying.

The man turned to look where Gabriel had, and Gabriel caught his breath. *No!* How could he have been so thoughtless? If Elena were found, it would be his fault. She stayed motionless now, terrified, but Gabriel could still make out her form.

"The night is dark, boy," the man said quietly. "Not even I can see everything."

He turned away from Elena and carried Gabriel down the path, back into the firelight of the orphanage. Gabriel stared at Elena's hiding place until the bush was nothing but a spot of blackness in the distance. The screams had ended and even the dogs had stopped barking. In the courtyard the loudest sound was the crackling of the fire.

"Two small boys are with Gwen," said the tall man who had bitten Mistress. Gabriel's stomach rolled over when he spotted her lying lifeless at the man's feet. "The rest were too old."

"This one fought like a warrior, but he's young," the man carrying Gabriel said.

"Did you see any others?" the tall man asked.

"No, Ernst." Gabriel knew he was lying. This man had seen Elena; he was sure of it. "But three boys is enough."

Ernst reached out and took Gabriel's face in his hand. Gabriel's pulse pounded in terror. Would he be bitten now? But Ernst simply nodded. "He's young. Bring him along, Sam."

As they followed Ernst toward a small group of people waiting in the darkness, Gabriel began to cry. Shay felt the shuddering sobs in her own body, felt Gabriel's anguish as if it were her own.

Mistress was the only mother he'd ever known, and now she lay on the ground. Fear coursed through Gabriel's little body—through Shay's body. The other adults at the orphanage—the teacher, the farmhand—they were dark lumps on the ground as Sam headed away from the buildings.

"It only looks frightening, boy," Sam murmured. "You will come to understand in time."

"Are they all dead?" Gabriel sobbed. "The older boys and girls?"

"No one is dead," Sam replied. "They will wake with the sun, and they will search for you. But they will not find you."

"He bit Mistress. She looks dead." Gabriel could not stop the tears, even when he saw Philo in the arms of a plump woman, Lysander being lifted onto a horse in front of Ernst. There were six of them, the attackers. Six horses. They would be moving fast.

"We needed strength, and we took it from your people by drinking of them," Sam told him. "But that is all. We do not take the Givers' lives."

"You're taking us, too," Gabriel said.

Sam smiled, a little sadly. "Yes. We take strength and youth. Tell me your name, boy."

"Gabriel," Shay said.

"What's that, honey?" her mom asked.

Shay blinked, confused, her mother's face melding with Sam's for a moment as Martin took the needle from her arm.

Shay gasped, bolting upright in her bed. "No!"

"It's okay, Shay, you were dreaming," her mother said, taking her hand. "This wasn't a regular transfusion, was it?" she hissed at Martin.

"The regular ones aren't—" Martin began.

But Shay's mother had already turned her attention back to Shay. "You're okay."

No, I'm not, Shay thought. I want more.

FIVE

○ ○ ○ ○ ○ ○ ○ ○ ○ ○ ○ ○ ○ ○ ○ ○ ○

"MOM, I JUST READ AN ARTICLE about this great meditation CD. A scientist and a Buddhist worked on it together. It uses a lot of the new information on neurolinguistic programming," Shay said. She sat at the kitchen table as her mother rinsed the lunch dishes.

"Sounds interesting," Mom said, exactly as Shay had known she would. Her mother was into pretty much anything that involved using the mind to help the body.

"Yeah," Shay agreed. "I was thinking I might try it. Maybe I'll order it on Amazon."

"I'll run out to Light and Enlightenment," her mother offered—exactly as Shay had known she would. Her mother wanted to do anything possible that might improve Shay's health. She also loved the New Age-ish book store. "What's it called?"

"*Science of the Ages.* There's some subtitle about combining ancient wisdom and cutting-edge research," Shay answered, a little ashamed at how easily the lie tripped off her tongue. As far as Shay knew, there was no CD with this title. Which meant her mother would be gone for a while, trying to find something that didn't exist.

She left as soon as the last dish was stowed. Shay waited until she saw the car pull out of the driveway, then she jogged in place until she had a tiny bit of sweat going and her pulse was elevated—which didn't take long.

Here goes, she thought as she headed to Martin's study. Playing Martin wasn't quite as easy as playing her mom, but she had to make it work. Tonight was too important. Shay gave a quick knock, then stepped inside. She let herself flop down into the nearest chair. Martin looked surprised to have a visitor.

"How goes it?" he asked.

"So-so," Shay answered. "You?"

"I'm more interested in you right now," Martin said. "You look a little off."

"Please don't turn into my mother," Shay said. She wanted Martin to bring up the idea of a transfusion, without having a clue that the idea was really hers. It wasn't as if she was lying. She *was* weaker. The jogging to up her pulse was simply a precaution, to make absolutely sure Martin said yes to a transfusion today.

He stood and walked over to her. He placed two fingers on her wrist and looked at his watch. "A little fast," he commented. His eyes flicked over her face and Shay knew he took in the beads of sweat along her hairline. Martin noticed pretty much everything, all the time, like some kind of machine that stored data to be evaluated later. Some part of him was always scanning, interpreting, researching.

Say it, Shay silently begged. *Say it; say it.*

"A transfusion on Monday and then again on Thursday," he said slowly. "I know that's a lot this week already. But I think it might be time for another one."

His tone was tentative, as if he were giving her bad news. And in a way he was. Shay knew what he was thinking—the new blood worked better, but it didn't work for as long. Maybe it wasn't the new blood. Maybe it was just her body. Maybe nothing would—or could—work for as long anymore. Even the effects of the old blood had started wearing off more quickly.

Martin never said anything like that out loud, and neither did Mom. What was there to say? That Shay was dying? They all already knew that.

"We could probably hold off until tomorrow," Martin added.

"May as well get it over with now," Shay said, trying to sound sad. Trying to sound as if she hadn't planned this entire thing. "I *could* use some more energy."

"You get in bed. I'll go get the transfusion equipment," Martin said.

And then I'll definitely have enough strength for tonight, Shay thought. Because tonight, she was going to the dock.

Everyone at school hung out at the dock every weekend, even when it got incredibly cold in the wintertime. Shay wasn't really sure why, or what happened there, she just knew that she was the only one who had never gone. And she was going to go, even if it was the last thing she ever did.

But she couldn't tell her mother about it. And even Martin had started getting on her case about not pushing herself too hard. His worry wasn't the same as Mom's though. Martin seemed more concerned that he was running out of time to help her, to figure out how to capitalize on this new blood treatment. The more Shay exhausted herself, the faster the strength of the transfusions wore off. He needed more time to research. Shay sympathized, but that wasn't going to stop her from living her life while she could.

And after Martin gave her this transfusion, she'd be able to live it to the fullest.

"Why are you in such a rush?" Millie asked. "Hot date?"

Shay shook her head—*Gabriel* shook his head—and shoved down the feelings of sadness and guilt that filled him at those words. Millie was joking, of course, but her words had reminded him of his last conversation with Sam. It was years ago now, but the memory was as painful as if it had been yesterday. The price of a long life was that years felt like hours.

But why is he sad? Shay wondered. *Did something happen to Sam?* Her thoughts were fleeting, disappearing as soon as they came. While the blood flowed into her veins through the transfusion tube, Shay wasn't in control.

"I can't be late. I'm meeting with the Duke University people tonight," Gabriel said, trying to match Millie's conversational tone.

"Right—how could I forget? Ernst has been lecturing me about staying out of sight and how to act if one of them stumbles across us." Millie shoved a lock of her curly red hair behind her ears and slipped her night-vision glasses back onto her face. Then she took them off. "Why do we even bring these things?"

"In case some lost hiker comes across us, or the state sends a regulator to check up on our work," Gabriel replied. "We can't be too careful."

"I see twenty times better without them," Millie grumbled, but her quick smile told him she understood. When it came to humans finding out about the family's true nature, every precaution must be taken.

Gabriel ignored his own glasses and peered through the darkness of the cavern. No sunlight had reached this place in thousands of years, but he could see each stalactite clearly, each boulder and pebble and drop of water.

The bats were sleeping. Hibernating. The sound of their slow heartbeats soothed Gabriel. Sometimes he wished he could do that, hibernate for months, when his memories became too hard to bear—of Greece, and of his family, and of Sam.

"I think I should be insulted that Ernst never chooses me to face-to-face with the humans," Millie said, jerking him back to reality. "I can't even remember the last time I talked to one."

"It's not an insult. Be flattered that he spares you," Gabriel replied. "Ernst considers it a chore to make me interact with them. He'd like us all to avoid any contact with people."

"Then why make you meet with them?" Millie asked. "I don't get him."

"Zero contact is too suspicious," Gabriel answered. "As a bunch of bat-obsessed scientists, people are okay with us keeping to ourselves most of the time. But if we never had any contact with outsiders, it would cause too much speculation."

"I guess." Millie sounded doubtful.

"And we need to make money. It's pretty much impossible to do that without at least some interaction with humans," Gabriel said.

"Well . . . it's impossible to do it *legally*," Millie joked.

What is going on? Shay wondered, her mind struggling to understand. Night-vision goggles, and Duke, and a vampire girl dressed in jeans . . . it was too strange. For the first time, Shay felt her own mind trying to push its way into the vision.

Gabriel suddenly jumped, leaping in one move from the cave floor to the top of a rock spire twenty feet in the air. The rush of air past his face, the brief feeling of weightlessness . . . it made him smile. It made Shay smile. She was clinging to the rock now, a mere foot or two beneath the upside-down bats. Her own thoughts vanished as she peered at their wizened faces, searching for any signs of the white-nose syndrome that was spreading through America's bat population.

Millie had jumped up next to her, silent in the cool air of the cave.

"No signs of the fungus on these little guys," Millie murmured, studying the faces of the sleeping animals. "There's another colony up in the crag there. We'll need climbing equipment to get to them—if we're worrying about hikers. A twenty-foot climb we can explain. Not a fifty-foot one."

"No time tonight, I have to get back to the lab. We'll send Richard and Luis tomorrow." Gabriel turned away from the bats and let go of the rock. Down was even better than up—like flying. He didn't bother preparing to land. He knew the strength of his legs would absorb the impact.

Shay gasped with pleasure right along with Gabriel. To fall

through the air with absolutely no fear . . . it was exhilarating! *But is that my feeling, or his?* she wondered. This vision felt so odd, so different from the others, that there was a creeping sense of confusion in Shay's mind. Or was it Gabriel's mind?

He's more closed-off than usual, Shay's thought told her. But then Gabriel took a deep breath, and a dozen different scents filled her nose. Shay's thoughts vanished, melting into the sensations Gabriel was experiencing.

The entrance to the cavern was a ten-minute hike from here, following a trail they'd marked fifteen years ago, when the family first came to Tennessee. The scents coming from outside the cave were so familiar to Gabriel—pine, sandy clay, oil, dogwood, algae from the lake—and, yet, somehow forever fascinating.

"What are you going to tell the Duke people?" Millie asked, landing beside him.

"It's just the quarterly update on our research. They want to know that their money isn't being wasted." Gabriel shrugged. He wasn't like Sam had been. He didn't *enjoy* interacting with humans. But he could handle it. The scientists from the university were passionate about the bat project, interested in the sonar applications. It wasn't hard to talk to them. And as long as he had fed recently, the scent of their blood didn't bother him.

"I could do that. I could absolutely do that. Tell Ernst to give me the chore," Millie coaxed. "I know you don't like it."

"You're young. It's easier for me to withstand the temptation of their blood." Gabriel was old enough now that he could go for weeks at a time without feeding. Millie had given up the sun less than a century ago. She still needed human blood at least once a week. Perhaps that was another reason Ernst trusted only Gabriel with the scientists. The rest of their new family was still so young that they might lose control, do something . . . *inhuman* . . . and put the whole family in danger.

Shay shivered at the fear that spiked through Gabriel just thinking about humans. He didn't want Millie to see how frightened he was by this meeting, by every meeting with their university colleagues. It was always Gabriel, alone, who did it.

Ernst hated humans too much to trust himself near them. He could control his hunger, but not his raw fury. He couldn't bring himself to have a civil conversation. And for other members of the family, like Millie, there was a temptation to be too friendly, too curious about the outside world. Gabriel was the perfect spokesman. He hated the humans as much as Ernst did, but he could control himself enough to present the facade of a genial colleague. And he would never be tempted to get too close.

He knew the consequences.

Another wave of guilt, hot and nauseating, swamped Gabriel. *Sam* . . . Shay caught a flicker of Sam's face, but Gabriel pushed the thought away. Had it been his thought or hers? She couldn't tell.

"How many people are coming?" Millie asked. "I like to know just who I'm hiding from."

"It's not hiding; it's simply staying in the private quarters," Shay said with Gabriel's mouth. In the living facility, it was only the family. Most of the time, it was just family in the labs, too. All they needed was each other. The only time they even ventured into town was if they needed to feed and the blood shipment that they ordered through the Internet was late.

"Say hello to the world for me." Millie sounded sad, so Gabriel slipped an arm around her shoulders.

"You aren't missing anything. I'm just going to give a tour of the lab, answer some questions," Gabriel told her. She sighed. "You weren't one of us yet when it happened. You don't understand," he continued. "But the isolation is necessary for our safety."

"I trust you and Ernst," she said. "I just get cabin fever sometimes, all alone up here. Luis says some families live in cities."

"He doesn't know any more than we do. He grew up in our family." Gabriel could feel by the pull of the moon above that it was getting late. "I need to run, Mils." He gave her shoulders a squeeze and took off through the darkness.

The trail was marked, but Gabriel didn't need it. He knew the twists and turns of these caverns by heart. They were his whole world now. He was running fast, jumping over the biggest rocks, almost flying. The ten-minute hike would take about two minutes this way, and it was fun. It got his blood pumping to run.

Fun. The pounding pulse, the air rushing past my skin. It is fun, Shay's thought whispered.

Outside, the moon was rising. The scientists would be here at eight o'clock. Gabriel rushed into the lodge, where Ernst was waiting.

"They'll be here soon, I can smell them," Ernst said. "Here's the paperwork, numbers on the diseased colonies, updates on the sonar findings." He handed Gabriel a binder full of charts and papers.

"Ernst . . . in another year or so, I'll have to go back to school. The date on my doctorate doesn't exactly match my face anymore," Gabriel said. "Even though, as we all know, I was a savant who skipped most of high school."

Ernst sighed. He hated moving the family, establishing new identities. But it was necessary every few decades, to avoid detection by the humans.

"It's different for you. You're elusive, with a reputation for eccentricity. No one has seen even a picture of you in years," Gabriel went on, choosing his words carefully. "We can all ride on *your* degrees for another ten years, since none of the humans see you—they'd probably be willing to do a conference call instead of coming in person. If we say that the famous Dr. Ernst Geiger will be on the call—"

"No." The word was like an angry bark. "We need the humans, my son, but I am not ready to interact with them, even to that degree," he added, his voice softening. "I can't bear to put on a show, the way you do when the scientists insist on visiting here."

The alarm sounded from the laboratory building, signaling that the Duke people were at the door. Ernst turned and vanished into his private rooms, and Gabriel headed toward the hallway that connected the lodge to the main lab. Out of habit, he stopped at the mirror, just to make sure he looked normal enough for the humans.

His hair was a mess, and there was a smudge of dirt on one cheek—

"All done," Martin's voice sounded harsh.

Shay gasped, grabbing for the needle as he pulled it away. Martin frowned down at her hand, clutching his like a claw.

"I need more," she whispered. *Just enough to figure out what's going on with Gabriel.*

"No, that's enough." Martin pulled away from her. "I think you're still half-asleep. I'm not sure yet why this treatment makes you so fatigued initially. You conk out every time."

Shay collapsed back against her pillows as he left the room. She felt stunned. The blood had left her strong, like it always did. But the dream this time . . . it was bizarre. Gabriel in modern clothes, with different people, in America. It had seemed like a different world from the previous visions.

Shay grabbed the journal from her nightstand.

I saw him! I saw Gabriel! I mean, in the vision I was looking at myself, because in the vision I am Gabriel. But I remember how he looked. And wow. Seriously, wow. He's got this incredible hair, dark and curly and thick. And his eyes are almost the same color, this rich dark brown, sort of a chestnut color. I sound like a dork. But he's gorgeous.

Okay, that's creepy.

It's creepy, right? I was looking in the mirror, at myself, but at the same time I was also thinking, "Damn, he's hot!" That's how it is in those visions, or dreams, or hallucinations. Whatever they are. I am Gabriel, I'm in his body, I feel what he feels, and I see what he sees. But on some level I'm also myself, kind of. It's as if I'm watching from somewhere way in the back, and I can't say anything or do anything, or even really think my own thoughts very much. But then, when it's over and the transfusion is done, I remember it all and I can make my own judgments. So it's not like I was actually feeling attracted to myself. But still. Weird.

I know I should be worried because I'm seeing things. I should tell Martin what happens every time I have a transfusion of this new blood, because it's obviously a side effect. I never had visions or dreams during my treatments before. But it seems, I don't know, private.

And I don't want to bring up anything thing that will make Martin—or my mom—decide my new transfusions should be stopped and re-evaluated. I have to have my visions. There's so much I want to know about Gabriel. So much I don't understand.

Like Sam.

In this last vision, Sam was gone. I don't know what happened, but I could tell he wasn't part of Gabriel's life anymore. Whatever it was, it made Gabriel feel overwhelming grief and guilt. Maybe they had a fight? Do vampires do that? It seems so mundane. But I still want to know! It's as if every vision gives me a different piece of a puzzle. Is Sam the good friend who was there to support Gabriel's decision to join the vampire family? Or is he the scary man who kidnapped Gabriel when he was small? (Although he seemed gentle, even in that vision. But WTF? How could someone do that to a little boy?)

And the same with Ernst. Sometimes he's frightening, like when he attacked the orphanage and when he talked about how he hates humans. But then when I had a vision during my transfusion on Thursday, Ernst was so compassionate toward a little human girl.

In that one, Gabriel and Ernst were by themselves, watching a house at night. I don't know when it was, but the air was cold enough that I could see my breath. I mean, Gabriel could see his breath. So maybe they'd already left Greece? Anyway, someone in the house had died of influenza. The father. And Ernst thought the mother might die too. If she did, they were going to sneak in and take the little girl who lived there. They would make her part of their family, just like they had with Gabriel when he was little. Ernst terrified me in that vision when he attacked Gabriel's orphanage. But this time, he was incredibly thoughtful. He kept saying that he hoped the mother lived, that he didn't want the little girl to experience such a terrible loss. To lose both parents, such a tragedy.

What's funny is that Gabriel couldn't quite get it. He'd never known his own parents, so he didn't mourn for them. He kept thinking how Ernst was basically his father, and how he loved Ernst and would hate to lose him. That was the only way he could relate to the idea.

It's how I feel about my father. I never knew him, so there's never been anything to feel sad about. I know Mom hates him. She never said so, but I could always tell. Her mouth gets all pinched whenever she even mentions him and she never wants to talk about him. He left her, abandoned her—and me, I guess. So I get that she hates him for it. But I don't. You have to know someone in order to feel anything for them, and I don't know my dad.

That's what Gabriel said, to Ernst. That he'd never known his parents. Then he asked if that meant he didn't really know himself.

But Ernst just smiled. He said that even if your conscious mind doesn't hold memories of your parents, your soul holds on to them. Your body knows who they were; the knowledge is written in your very cells. Who they were is who you are, so there's no need to trouble yourself. That's what he told Gabriel, and Gabriel thought it was so beautiful.

I think it's beautiful too. Maybe my soul knows my father, the way my conscious mind knows my mother. I always think that all I have of my dad is the locket he gave Mom and maybe my disease.

But now I think Ernst was right. I think my dad is inside me, all the pieces of him, somewhere.

That makes it easier. I might die without ever even meeting him. I probably will. But that doesn't mean I don't know him down in my soul.

See—Ernst was very cool that night.

I guess if you look at somebody's life over hundreds of years, they're nice sometimes and scary sometimes, but it makes the visions kind of hard to track, especially because I'm seeing all these snippets out of order.

When Gabriel was young, in Greece, the clothes were strange and the places were simple. Old-fashioned. I don't know when it was that Sam took him from the orphanage, but it was definitely a long time ago. But then today, I had a vision of Gabriel wearing normal clothes, living in Tennessee, using modern technology.

I have no idea if whatever it was that happened between him and Sam took place hundreds of years ago or just last week. Vampires are immortal, at least in the movies. How long has Gabriel even been alive?

Okay, I know he's not actually alive, but still . . . I want to know more. I want to know how the puzzle fits together.

I'm sure I'll have another vision—another transfusion—in a few days. Soon enough, I'll need them every day, and then every hour, and then not at all.

I'm dying.

Could that be what these visions are? My brain's way of dealing with death? Maybe my neurons are firing like crazy, giving me something interesting to think about, to distract me so I don't freak out.

Or else it's metaphysical—they're memories of another life, a past life. Maybe I was Gabriel once. When you're dying, it makes sense that you might start to remember your past lives, doesn't it?

Or maybe the visions are just a way to make me happy before the end. Because in them, I'm strong. Gabriel is so vibrant and alive. His life—and I get to experience it—is more robust than anything I've ever known. His heartbeat, his stamina, the power of his muscles—the health of that body is like a dream come true for me. Each of my senses is cranked up to an insane level. When I'm Gabriel, I don't have to think about my body at all. I just use it; I just live in it. I don't worry about how much strength my body has in reserve, and it never lets me down.

The point is, I don't care what the vision-dreams are, and I don't want Martin trying to make them go away like they're some annoying side effect. Because I love them. Because of the visions, I'm having the best time of my life.

(And real life isn't bad either. When I'm on the transfusion high, I can do anything. Yesterday I cut class and went to the Dairy Queen with Chris Briglia. Another dream come true! And Lai-wan is like my new BFF, which is hilarious because she's a total flake. It's fun, not caring what the consequences are. Why should I care? If I'm not going to be here for much longer, there aren't any consequences. I'm sure Olivia is going to be there at the dock tonight. I'm sure she'll still be giving me the silent treatment. But I don't care. Life's too short to care. My life is too short.)

Shay stopped writing. It was getting kind of heavy, and she hadn't meant to go there. She'd wanted to write about Ernst, about how much Gabriel loved him, then she'd gotten sidetracked.

Gabriel's relationship with Ernst had been making her really think about her own family lately. Ernst was essentially Gabriel's stepfather. He'd raised Gabriel after taking him from the orphanage. He'd taught Gabriel how to drink blood. And Gabriel adored him, the way Shay adored her mother.

Martin is my stepfather, she thought uneasily. *But I don't love him like that.*

Shay sighed. She was grateful to Martin. That's what she always felt. Gratitude. Life was easier since they'd found him, because she and Mom weren't traveling all over looking for new doctors anymore. Because Mom didn't have to work three jobs just to keep up with the minimums on Shay's medical bills. Martin took care of them, both of them.

And she was grateful. But love? Not really.

"Maybe the visions are my inner shrink," she murmured. Maybe she'd made Gabriel up as a way to unravel all her own issues—her missing father, her stepfather, even her own weakness and the way the strength of this new blood was like an addiction to her. She glanced down at her journal. Past lives, psychobabble, brain chemistry gone crazy . . . did it even matter what the visions were?

Shay tossed her journal aside and stood up. Enough living in her dreams. Tonight she was going to live for real.

CHAPTER
SIX

° ° ° ° ° ° ° ° ° ° ° ° ° ° ° ° °

"ARE YOU GUYS OVER FOR GOOD?" Lai-wan asked, leaning back on her elbows. She blew a stream of smoke into the night air.

Shay glanced over at Olivia, snuggled in Kaz's arms at the far end of the dock. She could hear the rushing water, but it was invisible in the darkness. "Who knows?" she replied. "Kaz won't even look me in the eye."

"He's just scared," Brian Kiley said from the other side of Lai-wan. "If I got caught kissing some other girl, I'd be scared too."

"I heard that!" Jacey yelled from the reeds along the river's edge, where she was peeing or puking or God knew what. "You better not be kissing anyone else."

"See?" Brian said.

Lai-wan giggled. "I was talking about Olivia," she said. "I thought you guys were practically sisters."

"Nope," Shay said. "She's more like my lifetime chaperone, and I don't want one anymore."

Next to her, Chris Briglia lit up the pipe they were all passing around, taking a big hit. "That's pretty obvious, Shay," he wheezed.

"Seriously. You are adrenaline girl lately." Lai-wan reached for the pipe. "But still no pot, huh?"

"I don't need drugs," Shay said. "I'm high on life!"

The other three burst into the kind of druggy laughter that was only half-real, and Shay grinned. She'd been kidding, but it was actually true. Being stoned couldn't be better than feeling the health and power of the blood pumping through her right now. Anyway, fog in her mind wasn't what she wanted. She wanted to be aware, to feel every bit of every experience, and to remember every single second. Maybe these guys could afford to waste their time floating around in a drug haze, but she couldn't.

Lai-wan lay back, stretching out on the wooden dock. It extended all the way from the nearest street, across the scrub grass of the shoreline, and out at least thirty feet into the rushing Black River. There was nothing else. No houses nearby, no stores or restaurants. Not even any boats tied up to the end of the dock.

"I don't get it," Shay said. "What's the big deal about this place?"

Jacey came clomping back to their spot halfway down the dock, her footsteps making all the wood slats shake. "It's fun," she said.

"No parents," Brian added as Jacey sat down in his lap and took the pipe from him.

"And lots of stars." Lai-wan sounded dreamy, gazing up at the sky with a goofy smile.

"That's it?" Shay felt a stab of disappointment. She'd been hearing about the dock for years. People talked about it like it was Vegas or something—things happened at the dock, but nobody would ever say exactly what. And younger kids weren't allowed there. No losers, geeks, or kids without cars—or friends with cars—either. It was a cool place for cool people. Shay had been expecting . . . well, she didn't know. But not just sitting around on the damp wood, watching other people make out. "Why exactly is this fun?"

"Um, because we're stoned." Brian held out the pipe toward Shay. She shook her head again. "Olivia and Kaz aren't."

"I'm not, either. Not much," Chris said. "You don't have to be; you can still have a good time." He inched closer to Shay, his hand brushing against the side of her thigh. Shay let it stay there, but she felt like laughing. She'd practically thrown herself at Chris during Kaz's party, and he'd been too afraid of her to do anything about it. But now that she just treated him like any other guy, he was always flirting.

"So that's it? People just come here and hang out?" Shay asked. "It sounded more glam when I'd never seen it."

"Well, there's always the island," Chris said.

"That's a load of crap," Brian replied. "Total myth."

"What is?" Shay asked.

"Supposedly people swim out to the island in the middle of the river," Lai-wan said. "You know that little spit of land you see when you take the Route 5 bridge?"

"I guess." Shay couldn't remember ever noticing any island in the river, but then, she couldn't remember ever looking, either. What else had she missed by not really seeing? When she was Gabriel, she noticed everything.

"There's all kinds of stories about kids who swam out there from the dock," Chris said. "You swim to the island and you carve your name in this big rock there to prove that you did it."

"I heard John Fox did it three years ago," Jacey said. "Remember him? He was a senior when we were freshmen."

"He was hot," Shay said. She'd never even said hello to him, but she remembered that much.

"He was on the swim team," Brian put in. "If he did it, that's why. But I doubt it. You know how fast the current is?"

"My sister says it's just an urban legend," Lai-wan agreed. "And that she'd kill me if I ever actually tried it."

"That's because of the kid who drowned." It was the first thing Olivia had said all night, and Shay jumped, surprised to see that her best friend had come over to join the group. "Back in the nineties, some sophomore tried to get to the island and got swept away."

"No way. *That's* the urban legend," Chris replied. "If somebody actually died, they would've ripped out the dock and put up barbed wire."

"Is the river really that fast? How far is it?" Shay asked.

Brian shrugged. "Far enough that you can only barely see it from the end of the dock."

"I want to try it." Shay stood up.

Everybody gaped at her. "Can you even swim?" Lai-wan asked.

"Of course." Shay ignored the trickle of worry making its way up her spine. She'd taken swimming lessons as a way to exercise without overexerting herself. It kept her heart strong; that's what Mom had always said. But that was in a pool, always. Shay had never even swum in a lake, or the ocean, or anywhere nonchlorinated.

But Gabriel did, she thought, remembering the salty taste of the ocean in Greece. He'd been able to swim through the waves with no effort at all, and that was even before he gave up the sun. How fast could he swim once he was a vampire? As fast as he had run in her last vision?

"Shay, we are not going to have this fight again." Olivia sounded tired. "Even if you weren't you, nobody would let you go to the island. Regular people don't try it, so you definitely can't."

So the silent treatment was done. Unfortunately, Olivia had taken back the role of Shay's second mom. And right now, Shay didn't even really want the first one. Her mother turned into more of a Hovercraft every day.

"Since I'm so irregular, I might be the one to make it," Shay said. "My new treatments are like being on speed or something. I'm stronger than ever. I'm doing it."

She headed off toward the river, the night growing darker around her as the dock left land and went into the water. Shay smelled it, sort of a muddy scent, and she heard the plunking sounds of the waves slapping against the supports underneath her. The footsteps of her friends weren't far behind.

"You're being an idiot," Olivia practically screamed.

"Shay, everybody who tries this ends up turning around," Chris told her, jogging up to Shay's side. "It's actually dangerous. And the water's really cold."

"So I'll swim fast," she said. "Come on, aren't you curious? I want to see if anyone's name is really on that rock."

They'd reached the end of the dock, and Shay peered into the darkness. She didn't have Gabriel's night vision. She couldn't see a thing.

"It's straight out," Brian said, "but you can't get to it if you can't watch it while you swim."

"There." Shay smiled as her eyes adjusted to the darkness over the water. It wasn't as clear as Gabriel's sight, but she could make out the top of a tree, black against the sky. "I see it."

"I don't," Kaz muttered, peering over the river.

"Oh my God, I'm getting a flashlight from my car." Jacey took off running back toward shore. Shay sat down on the end of the dock, dangling her legs over the edge, and pulled off her sneakers.

"Should I call the cops?" Kaz asked. She didn't know if he was asking her, or Olivia, or just the universe.

"You guys are freaking out because you're wasted. How hard can it really be? I bet it's much less scary during the day," Shay said.

"If you get there, you'll be famous," Lai-wan said reverently. "*Everyone* will know."

"That's worth it," Shay said. Worth any danger. Worth drowning. Worth trying. It would be worth it to go down having fun and trying something new instead of lying in a bed waiting for her own blood to betray her. "Anyone coming? Buddy system, you know."

"I'm your buddy," Chris said, shocking her.

She grinned at him, completely forgiving him for Kaz's party. "Thank you!"

"If you're sure . . ." Chris began.

"Let's go." Shay launched herself off the end of the dock before she could think anymore, before Chris could chicken out, and before Olivia could grab her. She heard a few gasps, and Olivia yelling, and then the black water closed over her head.

Freezing.

Shay came up for air, treading water and already regretting her jeans, which felt like wet cement stuck to her legs. It was cold. Beyond cold. "I'm in," she called up. She had to move or she'd sink. Kicking as hard as she could, she turned herself toward the opposite shore and started swimming.

Two seconds later there was a splash behind her. Shay didn't stop. Maybe it was Kaz or Olivia coming to drag her out. Maybe it was Chris. Either way, she was going. A quick glance at the sky showed her the tree she was aiming for.

"Jesus, the current is strong." Chris swam up beside her, his teeth chattering.

"Yeah." Shay tried to ignore the insistent pull of the water. She had to swim left just to go straight. It was hard to keep track of where the island was. This was why people couldn't do it, she realized. If they couldn't see that tree, they didn't know where to aim. The current pulled them to the side and they probably swam right past the island. "This way," she sputtered. "Pull left."

Chris just grunted, swimming for all he was worth.

Shay pumped her arms, kicking as hard as she could, powering herself through the water. Her muscles did exactly what she wanted, her heart beating as steady as a drum. Like Gabriel's.

What if my strength goes—like it did on the track?

The thought made the water feel even colder. For a moment,

Shay could picture herself sinking, sinking, sinking, her muscles too weak to get her back to the surface.

"I'm too tired," Chris gasped from beside her. "We have to turn back."

"No, we're close," she said. "I see it." She did, a deeper darkness looming above the choppy water. Twenty more feet and they'd be there.

Shay's body wasn't showing any signs of fatigue. Her fear was only that—fear. But Chris was slowing down. Shay reached out for him and grabbed his hand. "We're almost there and we can rest," she cried.

He nodded, his eyes frightened.

Shay let him go and swam forward, smooth, even, wonderful strokes, enjoying the push of the current against her body. She kept her gaze fixed on the tree in the darkness, hoping Chris could follow her. In a few seconds she felt her arm hit something hard and slimy—a rock. Shay felt a burst of relief. She ran her hand across the rock until she found the top, then pulled herself up on it. "Chris!" she called. "Give me your hand!"

Leaning out over the water, she caught hold of him and held on until he could make his way up the rock. Together they crawled across it and onto a narrow spit of land, rocky and barren except for the one twisted tree Shay had seen.

"We did it!" Shay let out a whoop, yelling so they could hear her back on shore. But if they answered, their voices were lost in the rushing sound of the river. "Where's the rock?" She scrambled over the hard ground, looking for a boulder.

"Over here," Chris said. He flopped down on the ground next to it, panting. "This may be the stupidest thing I've ever done."

"Worth it though, right? What a complete thrill. Whoo-hoo!" Shay cried.

"Whoo-hoo," Chris echoed, without a lot of enthusiasm.

Shay went over to him, shivering in the night air. There was a huge rock sticking up from the water on the far side of the island. She ran her fingers over it, feeling for carvings. "There," she said. She leaned closer, peering at the place where she felt an indentation. "Initials."

"John Fox?" Chris asked.

"I don't know. It's too dark." Shay frowned. "How are we even supposed to carve? Do you have a knife?"

"We could use a smaller rock," he said. "Or we could just tell everyone we did it. They're not gonna check."

"Wimp," she teased him.

"You know it," Chris answered. Shay threw herself down beside him, grinning.

What Sick Girl? she thought. *I'm famous! Anyone who can make it to the legendary island can't be just a sick girl.*

"Look at the stars!" Shay urged. "They're like a million times brighter on this side. Or maybe they just look that way because I'm so pumped!"

"I can't believe we have to swim back," Chris groaned. Shay didn't think he'd even glanced at the sky.

Shay lifted herself up onto her elbow and leaned over him. "It won't be as bad. We can let the current take us downstream if we want, we'll still hit the shore. We can walk back to the dock."

Chris chuckled. "I wouldn't have thought of that."

"I can't believe you came with me," she said.

"I can't believe *you* did it at all," he told her. "You're not who I thought."

"Not Sick Girl," she murmured. "I never was, inside."

"Not Sick Girl at all," Chris said, pulling her face down to his. He kissed her, his lips cold from the water. But when he opened his mouth it was warm. Shay relaxed into the kiss as he moved his hands across her back, into her hair.

Gabriel would have looked at the stars, Shay thought absently.

She opened her eyes, surprised. That was not a thought she needed to be having right now. This was a real kiss. Not like Kaz. That was just an experiment with a friend, a drunken experiment. This was an actual, hot makeout session with a guy she'd liked for ages. All alone, in the dark, with adrenaline pumping through them.

So why am I bored? Shay wondered.

Chris held her tightly, their bodies warming each other up from the cold. He was as cute as ever, and he was finally acting the way she wanted . . . but she just didn't care. His blond hair was short and straight under her fingers, not thick and curly the way Gabriel's hair was. His arms around her were muscular, but not lithe like Gabriel's.

Gabriel. Shay caught her breath, astonished. It wasn't Chris Briglia she wanted. It was Gabriel. Gabriel, who wouldn't start worrying about swimming back before he'd even taken in the enjoyment of being on the island. Gabriel, who would absolutely have looked at the stars.

Gabriel, who didn't exist.

"I still say we could've stayed there longer," Chris griped as they picked their way along the riverbank, heading for the dock. "What are you afraid of?"

"I think it's pretty clear that I'm not afraid of anything," Shay told him. She knew he was talking about how abruptly she'd stopped kissing him, but she didn't feel like discussing it. What could she say? *Sorry, but I've decided that I'm more attracted to my imaginary vampire friend than I am to you?*

"There they are!" Jacey's shriek came floating on the wind. Shay had seen the thin flashlight beam as soon as she'd crawled ashore, but it had still taken almost twenty minutes to walk back upstream to the dock. Now Jacey was shining the light on them.

Chris held up his hand to block it. "Point that thing somewhere else!"

Lai-wan clambered down off the dock and ran toward them, throwing her arms around Shay. "Oh my God, you're okay! Did you do it? Did you guys make it there?"

"Yeah," Shay said.

"But we didn't carve our names in the rock. Shay was in a hurry to get back," Chris complained.

"Right, and also there was nothing to carve with. Next time I'll remember to bring a pocket knife," Shay said, annoyed.

"There's no *next time*." Olivia stood on the dock above them, arms crossed. "You guys are lucky you're not dead."

"You really did it?" Brian asked.

Shay shot Chris a look, and he finally smiled. "We did," he said. "We did the island!"

"Legendary!" Lai-wan cried. "What's it like out there?"

"The water's freezing, and the current is really fast," Shay said, letting Brian pull her up onto the dock from the riverbank. Chris climbed up behind her. "It was scary, and exciting, and definitely something to experience."

"And the island is tiny. It's like four boulders and a tree," Chris reported.

"With a great view of the stars. Anyone have a blanket?" Shay's teeth chattered as she spoke. She'd been so high on adrenaline ever since they'd jumped back in the river that she hadn't noticed the cold. But now her wet clothes felt like they were freezing in place, encasing her body in ice.

"Here." Kaz took off his jacket and handed it to her.

"We can go sit in my car," Jacey offered. "I'll turn on the heat."

"This is ridiculous," Olivia exploded. "Shay needs to go home and wrap herself up in heating pads or something. She's probably got hypothermia on top of her blood disease, and you guys are all acting like it's cool."

"It is cool," Shay insisted, although her head was beginning to ache. The swim out hadn't been bad, but the swim back had clearly used up a lot of her new-blood strength. "I'm putting it on the list of things I never thought I could do."

"Oh yeah, what will you say?" Olivia snarked. "Acted like a moron by risking my life?"

"Why do you even care?" Shay yelled. "Jeez, let me have a few moments of fun, will you?"

"No," Olivia said. "If it means watching you kill yourself, I'm not going to do that."

"Fine. Don't watch." Shay turned her back on her so-called best friend and held her hand out to Jacey. "I think we should go sit in your car."

"Great." Jacey pulled the keys from her pocket and headed down the dock. Shay followed without a glance at Olivia. But when they got there, she would ask Jacey to drive her home. Olivia was a buzz kill, but she was also kind of right. Shay couldn't stop shaking, and if she didn't get warm soon, she didn't think her body would recover.

Besides, it wouldn't matter if she left now. She was still a living legend.

"Can you climb up and sneak through your window?" Jacey asked, studying Shay's house from their parking spot at the curb. "There's no way your parents will miss the fact that you're dripping wet."

"I can't," Shay said. She physically couldn't—she felt too weak, too close to Shay-normal. But Jacey wasn't Olivia, she didn't know the limits of Shay's strength and she didn't recognize the signs of weakness. Maybe Jacey would think it meant there was no way to climb up to the second floor. "But it's only my stepfather. My mom was going to some Neighborhood Watch meeting."

"Men never notice anything," Jacey said with a shrug. "Just run for your room and tell him you're having girl problems."

"Good plan." Shay hid her smile. If she tried the girl-problems excuse with Martin, he'd probably die of embarrassment, even though he was a doctor. "Thanks for the ride."

By the time she got inside the house, Shay felt like an icicle. The cold was so complete that her insides were numb.

"Shay, you okay?" Martin asked, glancing up from the medical journal he was reading.

"When's Mom getting home?" she whispered, hugging herself to stop the shivering.

Martin was on his feet in an instant. "Not for another half hour."

He took Shay's arm and pointed her toward the stairs, helping her up to her room.

"I feel weak," she mumbled.

"I'll get the IV supplies. You put on something dry." Martin closed her door behind him. Shay stumbled over to the dresser and pulled out her warmest sweater and a pair of cords. It took forever to get changed because her fingers were so cold, but finally she was dry and the shaking had stopped. By the time Martin came back, she was in bed and under the flamingo comforter.

"Two transfusions in a day is pushing it, Shay," he said quietly.

Shay nodded. It was the closest Martin would ever get to yelling at her, she knew. There was an unspoken rule between them that he couldn't reprimand, lecture, or guilt her. That was a job for her real parent, Mom. "It's not because the effects wore off superfast. I just . . . used them up," Shay said.

"So it goes into my research as an aberration?" Martin asked.

"Yeah," Shay promised. *Translation: I abused this new treatment, and I promise not to do it again.*

Martin swabbed a spot on the back of her hand. Shay hated to have needles there, but her arms were like pincushions now. She gritted her teeth, closed her eyes, and waited for the blood. For the vision.

When I feel Gabriel's strength, it will be better, she thought. *I'll forget all about the cold, and the weakness, and I'll be healthy again for a little while.*

But there was only darkness. She could see in the dark—Gabriel could see. But he didn't know where he was, and the various cabinets and counters he was able to make out didn't give him any sense of what the place looked like.

Besides, all he could see was part of the ceiling and one wall. He lay flat on his back, and something held his body down. Or else he'd been paralyzed. He couldn't tell, couldn't feel his arms or legs. Couldn't even turn his head. It lay there, facing to the right, his eyes focused on that one wall. On the door in the middle of it.

For all he knew, there was someone behind him, getting ready to attack, and he couldn't even see them. He was helpless, defenseless. Was this how it had been for his family?

His pulse was loud in his ears, like a drumbeat. His heart slammed against his chest. He could feel that much. He felt the fear.

The door opened, spilling a shaft of cold light into the room. Not the sun. Fluorescent. A dark figure silhouetted in the doorway, a painting on the wall behind him. Sunset over the water.

Gabriel felt a stab of bitter anger. *Sunset.* If only he could move, he would attack. He would feed and not stop. He would—

"Never again!" Shay's mother jerked the needle out of her hand. Shay cried out in pain, the breath rushing out of her. "How dare you do this without even telling me?"

"She was ready to collapse," Martin retorted.

Shay's mind was reeling from the suddenness of reality crashing back in on her . . . and the strangeness of that vision. "What's happening?" she whispered.

"These treatments are ruining you!" her mother yelled. "What do you think you were doing in that river, young lady?"

Shay just gaped at her, trying to make sense of it all.

"Olivia called me on my cell," her mother continued. "She told me what you did tonight."

"I'll kill her," Shay gasped.

"You'll kill yourself!" Her mom whirled back to Martin. "Shay would never have even thought of pulling this kind of thing before we started the treatments."

"What did you do?" he asked Shay. "You jumped in the water?"

"She and some lamebrain boy swam out to an island in the middle of the Black River," Mom said. "On a dare."

"Nobody dared me; I wanted to." Shay tried to sit up farther. She wanted to get out of bed, but her legs felt heavy. She hadn't had enough blood.

"You swam there and back? Isn't there a fast current?" Martin sounded excited. "How long were you in the water? Did you do a self-check when you got out?"

"No," Shay said. "I felt fine. It was the cold that bothered me, and then I started feeling weak."

"But you were able to swim with no complications?" he pressed.

"Enough!" her mother yelled. "This is not a good thing, Martin. It's reckless, dangerous behavior. The blood is making her psychotic."

"Jesus, Mom, I'm right here. I can hear you." Shay forced her legs off the bed and stood up. She was stronger than before, just not as strong as usual after a transfusion. And her head was still foggy from the vision. Gabriel had felt more like Shay than like himself. So weak . . .

"It's working, Emma. It's the first thing that's even made a dent in her deterioration," Martin was saying. "There's no coincidence—"

"The aggression is going to kill her faster than the disease." Mom was crying as she yelled at Martin. Shay watched it all with a strange buzzing in her head. She couldn't process anything. It was as if she were still stuck in that dark room with Gabriel.

"You had to expect some side effects. With time, I can try to isolate the specific—"

"Shut up!" Shay said, cutting Martin off mid-sentence. "Both of you! I'm still too weak. I need to finish the transfusion."

"No." Her mother's tone was more decisive than Shay had ever heard. "No more of that blood. It's turning you into a stranger."

"It's letting me be who I want," Shay said.

"I've known you since the day you were born. You are not a girl who takes needless risks and puts herself in danger," her mom replied.

"Then you don't know me as well as you think," Shay snapped.

"No more of these transfusions, and that's final," her mother insisted, looking at Martin as well as Shay.

"Then I guess I'll just have to die," Shay said.

Her mother reached for her, but Shay shoved past. In the bathroom, she'd be alone. She could lock them out. She stalked inside and slammed the door. By the time she hit the lock button, Martin and Mom were already fighting again.

"...more time, or this has all been for nothing," Martin was saying.

"The blood is tainted. It's turning her—"

Shay turned on the faucet in the tub full blast, drowning out their voices. She sank down to the cool tile floor and dropped her head in her hands, trying to think. She needed blood. They could fight all night, but she didn't care. If she could just get them out of her room, she could give herself a transfusion. She knew how, after all these years.

"Martin won't leave the equipment in my room," she murmured. And even if he did, Mom definitely would notice and get it out of there.

But without the blood, even the strength she had now would disappear. She felt all right, but it wasn't enough. It wasn't what she'd gotten used to these past two weeks. And that vision . . . Gabriel so afraid . . . she had to see the rest. What had happened to him? It was the first time she'd seen him weak. Like her.

What did it mean? Her visions were usually inspiring, interesting. Not scary. Not bleak. Did it mean this was it? If Gabriel was weak, did that mean even her mind had accepted her sickness? Was she dying now?

Shay pulled herself up to the sink and stared in the mirror. Her long dark hair was a mess from the water. Her light blue eyes looked almost electric against her pale skin. But she wasn't dizzy or out of breath, and her hands weren't shaking. This was better than she'd felt for most of her life. And if Mom had her way, this was the last time Shay would feel it.

It's not enough.

She'd loved the strength of the new treatments. She wasn't ready to let go of that feeling. She wasn't ready to die. Not yet.

Maybe if I finished the vision, Gabriel would've gotten better, she thought. *Maybe that person was coming to help him.* She remembered the dark figure in the doorway, the sunset painting behind him.

"Sunset over the water." Shay shook her head. It seemed so unfair, almost as if it were there to remind Gabriel of the last time he saw the sun. No wonder he'd been angry. But there was something else. Shay frowned at her reflection. The painting—she had seen it before. Seen it lots of times, in fact. It was a watercolor that hung in Martin's office.

The realization stunned her.

"Thank you, subconscious," Shay whispered. The visions had never given her such a clear message before, but there was no mistaking it now. Martin's office—where he kept his medical supplies. Where he kept the blood he used to treat her. They never had more than a few bags here at home, and sometimes Martin went to the office before a transfusion, to get more blood.

If Mom wouldn't let Martin give her a transfusion here, she'd go to the lab and give herself one.

Shay turned off the water. It was quiet outside the door. Mom and Martin must've moved their argument downstairs, probably thinking Shay was taking a bath to calm down.

She inched open the bathroom door and tiptoed into her empty room, closing the bathroom door behind her. They wouldn't come to check on her for ten minutes or so. Enough time to get out.

Martin always left his car keys in the ignition once he was home, so he wouldn't ever lose them. It drove her mother insane, since Mom was a lock-every-door, check-every-window kind of person. But Martin figured if someone was going to break into the house, they probably weren't after the car. And the house had an alarm, after all.

He'd probably never thought that it would be someone inside the house taking the car.

Shay pulled her window open, slowly, wincing at every squeak and bump it made. But judging from the volume of the voices downstairs, she figured no one would hear a couple of odd noises.

Easing herself out onto the eave was simple. Getting over to the brick chimney was a little tougher. The roof slanted at a steep angle there, and once or twice her feet slipped, threatening to send her flying off the edge. But finally she was able to grab on to the bricks. She inched her way around, hugging the chimney for support. On the far side there was a branch that grew within a foot of the roof.

The tree limb was almost bare now, just a few yellowed leaves clinging on. Shay closed her eyes for a second, trying to steady her nerves. She would have to let go of the chimney in order to grab the branch, and if she missed she would probably fall.

It's either that or give up on ever feeling healthy again, she thought.

Shay got herself out to the very edge of the roof, hanging on to the chimney for support. *Gabriel just let go of that rock spire,* she thought, remembering her vision. *No fear. He just let go and jumped.*

She stretched her right hand out . . . closer to the branch . . . closer . . . and finally she let go of the chimney, and jumped.

One brief second of falling through the air and then she was hanging from the tree limb. She quickly grabbed on with her other hand, then pulled her legs up so she was straddling the branch. Did people really do things like this all the time? Her friends talked about sneaking out of their houses whenever they were grounded. It seemed like way too much trouble.

When Gabriel did it, it was fun. But for Shay, it had been kind of terrifying.

She gave herself only a few seconds to catch her breath, then she shimmied along the branch to the tree trunk and clambered down. She had to duck under the living room windows so Mom and Martin wouldn't see her—not that they were looking. As far as she could tell, they were having the biggest shouting match of their entire marriage. She made it to the garage, punched the alarm code into the keypad, and opened the door.

Inside Martin's Range Rover, Shay quickly adjusted the seat and the mirrors, and glanced at the gear shift and the displays. She knew how to drive, because she'd insisted on taking Driver's Ed with Olivia. It was one of those things sick girls were supposed to just opt out of, like gym and a love life. But Shay couldn't bear to be the only one who didn't know which pedal was the gas and which was the brake. She'd even gotten her learner's permit, because you just had to take a written exam for that.

But never her license, because she'd always been too weak to take the test. She could never be sure she wouldn't suddenly pass out while driving along with the examiner.

She was breaking rules all the time these days, though, so if she had to break the law by driving, what was the difference?

"Okay. Reverse." Shay started up the car and shifted as fast as she could. Mom and Martin might hear the engine, and she wanted to be gone before they came running out here. She hit the gas and tore backward down the driveway, managing to stop at the street with a jerk. Her heart pounding, Shay looked back at the house. Nobody there.

Not the smoothest start, she thought. *Must be because I only managed to get to half the Driver's Ed classes.* She shifted into DRIVE and pressed the gas more gently this time. The car felt heavier than she'd expected. Somehow, she'd thought it would be more like a video game.

Martin's office was about five miles away, but she could get there without going on any major roads. It would take longer, but the last thing she needed was to get into an accident right now.

After a moment, Shay realized she'd been holding her breath. She chuckled. Swimming to the island, sneaking out, stealing Martin's car . . . a lot of living for one day. Maybe her mom was right about this all being out of character, but only because she had a lot of living to make up for. She wouldn't usually be a car thief. But she needed the blood. She could apologize once she felt strong. And maybe she'd have to stop taking so many chances, to prove to Mom that these treatments weren't making her crazy.

Maybe then she could keep getting more transfusions. More strength. More Gabriel visions.

Shay turned the car into the parking lot of Martin's office. It was a low brick building with a yard all around it. It used to be a diagnostic testing facility or something like that. It was way too big for Martin, but he'd bought the entire building anyway. Shay figured that was just how famous doctors rolled. Big car, big house, big office.

The place was dark. She turned off the car and breathed a sigh of relief. Her hands were gripping the steering wheel like claws, kneading the leather the same way her mom did.

"I'm okay. The car's okay," she said out loud, her voice shaking. "Martin won't murder me if I bring the car back in one piece."

Shay forced her hands off the wheel and climbed out of the car. She didn't even realize until she got to the office door that the place was locked. She had Martin's key ring, but it wouldn't help. The door had an electronic lock that required a password.

Oh my God, I'm an idiot, Shay thought, staring at the glass door. She could see the waiting room inside and the doors to the lab rooms, so close. The blood that she needed was right in there, and she couldn't get to it.

Maybe she could figure out the password. Her mother's name?

His own name? Martin acted all humble, but she knew he had a healthy ego. He had entire rooms full of awards to prove it—and nobody got to go on *Oprah* unless they had a pretty high opinion of themselves.

Tentatively, she reached out and typed MARTIN onto the keypad. It flashed red, gave a disapproving beep, and stayed locked.

What else? EMMA? SHAY? The idea of it seemed absurd. Martin had joined their family, had married her mother . . . but they weren't central enough to his life to be his password. Shay lowered her hand. She didn't know how, but she was absolutely sure that their names wouldn't work.

"NOBEL PRIZE?" she whispered. That made more sense. If it ever came down to a choice between family and science for Martin, science would win. "CANCER CURE? SHAY'S CURE?"

Desperate, she typed in CURE and got the same red beep.

The lock probably wouldn't let her have many more tries before it set off an alarm. *Screw it,* Shay thought. She hadn't come this far for nothing. She returned to the Range Rover and got a tire iron. She wasn't at her post-transfusion peak, but she was strong enough to smash through this door. She could use all the strength she had. More blood was waiting for her inside.

Shay raised the tire iron high and slammed it into the glass— again, and again, and again—until she'd made a hole big enough for her to slip through. Thank God this place was so far from any other buildings and any other people who could hear her.

It was dark in the waiting room, the only light coming from the EXIT sign over the door. Shay reached for the light switch, but stopped before she flipped it on. It was late at night. She didn't want to draw any attention to herself—or the smashed-in door. Besides, she could see well enough.

The blood will be in a fridge, she thought. She remembered one room that was basically filled with refrigerators. It was one of the smaller rooms, not a big lab. Shay knew that the first door along the hallway was Martin's personal office. Beyond that, she wasn't sure. She hadn't been here in a while, and she'd never paid much attention. She had no interest in hearing the details of his research. She already knew more than she'd ever wanted to about blood and the many things that could go wrong with it.

The only thing she wanted to know now was how to get that new blood into her veins.

There were two labs, she remembered. Plus the cold room and an exam room. Maybe another storage room. She stood in the hallway for a moment, trying to remember which one was the cold room. The blood would be in there, but the IV supplies would be somewhere else. Martin might not even keep them in the exam room anymore, since he never saw patients. They might be in a supply closet. Shay glanced around as she thought. Her eyes were adjusting to the dimness in here, and light from the streetlights shone through the narrow windows that lined the top of the hall. The watercolors hung between the doors.

Shay's eyes automatically went to the sunset picture. Sunset over the water. The colors were invisible in the dark, but she could see the lines that formed the clouds. It was usually pink and orange, but now it just looked like shades of gray.

A strange tingly feeling crept up the back of her neck, as if someone were watching her. She stepped closer to the picture. Gabriel could see colors at night; she knew that from her visions. He'd seen this painting in color, even though he was in the dark. He'd seen it through the doorway. . . .

Shay's entire body felt numb even before she turned around.

She moved slowly, almost afraid to see the door right behind her. Across from the painting. Right where the door was in her vision of Gabriel.

Shay's heart slammed against her ribs, but she hardly noticed it. Strength, weakness . . . she wasn't even sure what she felt. Mostly it was just fear.

Her hand reached for the door handle, and she watched it as if she wasn't even controlling it. It was locked, of course. But there wasn't a keypad. There was a reader for a security card. And on Martin's key chain hadn't there been . . .

Shay pulled the key chain out of her pocket. A small plastic card—about the size of the ones for the grocery-store bonus programs—hung from it. She swiped the card, and the lock clicked. Shay grabbed the knob with shaking fingers and pulled the door open.

The darkness inside was deeper than in the hall. There were no windows to let in any light. But Shay could see the table. It was a regular exam table, but there was something wrong with it.

Chains.

Her brain couldn't process that. Chains stretching from the exam table down to metal loops in the floor. Why would Martin need chains on the table?

Bile rose in Shay's throat, and suddenly she noticed just how hard and fast her heart was beating. The hair on her arms stood up as she fumbled for the light switch and turned it on.

The overhead lights sputtered to life, throwing a cold white glow over the room.

Over the table.

And over the man who lay there, chained in place.

Shay didn't want to look. She didn't want to know. But really, she already *did* know. With halting steps, she moved closer, close enough to see him.

Thick, dark, curly hair. Skin a tawny bronze. Eyes as dark as his hair, sort of a chestnut color . . . staring right back at her.

"Gabriel," Shay whispered.

TWO

○ ○ ○ ○ ○ ○ ○ ○ ○ ○ ○ ○ ○ ○ ○ ○

REALITY

SEVEN

○ ○ ○ ○ ○ ○ ○ ○ ○ ○ ○ ○ ○ ○

THE SMELL WAS NEW. Not the scent of the human man or the woman who'd been there the day Gabriel was captured. He jerked his head toward the door. Too fast. The motion sent a wave of dizziness through him. He was getting weaker every day. The man brought him blood, but not enough to compensate for all the blood he drained from Gabriel's body.

Gabriel blinked, and the figure at the door became clearer. A human girl. Young. An expression of horror on her face. What else would a human feel at the sight of him?

In the quiet room, he could hear the beat of her heart, as fast as a rabbit's. He expected her to turn and bolt; instead she took a few steps toward him, hesitated, then moved right up to the edge of exam table he was chained to. She stared down at him, her blue eyes wide. "Gabriel."

Gabriel's brain felt as weak as his body. She shouldn't know his name, should she? No, it was impossible. He hadn't told it to his captors—not even in the initial e-mails that had lured him to them. So this human shouldn't know it either.

"What are you doing here?" With shaking fingers, the human girl touched the chain wrapped around his chest. "Why . . . why are you chained?"

It felt as if there was compassion in the question, in her tone, but that was impossible. It had to be some sort of ploy. Was her scent part of it? He took a deep breath, filling his lungs with it. It was as if the smell of her had been engineered to invite him. It was almost maddening, almost painful in its perfection.

She shook her head. "I feel like I fell down the rabbit hole. You're real?"

Gabriel felt light-headed from her nearness, the overpowering scent of her. It acted like a drug on his weakened senses. Something in the smell was so familiar. . . .

"You're real and in Martin's office." Her tone of voice had changed. She bit her lip, thinking. Gabriel stared at her mouth, fascinated by its youth, the blush of blood lending it a perfect pink color. "Why? Is he treating you? Are you sick?"

Martin. That must be his captor's name, the human man.

"I saw you here. You were paralyzed, you couldn't move. . . ." Her gaze focused on the thick chains for a moment. Then she looked right at him, horror in her eyes. "You were afraid."

Gabriel couldn't understand her words. How had she seen him? Was there a camera somewhere in this room, recording this torture? Did this Martin have people watching his experiments?

The girl turned away, frantically glancing around the room at the IV supplies—the pole, the bags, the tubing. Suddenly she grabbed Gabriel's hand, chained down at his side. Her fingers, cool and slim, lingered over the shunt that the man had put there. Easier to harvest his blood that way.

"No . . ." her voice trailed off, her blue eyes clouding with worry and confusion.

God, he wanted her. He was so weak, and the smell of her blood was so strong. Gabriel took another breath of her, and smelled a new odor mixed with hers.

The man. Martin.

He was close, very near the building. Had he brought this girl, then? What kind of game were they playing with him? Gabriel studied her face—pointed chin; eyes a light, pale blue; lips as soft-looking as rose petals—trying to figure out what was happening. He saw pain, anger, and fear in her expression, but no guile.

Gabriel heard the front door open, sliding over what sounded like shards of glass. The girl heard it too and gave a start. The scent of her fear intensified. She'd been frightened of him, but now she was terrified. Was she afraid of his captor? If she was . . .

"Help me." His voice came out ragged from disuse. "Please," he begged, although it went against everything in him to seek help from a human.

The girl fumbled with the ring of keys in her hand. She found the smallest key and tried it in the lock that held the chains tight around him. It worked. Gabriel struggled to shove the chains away. He was so weak. The man was so close.

The girl grabbed one of the loose ends of the chain and began to unwrap it. When his arms and hands were free, Gabriel was able to slide himself up on the table, releasing his legs from the chain. He climbed to his feet. The floor rolled beneath him, and his knees buckled. For a moment, Gabriel thought he'd fall or pass out and all chance of escape would be lost, but the girl took his arm and steadied him.

He had to get out before Martin reached him. Gabriel wasn't strong enough to battle even a human right now. He staggered to the door and wrenched it open. Martin was at the end of the hall. He held a knife in his hand.

There was no window in the room where he'd been held captive. There was no door at the other end of the hall. The windows along the top of the hallway were too small to fit through.

No way out.

Martin moved closer, wary, but ready to use the knife.

"Martin, what are you doing?" the girl cried. Gabriel hadn't realized that she was following him. She was at his side, her hand an inch away from his arm as if she thought he might fall.

"Shay, step away from him," Martin said in that cool, detached voice of his. "You don't know what he is."

So his captor wanted to protect the girl? That meant that he cared about her, that she meant something to him. That he wouldn't hurt her.

Gabriel grabbed the girl by the arm and yanked her in front of him. "I'll kill her if you don't drop the knife and let me walk out of here." Martin stopped where he was, but he didn't drop the knife. "I'm weak—you saw to that. But I have enough strength left to snap her neck," Gabriel growled.

A shudder rippled through the girl's body, and the smell of her fear intensified. Gabriel tried to ignore it, pulling her tighter against him.

"Martin, do what he wants," she cried. "Please."

The man advanced another step, raising the knife. Gabriel gasped, or maybe it was the girl. It was hard to tell where he ended and she began, with her this close to him and her smell in his head. He was so weak. . . .

"Martin, stop," the girl whimpered.

But he wasn't going to stop. Gabriel could tell by the cold look in the man's eyes. Martin didn't care if the girl got hurt. He was focused on Gabriel.

"Martin!" It was the woman, shrieking as she burst through the shattered front door. "Oh my God. Drop the knife. Do what he says!"

"I told you to wait in the car," the man barked.

"I heard Shay," the woman answered, her eyes wild. Her fear was so sharp that the scent of it overpowered everything else. Martin might not care about the girl, but this woman did.

Gabriel tightened his grip, digging his fingernails into the flesh of the girl's arm until she cried out. *It's necessary*, he told himself.

"Martin!" the woman cried again.

With a snarl, the man dropped the knife.

"Kick it away," Gabriel ordered. The man obeyed, sending the knife skittering down the hall. "Now face the wall, and plant your hands on it." The man obeyed again, shooting a look of fury over his shoulder.

"You too!" Gabriel told the woman. She instantly turned and placed her hands on the wall, tears running down her cheeks. "Good. Stay right there. Right there," he repeated as he started down the hall.

He pulled the girl along with him for security. She didn't struggle. She let him walk her past the man and woman without a word of protest.

"Shay . . ." the woman cried.

Gabriel jerked his hostage out through the shattered glass door. When the cold night air hit him, he was overwhelmed by its freshness and by the hundreds of scents that hit him. His prison had been climate-controlled and antiseptic. But he didn't have time to savor even one breath. "Which car is yours?" he demanded.

"Range Rover," the girl answered.

Gabriel plucked the keys from her fingers. He clicked the button to release the doors as he rushed her over to the vehicle. The girl opened the door before he did. He half-helped, half-pushed her inside, then climbed over her and into the driver's seat. It took him two tries to get the key in the ignition. So much time spent nearly motionless on that table had destroyed his coordination. When the engine purred to life, Gabriel sped across the parking lot. He paused for a second at the entrance, then pulled out into the deserted street. The ride was so smooth, it was almost like flying. He was free!

"We did it!" the girl exclaimed, her voice full of joy and triumph. It was as if her emotions matched his own, but that was impossible. "Thank God my mom walked in right then. I didn't think Martin was going to back down. And he's big. I always forget how big my stepfather is, because he's usually such an all-about-the-brain guy."

She sucked in a deep breath. "Sorry. Talking too much. I'm just so relieved."

So the woman was her mother, the man her stepfather. But this girl hadn't been aware that Gabriel was being held prisoner. Her shock when she saw him had been real—even though he still didn't understand how she knew his name.

Gabriel heard more traffic to the west, and he instinctively took the turn that would lead them toward it. He wanted cover and speed. The highway was his best option.

"Just stay quiet and do what I say," he ordered the girl. Shay, that's what they had called her. But he didn't need to know her name. She was a piece of his escape plan, nothing more. "If you do, you won't get hurt."

"I won't get *hurt?*" she repeated incredulously.

"I'm not like you people—I don't hurt simply because I can," Gabriel spat. "I'll let you go when I don't need you anymore. Unharmed, if you follow my orders."

"I'm the one who helped you escape. I unchained you and stopped you from landing on your ass when you couldn't even stand up. And you're threatening me?" the girl cried.

Gabriel ignored her. True, she had released him, but Gabriel hadn't had the chance to figure out what was going on with her. And it didn't matter. She was a human. He couldn't trust her.

The sound of the passenger window sliding down snapped him out of his thoughts. Before he could make his weakened body react, she'd leaned out the window and begun yelling for help. They were moving too fast for anyone to hear her, but if somebody caught a glimpse of her face, they would know she was in trouble. Gabriel couldn't let that happen. He grabbed her arm and jerked her back inside, then used the driver's controls to roll up her window.

"What did I tell you?" he demanded.

"Screw you. I just saved your life back there," the girl snapped, eyes bright with fury. "And now you expect me to be scared of you?"

He couldn't have this. He needed to subdue her. Now.

Gabriel moved his hand from her arm up to her throat and pressed down, not too hard, but enough to guarantee he had her attention. "If you knew what I am, you'd be scared—"

"You're a vampire," she choked out, cutting him off. "And you're a jerk."

Gabriel pressed harder on her throat, mostly out of shock, but it shut her up. She knew his name, she knew what he was . . . and she wasn't terrified. Even the man, Martin, had been afraid of him until he was in chains.

Who was this girl? How could she know so much about him, but not have been involved with his captivity?

She began to squirm, trying to free herself from the pressure of his arm. Gabriel swerved the car over to the side of the road, skidding to an abrupt stop on the dark shoulder. He threw it into PARK and turned toward the girl, releasing his true eye teeth, allowing them to extend beyond the human ones that kept them hidden.

Fangs. That's what humans called them. Fangs, like the teeth of animals. Carnivores. Man-eaters.

She wasn't moving anymore. She sat still, her body trembling as she stared at his teeth. Finally, she was afraid. He could smell it. Good.

"I'm a bloodsucker, a fiend, a demon," he said, throwing out some of the words he'd heard that dreadful night in the family's sleeping cave, so long ago. The words the humans used as they unleashed a greater hell than he was capable of. "I will not hesitate to kill you if you don't obey me."

She didn't respond. She just turned her eyes away from him.

"Understood?" He increased the pressure on her throat just a fraction.

She nodded.

Gabriel waited a few seconds, then returned his hand to the wheel, releasing her. He pulled back out onto the road, and the girl stared silently into the darkness. Her fear sharpened the intoxicating, familiar scent of her blood. It filled the car, filled him, driving him mad. All he wanted was to feed from her, drink, and drink, and drink until he was finally satisfied.

It would be the same with any human, Gabriel told himself. *She smells so enticing because I've been starved.* He promised himself that he would have her blood once it was safe to stop. He needed his strength and power, and this girl would give back what had been stolen from him.

But first he had to get away, as far as possible from the people who had held him captive. He stepped on the gas, speeding up as the highway ramp appeared in the headlights. West. South. Whatever road would take him in the direction of Ernst and the rest of his family.

Gabriel reached for the shunt in his hand, digging it out of his vein. Blood spilled from the wound, but he didn't care. It would heal as soon as he regained his strength. As soon as he fed.

His hunger for the girl mounted as they drove. Two hours later, when the road began rippling in front of his eyes, he was forced to admit that he was too weak to continue. He'd wanted to drive until sunrise forced him to stop. He wanted as many miles as possible between him and that room with the chains. But he had to stop. He had to rest. Most of all, he had to feed.

He glanced over at the human girl. She still held herself turned away from him, as close to her side of the car as she could get. Every muscle in her body was tight, as if she was poised to attack. *Or to fight for her life.* The thought came unbidden to Gabriel's mind. He shoved it away. He'd feared for his own life every day of his imprisonment. Why shouldn't she suffer the same?

Gabriel took the next exit that had a sign for a motel. It was just the kind of place he'd hoped for. Run-down. Not many guests. Clerk watching TV in the office. He parked at the back of the lot, against a chain-link fence in the darkness from a blown bulb in a streetlight.

"We're going in now," he told the girl. "Quietly." She didn't answer. She didn't even turn to him. "Did you hear me?" he asked, his voice sharp with menace.

The girl faced him and met his gaze with a directness that startled him. Then she laughed. "You don't get it. It doesn't matter what you do to me," she announced. "Everybody dies."

Didn't matter? What was that supposed to mean?

"No, not everyone," he said, although eternal life wasn't a guarantee even for him. "And death can come with or without suffering." She paled a bit, and it made the angles of her face even more striking. "Now shall we go?"

"Whatever you want. That's the deal, right?" she said.

In reply, he got out of the Range Rover and strode around to her door. She scrambled out before he opened it, but she didn't attempt to run. He wrapped his arm around her waist and pulled her tight against him as he walked her over to the door farthest from the motel office. He listened for a moment. The room was empty.

Gabriel forced the lock, the action taking much more strength than he'd anticipated. He realized that although he'd been holding the girl close so she wouldn't try to escape, she was also helping to prop him up.

He managed to pull her into the room and shut the door behind them. But now he had to feed. He didn't know how long he'd be able to retain consciousness. He took the girl by the shoulders and moved her in front of him, then brushed her long, thick hair away from her neck, his breath coming in ragged gasps. He hadn't wanted anyone this badly since the very first time.

Would he be able to stop himself?

"I won't take too much," he promised, as much for his own benefit as for hers. He unleashed his eye teeth, bending to the soft skin of her neck.

Shay gave a high whine of panic. Her body spasmed as his teeth entered her throat, then she went limp in his arms.

The warmth of her blood hit his mouth and he moaned. It had been so long. He pulled in a deep drink. The warmth turned to fire, to acid, eating away at the delicate flesh inside his throat. His veins suddenly felt like impossibly long shards of glass were shooting through them.

Vampire. Vampire blood.

It was too late. He'd taken in the blood, swallowed it down. Too much of it.

The agony eased as numbness invaded Gabriel's body, moving from his feet, up his legs. He pulled his mouth away from the girl, but the numbness continued. Gabriel managed a scream of horror before the paralysis took over his vocal cords.

He collapsed onto the stained tan carpet. Through his blurred vision, he saw the girl pick herself up from the floor. She bent down and took the keys from his pocket. Gabriel could do nothing to stop her as she ran from the room, leaving him to die.

Shay's fingers shook as she slid the key into the ignition. As soon as she heard the car whir to life, she slammed her foot on the gas. She had to get out of here. The engine revved, but the Rover didn't move.

PARK. *It's still in* PARK, she realized. She pulled in a deep, shuddering breath. *I'm not going to get very far if I don't get it together.*

Forcing herself to concentrate, she put the car in gear and slowly drove away from the motel. She got back on the highway, the first entrance she came to. She didn't care about north, south, east, or west right now. She cared about *away.*

A horn blared, and Shay realized she hadn't adjusted the rearview mirror when she had gotten behind the wheel. She'd completely cut in front of somebody. *Trying to save my life here, bud,* she thought as he sped past, flipping her off.

She reached up to fix the mirror, and the Range Rover started to slide across the line into the next lane. She wasn't up to driving one-handed. She wasn't up to driving at all. What was the point of escaping if she was going to die in a pile-up—a pile-up caused by her—five minutes later?

Shay got off at the next exit and parked in the lot of a gas station about a mile away. She put the Rover in park and turned it off. Then she crossed her arms over the wheel and rested her head on them. She needed a few. She just needed a few. And it was okay. She was safe. Even if Gabriel came out of . . . whatever it was that had made him pass out . . . he wouldn't know which way she'd gone.

Without lifting her head, she reached over and flipped the key, then turned on the radio. She needed music. Or even just voices from a commercial or someone ranting about politics. Anything at all to remind her that the real world was still out there, in spite of the turn into insanity her life had taken tonight.

A commercial for Pepto-Bismol came on. Shay choked out a laugh, even though there was nothing funny about the inane upset-stomach-diarrhea jingle. She was a fraction away from hysteria. Must be all the adrenaline pumping through her. That, and the fact that she had just been bitten by a goddamn vampire.

Shay listened to the next commercial and the song that came on after that. Then the next two. *I can't stay here all night,* she thought reluctantly. She raised her head, and noticed that she'd caught the attention of a couple of slimy looking thirty-something guys.

Don't even think about coming over here, she thought. *I've faced down a vampire tonight.* Well, sort of faced down. More like run when he'd gone unconscious.

Why hadn't she told him she was dying as soon as she realized he was taking her hostage?, she wondered as she checked to make sure the doors were locked. If there had ever been a time to play the Sick Girl card, tonight was it. But somehow, even in the horrific situation, Shay hadn't wanted Gabriel to see her that way.

She pulled her cell out of her pocket and punched the speed dial for HOME.

Her mother answered almost instantly. "Shay, where are you?"

"I'm—" Shay started.

"Are you still with that man? He's extremely dangerous. He's a killer," Mom cut her off. "Tell me where you are and I'll come get you."

"I got away from him. I'm okay, Mom. Try to calm down," Shay said.

"Oh, thank God. Thank God. I'm sorry. I should be telling *you* to calm down. Shay, honey, I was frantic thinking of you with him." Her mother's voice shook, and Shay could tell she was crying. "But I was afraid he might kill you if we didn't let him take you. I'm so sorry."

"It wasn't your fault," Shay said. "You didn't have a choice."

"And you're safe? Just tell me where you are." Shay could still hear the panic in her mom's voice, but she was clearly trying to take it down a notch. "I'll be right there and bring you home."

Home. Where Martin was.

A strange, cold feeling worked its way up Shay's spine. She'd been so freaked out by Gabriel—his anger, his violence, his very existence—that she'd put the rest of the night out of her mind. But Martin's name brought it all rushing back.

"Shay?" her mother said after a moment. "Say something. I'm afraid you're going into shock."

"Well . . . why wouldn't I be? I walked into Martin's office and found a man chained to a table. Chained there. Did Martin tell you that part?" Shay asked. "Or did he just tell you Gabriel was a killer?"

Her mother gave a little gasp. "Gabriel?"

"That's his name," Shay said.

"Sweetheart, don't listen to anything that man told you. He's insane. Martin had him chained up because he's so dangerous." Her mother tripped over her words in her rush to explain. "Please. Let's talk about all this when I have you safe at home."

Shay shook her head, even though her mother couldn't see. "That makes no sense. If he's an insane killer, why didn't Martin have him put into a mental hospital? Or why didn't he call the police? Why did he have Gabriel at all?"

"Shay . . ."

"There was a shunt in his hand. There was transfusion equipment all over that room where Martin had him," Shay went on. "And he's weak. He was never weak before."

"What are you talking about, Shay? What did he say to you?"

"Nothing. I just know he's always strong. But he's weak now, from lying on Martin's table with an IV tube stuck into him." The answer was so clear that Shay would have laughed if it weren't so horrible. "Martin was using his blood in my transfusions. Taking it from Gabriel and giving it to me."

Her mother sobbed on the other end of the line.

"That's why I was so strong afterward." There was a loud buzzing in Shay's ears or maybe it was in her mind. Maybe she had passed out from the Black River after all, and this was all some bad dream. "Martin was keeping Gabriel captive . . . for his blood."

"Shay—"

"What the hell was he thinking? I mean, that's illegal! It's *immoral.* It's insane," Shay burst out. "Martin's a doctor! He's supposed to help people, not steal their blood against their will."

"We were doing it for you, Shay." Her mother's voice had become small and meek.

We? We.

"You knew, Mom?" Shay whispered. "You knew Gabriel was there?" She'd assumed her mother had thought Gabriel was a drug addict or something who'd broken into Martin's lab. That Martin had spent the last few hours spinning some story to keep her mom in the dark. But no. Mom had known that Gabriel was a hostage, and she'd done nothing.

Nothing. What kind of person could do nothing? Her mother suddenly felt like a stranger.

"It was the only way to keep you alive. You were getting worse, and his blood was the only thing that has given me any kind of hope in so long," her mother said in a rush.

"Oh my God, you were in on this," Shay cried. "You didn't just know he was there; you knew what Martin was doing to him! Did you help kidnap him? Mom, what did you do?"

"Whatever I had to. You don't understand, Shay. He's not like us. It's not what you think. He's not—"

"He's a vampire," Shay interrupted. "I know that. So do you."

Her mother gave a muffled gasp, and Shay could picture her with her free hand pressed tightly to her mouth. "So you understand," her mom said. "It wasn't a human we kept in the lab. We'd never do that, Shay. Never."

"Why not?" Shay demanded. "What's the difference? You wouldn't need such thick chains for a human?"

"That . . . *thing* . . . is evil. Dangerous," her mother said. "It isn't like us."

Shay could barely think straight, she was so horrified. It was true, Gabriel was dangerous. She had seen that. But in her visions, he was also kind, and loyal, and more deeply connected to the world around him than anyone she'd ever met. More than that, she'd never seen him kill. In all the times she'd been inside him, she'd never felt evil.

But now, from her mother and Martin, she did.

"I don't even know you," she whispered. She'd always thought they were the closest thing to a Siamese-twin version of a mom and daughter. But the mother she knew would never do such a thing to another living being. The mother she knew wouldn't have lied to Shay's face every day.

"I'm the same as I've always been," her mother sobbed. "I would do anything to keep you alive. And I don't care if it means taking blood from a monster."

"He has a family. He has emotions. He feels pain."

"Don't start sentimentalizing. You don't know anything about them—him!" her mother said.

"I know a lot more than you do," Shay shot back. "Gabriel's not evil. What you did, *that* was evil. And you knew it, or you would have told me the truth. You knew I wouldn't have wanted to be kept alive that way."

"You can say that because you have been kept alive. It's easy to be noble now." Shay heard her mother take a deep breath and knew she was trying to calm herself. "Please tell me where you are. I don't want you driving home. You're in shock. You can yell and scream at me as much as you want when I get there."

"This isn't going to go away if you let me have a tantrum. I'm not a little girl anymore, Mom. When are you finally going to realize that?" Shay asked.

"I'm not going to apologize for doing what I had to do—"

Her mother's voice cut off, and Shay heard the sound of the phone changing hands. "Where is he, Shay?" Martin asked in his bedside-manner voice. "We have to recapture him."

"So you can chain him up again?" she demanded.

"You don't want to be responsible for him hurting anyone. Tell me where he is. I'll take care of the rest," Martin told her, calm and rational, all doctor.

He didn't even ask how I am, she thought. Usually the first question out of Martin's mouth was about Shay's illness. But he didn't care. He just wanted Gabriel back. Shay sank down into the big car seat, curling herself up into a ball. Martin's voice wasn't calm. It was *cold.* How had she never realized that before?

"Gabriel won't hurt anyone else," she murmured.

"Tell me where he is," Martin insisted.

Shay didn't answer. She'd run out of things to say. Maybe she was in shock, like her mother thought. She felt overwhelmed and numbed out at the same time.

"There's something else you should know," Martin said, frustration sneaking into his tone. "You can't live without his blood, Shay. I don't mean you'll die in a few years. I mean you won't survive the week." Shay heard her mother crying in the background. "We've got to get him back. Does he have the Range Rover?"

"No. I do," Shay replied. She focused on the sound of her mother's sobs. She'd always known that would be the last she heard of her mother's voice. She just hadn't expected it to be like this.

"How long ago did you escape? Where did you last see him?" Martin demanded.

Shay wasn't listening to any more of his questions. She hung up, tears stinging her eyes. She couldn't go home, not if Martin was there. And even though her mother's heart was breaking, Shay wasn't sure she could forgive her.

So she was on her own, with a week to live. Or less.

EIGHT

○ ○ ○ ○ ○ ○ ○ ○ ○ ○ ○ ○ ○ ○ ○ ○

SHAY REALIZED SHE'D BEEN SITTING in the parking lot, staring blankly out in the darkness, for almost half an hour. *Enough of this self-pity*, she thought, roughly brushing away the tears that hung off her lower lashes. She didn't have time for wallowing. She dropped her head back against the headrest. *Now what? Call the Make-A-Wish Foundation?*

She sighed. What would she even tell them she wanted to have for her last week on earth?

First, chocolate, she decided. She leaned over to the glove compartment and fished around inside. Martin always kept cash in the car for emergencies. She pulled out an envelope and peered inside. Two hundred bucks in a neat stack of twenties. More than enough for some junk food.

Shay got out and walked into the gas station mini-mart. She loaded up on M&M's—plain, peanut, almond, and even this weird strawberry and peanut-butter flavor she'd never seen before. After all, she was living it up. Having an adventure. Eating an unexplored kind of candy.

She added a few other things she'd never tried—fried pork rinds, wasabi-flavored peanuts, and a truly noxious-looking drink called Mountain Dew Code Red. The fat and cholesterol and artificial colors wouldn't kill her. They were too damn slow.

When Shay dropped her selections on the counter, the guy gave her a knowing grin. "Someone's got the munchies."

Shay tossed out her usual line. "I'm high on life, dude."

"Road trip, then?"

Road trip. Why not? See the world. Go out in a blaze of sugar-fueled glory. "Got it in two," Shay told him as he dumped her purchases into a plastic bag with a yellow smiley face on it. She grinned as big as the yellow ball as she headed back to the Range Rover. It felt good to have a plan.

Should she drag out the big atlas she knew Martin had stowed under the passenger seat? No. Road trips were for spontaneity. She was going commando. No maps, no plans, and unless she did some shopping soon, no clean underwear.

Shay pulled away from the gas station, her hands steady. She was absolutely, completely in control of her life for as long as it lasted.

That's the way it had to be. There was no one she could trust but herself. Not Martin, that was for sure. Not even Mom. Not Gabriel. He'd used her as a human shield.

She got back on the highway. When she found a town that had a funky name, she'd stop. On her road trip, she was going to stop only at places with funky names. She wasn't going anywhere she'd ever heard of. Unless she felt like it. Because who was making up the rules here? Shay was.

She'd passed only one exit before she saw something familiar. A sign with a white *H* on a blue background. *My first word was probably "hospital,"* she thought.

An ambulance passed her, silent. Shay hated the sight of it. She'd had a few rides in ambulances herself, and she always wondered who was in the ones she saw. Wondered if they were going to make it. In a way, the silent ones were the worst. Shay always imagined a body inside. Someone who couldn't be saved.

The image of Gabriel collapsed on the motel floor flashed into her mind. Was he still passed out? If he didn't come to before morning, somebody was going to open that door, and the sunlight would come in, and Gabriel would die.

Not my problem, she told herself. *He took me hostage. I owe him nothing.*

Nothing except running and swimming and kissing and living. Living her life more than she ever had before. And living his life, too, in her visions.

"What the hell am I doing?" she muttered as she cut across two lanes—getting honked at again—and took the exit, following the ambulance.

If I don't try to save him, I'm like my mom and Martin, Shay thought. *Exactly like them.*

She followed the ambulance for the few blocks to the hospital, then found a parking place in the fairly empty lot. So . . . the emergency room? If it was crazed, and a lot of times the ER was crazed, she could probably slip into a hospital-personnel-only zone. That's what she needed. That's where she'd find the blood.

But there was always at least one person at the front desk of the ER. If she timed it wrong, she'd get questions. Surgery, she decided. There'd be a few going on, but not many. Only emergencies that couldn't wait until morning. She started the Rover again and cruised around the hospital compound until she saw the surgical wing. She parked again and walked in.

The waiting room was big. It was also almost empty. A couple of little kids stared at the TV, while their mom stared into space. Or prayed. Shay wasn't sure which. She took a seat as close to the door leading into the unit as she could. The wait wasn't long. An orderly came out, heading for the alcove with the vending machines. The door slowly eased shut behind him. Shay had been counting on those slow-moving hospital doors. She caught the door before it shut and locked, and slipped inside.

She was in the prep area. There was a nurse behind the long counter, but his head was down as he entered info on one of the computers. Without hesitation, Shay walked over to one of the curtained-off sections and stepped inside. She sat down next to the bed, which happened to be empty. Even if it hadn't been, she'd probably have been okay. Family could usually stay with the surgical patient until they were taken into the operating room.

The bed was set up, complete with two neatly folded hospital gowns laid across the blankets. The first thing you did in any hospital was get into one of these hideous-but-comfy things. If anyone caught her walking around in street clothes, they'd kick her out of the restricted areas in a heartbeat. Shay put one on over her clothes with the opening in the back, then pulled the second one on like a robe, open in front. Hopefully no one would look too closely, or notice that she still had pants and boots on under her gown.

The next step—more waiting. She heard a patient being brought in. Thankfully, they weren't put in her little hideaway. They were given a nearby curtained cubicle. Shay heard the anesthesiologist introduce herself and start asking about allergies. The nurse would be taking some basic readings—blood pressure, for starters—and asking a bunch of questions of his own.

This is probably my best shot, Shay thought. She ducked around the curtain and headed down the hall, walking on her toes so the heels of her boots didn't hit the floor and announce her presence. She knew she wouldn't just be able to waltz in and take some bags of blood. If this hospital was like the other ones she'd been in—and it seemed to be, right down to the smell of bodily fluids not quite covered by the smell of industrial cleaner—everything would be computerized. A nurse would have to scan the patient's computer-coded wristband before administering the computer-coded medication. And to get the medication or the blood for a transfusion, the nurse would have to swipe a card. It wasn't as if Shay could just pick a lock, even if she knew how to pick a lock, which she didn't.

Still, nurses were humans, not computers. And sometimes humans weren't as careful as they should be. Shay ducked behind the counter. She could hear the nurse talking to the newly arrived patient. She had a minute or two. Staying low, she moved down the row of computers. There was a sweater hung over one of them. She checked the pockets. Nothing. She moved on, then turned back. She felt the front of the sweater. Score. A card was clipped to it. Shay grabbed it. One swipe, and she was through the door that led from the prep area into the hallway with the operating rooms.

There was a cart about halfway down the hall from where she stood. She knew those carts as well as she knew her own face. Everything in every hospital was basically the same, and in the course of her life she'd seen about a hundred nurses take blood out of a refrigerated chest like the one on this cart's bottom shelf. Shay hurried over and swiped the card through the slot on the chest. She pulled it open and saw four bags of beautiful, beautiful blood. She took them all.

Before she could even take a step, she heard the sound of a door opening. Shay shoved the blood bags under her hospital gown and crossed her arms over them to hold them in place. Then she turned. A man in scrubs was heading toward her, studying a chart.

"I know, I know. I'm not supposed to be back here," Shay said before she could be questioned. "But do you know how boring it is in a hospital at night? No good TV. And I don't have a private room, and the woman in the next bed keeps calling for the nurse. 'Nurse, nurse, nurse,' over and over again in this horrible voice. She keeps wanting her pain meds, says her pain is at a ten on the scale, but it isn't time for them, and the nurse can't get a doctor on the phone to see if she can get more, of course. The screaming was making the hair on my arms stand up."

She shoved up one arm of her gown, careful not to let the blood escape. She let the man see the marks of her many transfusions. She was now thinking he was medical personnel of the scrub nurse variety, rather than a surgeon or anesthesiologist. MD's usually wouldn't stand still for this many words. She'd seen her mother chase doctors down the hall just to get the answer to one question. "I thought I'd just duck into one of those observation rooms and get some peace. It would be like *Grey's Anatomy*."

"I'm going to get someone to escort you back to your room," the man told her. "This is no place for a patient."

"Unless they're being operated on, right?" Shay said cheerily. "I've put in some hours here. Splenectomy almost a year ago."

The man's pager went off.

"Listen, I'll get myself back upstairs. I know the surgery wing is insane. Sorry. Boredom made me do it!" She hurried away, and he didn't follow.

It was easier getting out than getting in. The nurse was behind the counter again, but since Shay was heading for the door, he didn't ask her why she was there. She ducked into the restroom and took off the gowns, leaving them on a hook on the back of the door. She dropped the card she'd stolen on the floor. Somebody would find it and get it back where it belonged. She didn't want to get the nurse in trouble or call attention to the missing blood anytime soon.

I'll give Gabriel the blood, then get out of there, she promised herself as she left the hospital. She repeated the promise several times as she crossed the parking lot, and quite a few more as she drove back to the motel.

Am I insane? she asked herself as she walked to the door of the room Gabriel had broken into. *He's a vampire. A vampire who threatened to snap my neck.*

A vampire who was kept prisoner and used against his will as my own personal blood bank.

There really was no arguing with that. Shay pushed open the door. Gabriel lay on the floor exactly where she'd left him. Was he even alive?

One way to find out. Shay set one of the blood bags on the bed. Later she'd wrap some ice from the machine in a towel to keep the rest cool so Gabriel could have them if he still needed more. If this even worked. If Gabriel wasn't already dead.

Shay studied him for a minute, then cautiously sat on the floor beside him. She rolled him onto his back without getting the smallest reaction. Well, vampires were technically dead, weren't they? As much as she'd seen in her visions, she still didn't know a lot about how it all worked.

Some things seemed the same as she'd read in books, like the sun being deadly. Some things seemed different, like the fact that vampires were evil killers. Gabriel hadn't been violent in her visions, and neither had Sam, or Ernst, or Millie.

So maybe he was dead, and maybe that was normal for him. All she could do was try.

Shay rooted around in the desk drawer and found the crappy pen they always left, advertising the motel. She used it to poke a little hole in the blood bag she held.

She didn't want to touch Gabriel again. But she didn't want him to choke, either. She knelt back down and cradled his head with one arm, raising his head several inches off the floor. With her free hand, she dribbled a little blood on his lips.

He didn't react.

"You know, I went to a lot of trouble for this," Shay muttered. She managed to hold on to the bag while using two of her fingers to part his lips. She tried dribbling the blood again, this time with the droplets falling into his mouth.

Was blood even going to help? He'd been drinking her blood when he collapsed. Maybe Martin had taken too much from him. Maybe Martin had weakened him to the point where he couldn't recover.

Martin and Mom. Shay had to keep reminding herself that her mother had known what Martin was doing. Even if she hadn't been the one actually taking Gabriel's blood, she had still been a part of it. She'd considered Gabriel nothing more than meat, or medicine, or a lab rat.

"Come on, Gabriel," Shay urged. She tore at the hole, making it wider, and let the blood flow down.

Gabriel coughed. His eyelids fluttered, but didn't open. Then his throat began to work as he drank.

Shay sighed in relief. "I owed you this much," she told him, even though she was pretty sure he couldn't hear her. "You did the same for me, whether you wanted to or not."

He's okay. He's just sleeping, Shay told herself for at least the twelfth time since dawn. *It's hard for vampires to stay awake during the day. Sam had to struggle to do it on Gabriel's last day in the sun.*

Still, it was unnerving to watch him—lying there so still under the bedspread she'd used to cover him. His chest did rise and fall, but very slowly. Was that normal? Vampire normal?

She wished there was something else she could do for him. She was afraid to try to give him more blood right now. If he didn't wake up—and it didn't seem like he *could*—he might choke on it.

He'd probably be more comfortable on the bed than the floor, but she wasn't strong enough to move him. Between the stress of finding Gabriel, and being bitten by him, and all that running around in the hospital, she'd used up almost all the energy given to her by the transfusion that Mom had interrupted.

I should check in, she decided. They'd gotten away with being in the room so far, but that didn't mean their luck would hold. Who knew how long Gabriel would be out of it? Maybe his day of sleep would energize him. Or maybe he'd wake up as sick and weak as he'd been last night.

Shay left the room, careful not to let the sun in far enough to touch Gabriel, then hurried down to the main office.

"Could I get the room all the way at the end?" Shay asked the motel clerk. "Less noise."

The clerk raised an eyebrow, clearly thinking, *What noise, crazy girl?*

"I'm very sensitive to sound. If there's a TV on in a room two doors down, I won't be able to sleep," Shay explained.

"Check-in isn't until noon," the guy told her.

"Please, can't you make an exception?" Shay asked. "I was up all night driving, and I'm whipped. Isn't there a room that's ready?"

The clerk snorted. "We're never full, if you want the truth, but the manager is a jerk about policies." He turned and plucked the key to the room Shay and Gabriel were already in from the Peg-Board behind him. "Thing is, the manager never comes in on Sunday."

"Thanks. Thanks so much." Shay paid in cash, glad that Gabriel had broken into a cheap place. Although money was the least of her problems. Well, maybe not the least, but it wasn't the top of the list. The top of the list was keeping Gabriel alive and keeping Mom and Martin from finding her.

She didn't think they'd be searching for her yet. Right now they probably figured that Shay was on her way home. Even after that big fight, they would still assume that she would come back, because where else did she have to go? Especially after Martin told her she would be dead in days.

She knew it wouldn't be too long before it sank in that she wasn't coming, but they had no idea which direction she and Gabriel had headed in. They could call the police, tell them the Range Rover was stolen, but Shay didn't think that would happen. Shay could just tell the cops that they had been holding someone captive in Martin's office, and that would start all kinds of badness. Even if no one believed her, there would be rumors about it. Martin was just well-known enough to land in the gossip blogs, especially for something as crazy as experimenting on an actual person. He wouldn't want that. And he definitely wouldn't want to risk the police finding out the truth about Gabriel.

Martin wanted Gabriel back; he'd made that clear. She was sure Martin was hoping that the vampire blood would lead to one of those go-down-in-history medical breakthroughs, the kind that won Nobel Prizes for the doctors who made them. If the blood could

help her, maybe it could help people with more common blood disorders as well. Maybe Martin had never given up on finding a cure
for leukemia after all.

He wouldn't risk losing that by calling the cops.

For now, she needed to concentrate all her attention on Gabriel.
She couldn't waste her time worrying about Mom and Martin, trying to guess what they might do. She needed a plan.

Shay opened the door to the motel room and slipped inside.
Gabriel hadn't moved, at least that she could tell. She put the DO
NOT DISTURB sign on the door and hoped that nobody would notice
that the lock had been broken. It didn't seem like the kind of place
where they'd check on the rooms too often. Shay crossed to the window and made sure the curtains were completely shut. Sam had said
vampires turned to ash in the sunlight.

Now what? She checked her watch. After nine. Early, especially
for a Sunday morning. But if Shay knew her mother, which she
absolutely did, her mom had already called Olivia.

Shay pulled her cell out of her pocket and hit speed-dial two.
"Where are you?" Olivia demanded before Shay could get a word
out.

"I had to take off," Shay answered, according to the only plan she
could come up with.

"Yeah, no kidding. Your mother called me at five o'clock this morning, wanting to know if I had any clue where you were. Which—as
you know—I didn't," Olivia told her.

"Mom and Martin were driving me insane. They keep treating
me like I'm still as sick as I was, which isn't true," Shay said. "I had to

get away from them for a while. And I need your help. I just need a few days, and you can talk them—"

"This is such bullshit," Olivia interrupted. "First of all, you *are* still sick. Maybe you're feeling a little better, but you're still passing-out-need-to-be-taken-care-of sick. And second, you're lying. I've known you forever, and I can hear it in your voice. So what are you really doing?"

Shay's mouth dropped open. Her brain revved as she tried to come up with something to say. It had never occurred to her that Olivia wouldn't believe her.

"You have two seconds before I hang up," Olivia snapped.

"You're right. It's bullshit," Shay burst out. "But I really do need your help, Olivia. That part is completely true."

"Oh my God, you are out of control!" Olivia shot back. "Why call me? All you've been saying lately is you don't want my help. It's obvious you haven't wanted me around, period."

"You're right," Shay said.

"Did you try Jacey first or Lai-wan?" Olivia went on. "What am I, the only one left?"

"No!" Shay cried. "I never even thought about calling anyone else, Liv. I'm sorry. I am. There've been a lot of things happening to me lately that I haven't told you about."

"We're supposed to be friends," Olivia said more quietly. "Best friends."

"I shouldn't have lied to you or kept secrets from you," Shay replied desperately. "I need to stay away for a while. That's the real truth, Olivia, but not because my mom and Martin are acting like they always do." Her voice began to quaver. She hadn't meant for it to, but it just did. She'd gotten herself in way over her head.

"So what's actually going on?" Olivia sounded a little more sympathetic, but only a little.

"Martin . . . he's not who I thought he was. Something happened with him, and I can't be around him, not until I figure out what to do," Shay told her. She couldn't bring herself to say that she felt pretty much the same way about her mother.

"Are you—did he touch you?" Olivia burst out. "That fucker. I always knew there was something weird about him. Shay, you have to tell your mom. And the cops."

Shay didn't think she'd ever heard Olivia say the word *fucker* before, and she couldn't believe how much she appreciated it. "No, not that," Shay said quickly. "But I found out . . . well . . . he did a bad thing. He really hurt someone."

Except he did it for me, Shay thought. *Well, me and a Nobel Prize.*

But not her mother. Mom had done it all for Shay. She would have let Martin drain her own entire body of blood if it would help Shay live longer. Her mother would literally die for her. But that still didn't make what she'd done right or even okay.

"So don't go home. Come here, Shay," Olivia urged her. "Come straight here. We'll figure out what to do."

"I can't. Not right now," Shay said. "My mom would find me at your place, and she's not going to be exactly easy to convince. She thinks Martin is practically a god. She thinks he's the only one who could have kept me alive this long. And she's probably right. But that doesn't mean he's a good person."

"She's your mother, Shay. She's going to believe you, whatever it is you found out about Martin." Olivia's voice was strong with conviction and anger.

"Please just help me, Olivia. I need a couple of days without Martin coming after me. Can you just tell my mom . . . tell her that I'm going to Miami," Shay begged. "That will send them in the wrong direction."

"Your mom is never going to believe that. That's not a Shay thing to do," Olivia said. Shay was surprised Olivia still thought she knew exactly what Shay would and wouldn't do.

"She'll believe it," Shay insisted. "I've been acting, you know, not-Shay lately."

"Really?" Olivia asked. Shay could almost feel the sarcasm dripping into her ear from the phone.

"So she'll believe almost anything. Tell her I know I'm dying, and that I want to have some fun before I do. That's why I want to go to Miami. Sit in the sun, look at cute guys, swim in the ocean, feel the sand between my toes. All that seize-the-day stuff."

"And where will you really go?" Olivia asked.

"I don't know. Not yet," Shay said.

Olivia was silent for a moment, and Shay knew that she was trying to decide if Shay was lying or not. Finally she sighed. "Look, I'll lie to Martin. I have no problem with that. I'll lie to your mom, too, which isn't going to be easy because she is completely losing her mind worrying about you," Olivia said. "But I'm not really on board with this, Shay. If you want my help, you have to check in with me every day—phone, text, whatever—and tell me whether or not you're okay. And you have to tell me the truth. I'll know if you don't. And if you lie or you skip a day, I'm calling everyone I can think of. Cops, your mom, reporters. Everyone."

It wasn't ideal, but Shay could tell it was the best she was going to get. "Thanks," she said. "You're a good friend, you really are. The best."

"You better believe I am," Olivia answered.

And Shay did believe her. But it didn't mean that Olivia might not call Shay's mother the second Shay hung up. She could imagine Olivia repeating every word of the conversation they'd just had. For Shay's own good, of course, because Olivia was such a good friend, because she did really care about Shay.

"I'll be in touch tomorrow," Shay promised. Then ended the call.

Shay yawned. Her eyes felt gritty, and her body ached with weariness. She had to sleep. There was nothing more to do for Gabriel right now. She'd done the best she could.

She wrapped the remaining blanket around her shoulders and curled up at the foot of the bed, staring down at Gabriel. Now that the insanity of the past several hours was over, she could finally take in the fact that he was real. He was here in front of her.

"I guess you weren't my brain misfiring after all," she told him. "Or some past life of mine."

She knew him so well. Or at least she'd felt that way until he took her hostage. Nothing she'd seen—no, not seen—nothing she'd *experienced* while she was Gabriel had prepared her for that.

But he'd been captured and held prisoner for his blood, Shay reminded herself. *That would change anyone.*

She studied Gabriel's face. Who was he really? The man who had threatened to kill her? The man who had mourned and savored his last sight of the sun? The little boy who had saved his friend? Could he be all those things? Evil and good?

"Live," she told Gabriel. "That's what matters right now. Just live, okay?"

∘ ∘ ∘ ∘ ∘ ∘ ∘ ∘ ∘ ∘ ∘ ∘ ∘ ∘ ∘ ∘

CONSCIOUSNESS SLOWLY RETURNED TO GABRIEL, and he knew it was sunset. It was the only way he could mark the passage of time since his capture. When another day broke, he sank into his death sleep. When another day ended, he awoke.

His arms and legs felt as heavy as granite. He wished the chains that bound him allowed him to change position. But if they were that loose, he'd free himself. And weak as he was, he would escape that man—

Martin.

His mind was flooded with memories of the previous night—it was the previous night, wasn't it? The girl, his captors, the knife, the escape, the searing pain in his throat and veins and heart. Gabriel's eyes snapped open. The first thing he saw was the human girl, sleeping on the bed above him. He tried to sit up, but realized that his limbs were still mostly paralyzed. *That's why I thought I was back in that room, chained fast*, he realized.

The girl's eyes opened, as if she'd felt his gaze, even in her sleep. They stared at each other in silence, then the girl looked at her watch. "Almost seven. I've been asleep all day. And you, you've been out about fifteen hours," the girl said. "How are you feeling?"

"Okay," he answered. Her name came to him again—Shay. He didn't care. She was an object he needed, nothing more. *An object that saved my life.* Gabriel shoved the thought down.

The girl stood and walked into the bathroom. She returned holding a bag of blood. "Is it okay if I . . ." She gestured to the spot on the floor next to him.

Gabriel nodded, glad to feel that the muscles in his neck were getting easier to move. The girl sat down cross-legged beside him. "Are you hungry again?" She held up the blood. He was hungry. His body ached for blood, but not the cold, sterile stuff encased in plastic. He wanted hers, warm and sweet and salty. The smell of it was overpowering.

She must have felt his desire in the intensity of his gaze. "Don't you remember what happened last time?" she asked. "You tried to drink from me, and you dropped like a rock. I'm sick. My blood must be poisonous to you. And even if it wasn't, you'd just have to deal. I'm here until I've gotten you back on your feet, but that doesn't include you feeding from me."

Poisonous. How could that be, when she smelled so enticing?

But as he stared at her throat, soft and creamy white, he saw the marks. Puncture wounds. The memory was vivid. His mouth on her skin, his teeth sinking into the soft flesh of her throat. And then—

"Vampire blood. You had vampire blood." He knew the taste, the feel of it. He'd experienced the effects before, once, during the blood ritual. But that time, he'd only had to drink a small amount. The pain to his heart had been more emotional than physical.

When he'd drunk from the girl, though, he had drunk deeply and greedily. Drunk too much. She was right; it had been like an injection of poison in his heart. "But you're human. I can smell it," he said.

Her brow furrowed. "Is vampire blood bad?"

"Deadly. To another vampire." Gabriel forced his eyes away from her throat. "I don't understand."

"You're hungry. Drink, and I'll explain." She held out the blood bag, but his arm and hand shook too badly for him to take it. The girl scooted around behind him and lifted his head into her lap. She pierced the bag and the smell of it intensified, though it was still nothing compared to hers. She cradled his head in one arm and held the blood to his lips with the other.

Gabriel sucked on the small hole, drawing the blood into his mouth. He couldn't drink without her arm supporting him, but he hated it. It made him feel like a little boy, helpless and vulnerable.

Why was she here, nursing him? He'd taken her hostage. Tried to feed from her. There had been nothing to hold her here once he'd lost consciousness. Any normal girl would've run away, would've brought the police, would've destroyed him. And this girl had obviously left—she'd had to, to get the blood. And then she'd come back to give it to him. Why?

He let the questions slide away for the moment, giving himself over to feeding. The scent of her, so close, surrounded him. If he closed his eyes, he could pretend that it was her blood sliding down his throat, her intoxicating presence filling him. Blood from a bag didn't bring the emotions that blood directly from a Giver did. The feelings were distant, vague. He'd always wondered if that was because part of the experience of feeding was missing. The smell, the warmth, the heartbeat.

He felt Shay's heart beating against his back. Pounding, really. Gabriel had the sensation of possessing two hearts in his body. As he lay cradled against her chest, the two hearts slowly came to beat in synch.

As soon as he drank the last of the blood, Gabriel shoved himself away from her, from the intimacy of her heart beating with his. She stood up without comment. "There's more if you need it," she said, throwing the empty bag in the trash.

He was still hungry. He'd been kept half-starved for so long. But he shook his head. "You said you would explain."

"About my blood."

"Yes."

She sat down in the room's only chair. There was probably seven feet between them, but she didn't move the chair closer. He was glad. The smell of her sharpened his hunger. He had the feeling that even if he'd drunk a dozen bags of blood, he'd still crave her.

"It's your own blood. My blood is yours," she said. "I've been getting transfusions of your blood for the last two weeks."

So that's what his captor had been doing with the blood he took. "Why?"

"I'm sick, like I said. Pretty much dying." She wrung her hands. "But I didn't know—I thought it was regular blood, just treated with something. I should've asked more questions, but I felt so good that I didn't even care. I swear, Gabriel, I didn't know what they'd done to you until last night, until I saw you. I thought you were just a figment of my imagination."

"My blood." Her answer only created more questions. His captor—Martin—had spoken to him sometimes, in that chilly voice of his. Always about immortality and strength, about isolating the unique protein composition that made a vampire's blood so powerful. About how it would change the world, ensure his place in the history books. Never about a sick girl. "It was for you?"

"I've gotten blood transfusions practically my whole life. I have a blood disorder—a weird, impossible-to-diagnose disease. My doctor, who is also my stepfather, he was the one who . . ." She swallowed hard, and his eyes followed the motion of her throat.

"The one who kept me chained to a table and took my blood by force," Gabriel finished for her, his anger blazing up for a moment as he remembered it.

"Yes. He must have thought your . . . your kind of blood might cure me." She pressed the heels of her hands against her forehead. "Although I don't understand that at all. Who even believes vampires exist? And Martin is a scientist, a famous one. How would he have come up with that as a possible cure? It's crazy."

"Not *so* crazy." Gabriel felt his mouth twitch, wanting to smile at her words. He stopped himself.

"Well, no, obviously . . ." Her voice trailed off as she looked at him.

"Somehow he knew of our existence, your doctor," Gabriel said.

"He came searching for one of us, he and your mother."

"Searching? How?" Her eyebrows knit together, her blue eyes clouded with confusion. "When?"

"I don't know when they started. They posted on every vampire-related website they could find. I saw one," Gabriel answered. "I've been curious about others of my kind, and I look at them sometimes, even though as far as I can tell, all the sites are created by pathetic humans who long to be something other than what they are."

If she heard the bitterness in his voice, she didn't comment on it. "So then why did you take Martin seriously?" she asked. "And my mom?"

"First, they weren't pretending to be vampires. Second, they knew details about . . . someone I loved. A member of my family. I didn't understand how that was possible, and I had to know. So I agreed to meet them," Gabriel explained.

He'd been so stupid. So arrogant. He'd seen firsthand what humans were capable of, and still he'd walked into a trap. "They were prepared," he continued. "They knew what my vulnerabilities were. The man—the *doctor*—injected me with an infusion of hawthorn. It's only a plant, but it paralyzes us, my kind. It left me awake, aware of what was happening . . . but I couldn't move. I couldn't lift a finger to fight him. I saw everything he was doing; I felt everything—" He struggled to keep his voice under control. He wasn't going to show this human how he'd suffered. "The effects lasted long enough for them to abduct me. Once he had me chained down, he began drawing blood, and that kept me weak."

"But how did they know all that—about the hawthorn, about your family?" she asked.

"You tell me," Gabriel replied.

She recoiled at the accusation in his tone. But she was his captors' daughter. Even if she'd come back here and saved him, he couldn't believe she knew nothing.

"You were surprised to see me on that table," he went on. "But you knew my name. I've never told it to a human. Your parents never bothered to ask." He'd managed to roll onto his side to face her, trying to show his anger, but it was all he could manage. He hated how powerless he felt.

"I have no idea how they knew about you, I swear," she said. "I was shocked to see you chained to that table, more than I've ever been in my life. But that's . . . it's because I thought you were . . . imaginary."

Gabriel just stared at her. This girl confounded him.

She opened her hands in an expression of helplessness. "Okay, I know this is hard to believe, but with every transfusion of your blood—what I later realized was your blood—I had a vision of you. Like a dream, but always about you and your life. That's how I knew your name. I heard Sam and Ernst and Millie say it."

Gabriel felt as if he'd been attacked again, as if she'd stabbed him with the syringe of hawthorn just like that so-called doctor had. *Sam? Ernst?*

"You know everything!" he exploded, dragging his weakened body up as far as he could, leaning against the bed. "Just like your mother did, and that—"

"No!" she cut him off. "I don't! I didn't know anything until I saw your family in my visions. That's how I found out about them. But I never told my mom or Martin. I thought it was just some weird side effect of the drugs Martin put into that blood."

"If I could move, I would kill you," he growled. "And your *doctor* would be next."

Her hand flew to her throat, and for one second she looked afraid. Then she laughed, as bitter a sound as anything he could make. "Don't worry, I'll be dead soon enough even without your help."

Gabriel felt his anger drain away. What was the use of it, when he could barely move and she wasn't frightened by his threats?

"You can believe me or not; I don't care," she said. "But I've been *inside* you, living parts of your life with you. That's what my visions were."

"Bullshit." It was the fantastical excuse of a child.

"I saw you when you said good-bye to the sun," she insisted. "You tried to memorize every color of the sky."

"That could apply to many of my kind," Gabriel scoffed. "And even your myths about us claim, correctly, that we'll die in the sunlight." But his chest tightened. Had she somehow truly been able to invade his thoughts, his deepest emotions?

She leaned forward in her chair. He noticed that her face had paled a bit, and there were tiny beads of sweat along her hairline. "You were nineteen, almost twenty." *She could have guessed that by looking at me,* Gabriel thought. "You weren't sure if blood would be enough to take the place of the sun." *That was it. That was it exactly.* "You talked to Sam about whether or not you were ready. He thought you might be feeling pressure from Ernst."

Sam. Ernst. He hated those names coming from her mouth. She knew about the ones closest to his heart. What else did she know? What else had she seen? Gabriel felt as if she'd stripped off his clothes and made him stand in front of her naked. He turned his face away from her.

"I'd hate it if someone knew about me like that," she said, her tone softening. "But being with you has been the most amazing experience I've ever had. I got to run. Run! Running in your body was . . ." she paused, seeming to search for the right word, ". . . exhilarating. And your strength stayed with me. For a while, at least. After every transfusion, I could do things I'd never done before. Run in my own body, swim to a place hardly anyone had ever been, kiss a guy. I'd never even kissed anyone before. I was always just the Sick Girl, not a *girl* girl. Your blood did more than just keep me alive. It gave me a life."

She pressed her hands over her face. "I know you don't care. But you deserve to know that you changed my life."

"And that's why you came back," Gabriel said.

"That's why I came back, even after what you did to me last night," Shay agreed. "You've been keeping me alive. Chained up in that room. It wouldn't have been right to let you die."

Honorable. She was honorable. And he'd treated her as if she was a pawn. *I did what I did to escape,* Gabriel told himself.

That's not all, though, he had to admit. Gabriel had taken her hostage because he wanted vengeance. He wanted his captors to suffer the same way he had. He wanted them to feel his hatred, his contempt for them.

The doctor didn't care about Shay; that much was obvious. But the woman, Shay's mother . . . she cared. She would come after her daughter, and Martin would come after his prize. His vampire. So Shay, hostage, would lure them to him, when he was strong, when he was ready, when he was surrounded by his family. It was a good plan. He would use her to extract his revenge on them. It's not as if he were treating her worse than he'd been treated. Not even close. And when he had what he wanted, he'd let her go.

Let her go. As if she couldn't walk out of this room right now. She was here of her own free will, and even so, he still planned to use her. *It's necessary,* he thought. He couldn't let himself get weak and sentimental. She was a human. Humans thought nothing of killing his kind.

She saved me, a small part of Gabriel protested. He ignored it. She was a human and he was treating her better than she deserved.

"I'll stay until you're strong enough to take care of yourself," Shay added. She stood up and walked over to the dresser. "I wish I had medicine with me. My head is pounding."

There was perspiration above her upper lip now, and her hands shook. Gabriel studied her thin form. This was more than a headache. "Do you need my blood?" he asked. She'd said it was what had been keeping her alive. Could it be true?

"No."

"You said you'd be dead soon."

She turned to face him. "Probably," she admitted. "Without your blood, I'd be dead already, I guess. But that still doesn't make it right."

Gabriel released his eye teeth, ignoring her sharp little intake of breath. He nicked a vein in his wrist and held his arm out to her in a silent invitation. It was the right thing to do, for him to give it, even if it had been wrong for her parents to take it from him.

Besides, he needed her alive.

She stood motionless for a moment, staring at the blood hungrily. Then she stepped over and knelt beside him. Slowly, she lowered her mouth to his wrist.

The sensation was like nothing he'd ever felt before. As she suckled, he could feel his blood transferring from his body to hers. It was like the blood was a hot, red current connecting them to each other. He gasped, overwhelmed by the power of the experience. It had been so long since he'd felt anything this intensely, so long since he'd allowed himself to. After what had happened to Sam, he hadn't wanted to feel anything ever again.

It had been Gabriel's desire to feel more, to experience more, that had led him out into the world. Sam, his brother, had come with him, of course. Sam would still be here if Gabriel hadn't—

Gabriel squeezed his eyes shut, allowing the sensation of Shay feeding to block out all thought. He didn't open them until he felt her mouth move away, breaking their connection. Her lips were stained by the blood, his blood. He had a wild urge to lean over and lick the blood away. His own vampire blood was poison to him, but it would almost be worth it.

"You've got—" Gabriel gestured to his mouth.

The girl blinked, slowly, as if she'd been drugged. "Oh." She reached up and wiped his blood away.

"What did you see?" he asked. There was a residual expression of horror on her face. She didn't answer. "Shay, what did you see?" He'd used her name without intending to. It made it harder to see her as just an object of use. But that was impossible now, anyway. What he'd experienced when she drank from him—those feelings weren't possible with an object.

"You were hunting," Shay said. Her voice had a tremor in it. "With Sam. You felt like an animal, ragged and dirty, with no home to go back to. Sam wanted to find a place to hide from the sun, but you said you had to get Ernst first. You and Sam, you'd . . . attacked a family in a farm. You drank from the mother and her son until they were unconscious. But then you looked for Ernst, and he—"

Her voice broke off, as if the thought made her ill. "He was in the stable with the goats, and he had drunk the father dry. He'd killed the man," Gabriel finished for her.

Shay met his gaze, tears in her eyes. "It made you sick. You threw up in the dirt while Sam pulled Ernst off the man."

Sick. It was exactly how he'd felt that day.

"Ernst is the one who taught me not to kill. I've never killed a Giver," Gabriel said quietly. "But he was mad with grief and rage. The humans had . . ." He couldn't go there, couldn't relive that night. "They had reduced us to that state."

"Not the farm family. Other humans," Shay whispered. "I felt a memory of terror, humans with torches."

"Yeah. The typical ignorant torch-bearing mob," Gabriel said angrily. "They think we're monsters. Only humans are deserving of life."

She backed away from him and sank down on the edge of the bed. "You were mad with grief, too. I felt that much. I still feel it. What happened?"

Gabriel turned his face away. He wasn't going to give in to this. Maybe she did see visions of his past—clearly she did. But that didn't mean he had to tell her more.

"Sorry." She got to her feet. "I didn't mean to pry. I got used to seeing pieces of your life and trying to fit them together like a puzzle."

"I'm not a puzzle."

"I know." Shay reached out to him, but stopped short of touching him. "I'm sorry."

He didn't answer. He would give anything to be able to walk away right now, but he was weak. Powerless. "I think I'll go take a shower," she said. "We could both use some time alone."

Gabriel nodded. He would definitely like some time without her around. Not that it would actually change anything. She was in control whether he liked it or not.

○ ○ ○ ○ ○ ○ ○ ○ ○ ○ ○ ○ ○ ○ ○ ○

By THE TIME SHE APPEARED AGAIN, Gabriel had managed to pull himself up into a sitting position. And he'd made his plans. Much as he wanted to push it, get up and get moving as soon as he could, that would be a bad idea. He was still far from his family's compound in Tennessee, and at any moment Shay's stepfather could come after them. If that happened, Gabriel would need enough strength to fight. Shay might not realize just how dangerous that man was, but Gabriel did. He'd experienced the intensity of Martin's ambition firsthand. These days, people threw around words like *sociopath* or *obsession*. A century ago, the word would have been *monster*.

It takes one to know one, Gabriel thought wryly. Maybe Martin hadn't killed anyone, but he was as much of a bloodsucker as Gabriel was.

The whole family would deal with him, together. It was their way—share the vengeance and the responsibility for the act of vengeance. Even though none of them could feel his fury—his rage at being kept chained, impotent, and used as a lab rat—Ernst and the others would still be angry enough to want revenge.

For now, though, he would give in to his weakness and allow Shay to nurse him back to health. He wouldn't try to move until he was truly strong enough. He would push down his resentment and play along. This girl wasn't the one who'd imprisoned him. He would focus on her and not on the memories of her stepfather.

Shay had put her clothes back on, but her dark hair was wet and her skin glistened. She sat down next to him and smiled a little shyly.

"So."

"So," Gabriel repeated.

She seemed to realize how close to him she was sitting, and she shifted away slightly. "So, you're a vampire."

He laughed. The way she said it, so casually—even though he could hear a little strain under the casualness—he never thought he'd hear a human make that statement in that tone. "Yep, I'm a vampire," he answered, channeling Ellen DeGeneres. Then he realized that Shay was too young to remember Ellen's *Time* magazine cover with the line "Yep, I'm gay" on it. She was too young to remember how big a deal Nirvana was at the beginning, or how shocking the OJ Simpson trial was. To him, her entire lifetime was nothing more than the blink of an eye. Shay hadn't even been born during the Watergate scandal or the Cold War or Vietnam.

o o I75 o o

She was so very young, too young to know much of anything, and yet she had experienced parts of his life that had happened hundreds of years ago.

"Okay, crosses: true or false?" Shay asked.

"You're not trying to figure out how to kill me, are you?" Gabriel said.

"No!" Shay exclaimed. "God. I saved your life twice. And I could run out the door right now, crossless. You're not exactly in tip-top shape. It's just the first thing that came into my head. Vampires—crosses."

He'd offended her. He hadn't meant to. He'd actually been joking—because, like she said, she'd saved his life twice. "Crosses don't hurt my family. Or holy water. But I've heard that there are some vampires who can be burned by either of them."

"I don't get it," Shay said.

Gabriel shrugged. "The mind is a powerful thing."

"So it burns because they expect it to burn?"

"As far as I know, all vampires are physiologically the same; so that's my theory," Gabriel replied. "If you truly believe you're an evil, God-forsaken creature, then a religious artifact burns."

"And you know you aren't an evil, God-forsaken creature, so it doesn't hurt you," she said. "So why does the hawthorn work?"

"I think it's just poisonous to us," Gabriel said, still reeling from her casual assertion that he wasn't evil. He'd practically choked her, he'd kidnapped her and used her as a human shield, and yet she didn't think of him as evil.

"Can I ask something else?" she said. "Actually, can I ask many, many questions?"

He smiled, despite himself. "Go ahead."

"Okay. What's the deal with Sam?" she began. "In one of the visions I saw, it was your last day in the sun, and Sam was completely awesome. But then I saw the night when Sam stole you from the orphanage, and that was terrifying. I mean, he didn't take Elena, because he knew how badly you wanted her to stay hidden. But he took you, and you were just a little boy. So what's his deal? Is he good or bad?"

Gabriel gaped at her. He hadn't been expecting something so personal. He'd figured she would ask about vampire slayers or if he could turn into fog.

Shay noticed his expression. "Sorry. I guess it's weird that I even know about Elena," she said. "I'm probably freaking you out."

Gabriel hadn't expected a human to try to see things from his perspective. Had being inside him, as she described it, actually made her willing to see him as a being with emotions equal to her own?

"It is weird. But it's not like you intentionally set out to pry," Gabriel said. He thought for a moment. "I'm so used to the way my family is formed, that it doesn't seem horrifying or even strange to me anymore. It's been almost four hundred years since the vampires came to the orphanage."

Now she gaped at him.

"I'm older than I look," he pointed out. "I haven't thought about that night in ages, literally. I guess it was terrifying. Looking back, though, I see it as the night I found a home, a real home."

He thought she'd begin to argue immediately, insisting he couldn't possibly feel the way he felt. Instead, she waited for him to continue. "I didn't have a family before that night. I almost had a sister, in Elena, but I didn't remember my parents. I don't know if I even have—had—any biological brothers and sisters. It's hard for me to imagine what my life would have been like if I hadn't been taken that night. I used to wish Elena had been taken too. But Sam knew I believed I was saving her, and he let me have that."

"Why did he take you?" Shay asked. "And the others?"

"We can't reproduce like humans. For us, having children means taking them." Gabriel sighed. "That sounds bad. In my family, we took only orphans. They had no family, so we would give them one. The child is raised with us, as if we are their parents, older siblings, what have you. When they're older, they serve as our eyes and ears during daylight hours. And when they're grown, they join us through the blood ritual. They become vampires."

"That's why they only wanted the youngest children," Shay murmured. "So they don't remember."

"Yes. For kids even a little older than I was, becoming a part of the family is almost impossible. The memories of human life are too strong. Mine had almost faded before I made the choice to give up the sun," Gabriel answered.

"Was it really a choice? I mean, I get that the timing was a choice. But could you really have kept your humanity, if you'd wanted to?" Her eyes were intent.

Gabriel's instinct was just to say yes—to say that nothing was forced. "To be honest, I don't know," he admitted. He tried to imagine Ernst's reaction if Gabriel had turned his back on the family. It was too painful to think about hurting the man who had become his father that way. "It never happened. No human is transformed until he or she reaches physical maturity. By that time—"

"By that time there's nothing to go back to. Like you couldn't go find Elena fourteen years after you were taken," Shay said. "She wouldn't have known you."

"I like to think she'd remember me. I never forgot her. But Elena wouldn't have been able to give me all that my family did. I loved them, and they loved me. That's why none of us ever considered rejecting the chance to transform."

"I saw you once, waiting for an orphan girl to take. You and Ernst thought her mother was dying of influenza."

Gabriel shook his head. He didn't recall that night.

"Her father was already dead. But Ernst said he hoped you wouldn't have to take her," Shay explained. "You were outside, watching her house. Waiting."

The memory rushed back to Gabriel. How strange that she remembered such detail about a moment he'd all but forgotten. "Millie," he said with a smile. "She was four, old enough to understand that her parents were gone. But the memory faded eventually. Ernst became her father after that. He's a father to us all."

"That vision made me think about my own dad. I never knew him. He left my mother before I was even born," Shay told him. "Ernst told you that your parents are in you, part of you, even if you never knew them." Gabriel watched Shay lightly run her fingers over her face, then down toward a necklace that hung beneath her shirt. "I'm not sure if that would be a good thing or a bad thing."

"I choose to think it's good," he answered. "Although I don't know anything more about my parents than you do about your father."

Shay snorted. "I know he left."

That's worse, Gabriel thought. It might be better to not know anything, like him.

"You said you had many, many questions," Gabriel reminded Shay, hoping to pull her out of the dark place she'd slipped into.

"Right. Okay." Shay thought for a moment. "So you study bats, is that right? Is that like an inside joke or what?"

"Ernst has always been fascinated by science—he's been there since its invention." Gabriel smiled. "Also, working as researchers in a remote location gives us the privacy we need. We've been doing it for two hundred years now, in various places. It's a good fit. As for why bats? I suppose there's an appealing irony. But mostly it's because they're nocturnal and so are we, and we were able to get a grant to study them."

"Wow. That is so much less interesting than 'We turn into bats at will, and so we surround ourselves with our bloodsucking brethren,'" Shay told him.

"I know. Sorry," Gabriel chuckled. "We are very comfortable in caves, for what it's worth. We lived in them in Greece."

Shay shrugged. "That just sounds uncomfortable if you're not a bat."

Gabriel didn't want to think about their cavern in Greece. He pushed the memory away, as he always did when it appeared. "Maybe when we leave Tennessee, we'll choose a new specialty. The children of the night, possibly."

"What?"

"You aren't up on your classic vampire lore. We're supposed to have an affinity for wolves. Dracula calls them children of the night."

He put on his best bad Transylvanian accent, and she laughed.

The sound startled him. This was wrong. He was feeling way too comfortable with her, perhaps because she was acting so comfortable with him. Did she truly believe she knew him after a handful of visions? Tiny pieces of a life that had spanned centuries?

If she did know him, she wouldn't be so comfortable. She'd be disgusted by what he had done. Maybe she would even have left him to die. Maybe he'd even have deserved it.

"Where did vampires come from in the first place, though?" Shay asked. "If you can't reproduce, then you need another vampire to make you."

"More than one. It's a ritual involving the entire family."

"But how did the first vampire come into existence?" Shay pressed.

Gabriel was suddenly tired of their question-and-answer game. He longed for the dark and oblivion of his daytime sleep. But it wasn't time yet, and he couldn't enter the state at will. Besides, he'd invited her curiosity.

"Where did the first human come from?" Gabriel countered. "Adam and Eve? Evolution? In China there's a story that says Pan-Gu, the first being, grew inside a big cosmic egg."

"Huh," Shay said.

"Yeah," Gabriel answered.

Shay yawned. "You must be tired," Gabriel said. "It's late for you." He wished she would fall asleep since he couldn't.

"I slept a lot during the day while you were unconscious," she told him. "I wasn't sure if you were going to wake up. But I remembered it's hard for you to stay awake during the day."

"It's called the death sleep. Some of the older vampires can fight against the impulse and stay awake during the daylight hours."

"Like Sam," she murmured. It was surreal hearing Sam's name on her lips.

"I haven't mastered that ability yet, although I've been trying to. Giving ourselves completely over to the death sleep makes us too vulnerable," Gabriel explained.

"So I shouldn't be worried if you're like that during the day tomorrow?"

"You shouldn't be worried." How did he get to this place, where he was telling a human not to worry about him?

"I've been up in the middle of the night a lot. In hospitals, they wake you up every few hours, for medication or to take readings or something," Shay said. "Sometimes there's a good old movie on. Wanna see?" She got up and grabbed the remote from the top of the television. "Although I guess there are no old movies for you."

"Not really," he answered. "I saw one of the very first movies. I snuck in, even though I wasn't supposed to have any contact with humans unless it was absolutely necessary."

"Unless you were drinking their blood," Shay commented.

Gabriel raised one eyebrow. "What part of *necessary* didn't you understand?"

"You sound so modern sometimes," Shay said.

"I am modern. I've just been around for a long time. If you aren't able to adapt, you'll die. It's something we teach the children in our family. Now, do you want to hear this story or not?"

"Yes. Pray continue. Please."

Was she actually mocking him? Teasing him? What kind of human was she?

He returned to his anecdote. "Anyway, it was this short little piece of film. A gunslinger turned toward the camera—so, toward the audience—and shot. People dropped to the floor, trying to find cover."

"What did you do?" Shay asked.

"You didn't have a vision of that day, clearly." One side of Gabriel's mouth curled up in a half smile. "I didn't do anything except think it was very cool."

Shay studied his face for a few seconds. "No, you screamed like a little girl in pigtails," she guessed.

"I might have made some sort of manly sound of surprise," Gabriel replied.

Shay laughed. Again, Gabriel was struck by how surreal it was to be sitting here with a human. Talking with her as if she really had known him for hundreds of years.

Stay focused, he told himself. *It's true; she's an innocent. And I'll make sure she's kept safe.*

But Shay's mother and stepfather, they were another story. They deserved to suffer for what they'd done to Gabriel. He'd make them pay for every hour they had held him captive. Then he would kill them both.

Shay reached out and ran one finger down Gabriel's arm, taking in the sensation of smooth warm skin over firm muscle. He didn't react. She hesitated, then swept his dark brown hair away from his forehead, letting her fingers tangle in the curls for a moment. She'd been wanting to feel the texture, and it felt the way she'd expected it to—soft and springy at the same time.

Abruptly, she jerked her hand away. What was she doing? Gabriel was out of it, as out of it as if she'd slipped him a roofie. More than that. His whole system had slowed down—his heart rate, his breathing. It was almost like he was in a coma, alive, but unaware of his surroundings.

Or was he aware, at some deep level, of everything he experienced during his daytime slumber state? Shay flushed at the thought of Gabriel feeling her light touch, knowing without being able to react, to push her hand away. That or capture her hand and hold it close.

Shay jumped up from the bed, where she'd been sitting next to Gabriel. *This is the guy who took me hostage*, she reminded herself, appalled that she imagined him touching her and liked what she was imagining.

Well, he was also the guy who'd kept her alive with his blood, who had completely changed her life, letting her experience strength and power and normalcy. He was the guy who had tried to protect his best friend, even at the age of five. Who loved Ernst even though he'd seen Ernst kill a man out of anger. He was sensitive. Powerfully connected to the people in his family.

And he was the guy she'd stayed up all night with, talking and talking. It had been, despite the circumstances that brought it about, one of the best nights of her life. Who was she kidding? It was *the* best. She'd never felt so close to anyone, except her mom. Mom, who had been lying to her, who had helped find Gabriel and take him captive. The thought brought up a mix of raw emotions. She felt betrayed, and angry, and as if the world had gotten knocked out from under her feet.

But still, this was the longest she'd ever gone without talking to her mother. Which was kind of pathetic, since it was only one day. She couldn't get the sound of Mom's sobs out of her mind.

Shay shook it off and turned her attention back to Gabriel. She didn't want to think about any of the other stuff right now. What she wanted to do was run her thumb over his lips. They were perfect. The top one perfectly molded. The bottom one just a little fuller than the top. She wanted to kiss that tattoo on his neck, a stylized phoenix that throbbed ever so slightly with his pulse.

I need to get out of here, she decided. She couldn't spend all day staring at him. Well, maybe she could, but she wasn't going to. Shay hurried over to the door. She opened it only a tiny bit, making sure no sunlight touched Gabriel, then slipped outside, into the sunshine. How would it feel to never have that warmth and brightness again? She looked up at the friendly yellow ball for a few seconds. She couldn't even imagine life without it.

I can go now, she thought. *Gabriel is alive; I've saved him. I don't have to stay.*

The thought seemed to freeze her, pinning her there in the sunlight. Why not get into the car and drive off? Her mind offered arguments—Gabriel couldn't even walk yet; maybe he wouldn't be able to reach the bags of blood. If someone came into the room, Gabriel was too weak to fight. But they were only excuses, not really the truth.

The truth was that Shay didn't want to leave.

I'm dying, she thought, knowing it was true even though she felt so strong. The strength wasn't hers; it was just borrowed from

Gabriel. It wouldn't last. But while it did, she wanted to do something worthwhile. Living with Martin and Mom wouldn't do. Going back to school wouldn't do. None of that really *mattered*. But being near a vampire, one who'd given her strength, one who she felt drawn to . . . well, that mattered. It was an experience that even people who lived to be a hundred couldn't possibly have.

I told Gabriel I'd stay until he was strong, and I will, Shay told herself. *I don't have to think about leaving until then.*

She scanned the area around their just-off-the-interstate motel and spotted an IHOP. All she'd have to do was cut across a couple of parking lots to get it. On the way, she passed a Dollar Tree store and impulsively headed in. She wandered around, looking at the mishmash of merchandise. She picked up a basket and tossed in a couple of toothbrushes and some toothpaste, then a pack of *High School Musical* playing cards. It was easy to figure out why some things had ended up in the bargain store.

It's a little like the Island of Misfit Toys, she thought. There was one hospital stay when she'd watched *Rudolph* every day, multiple times a day, even though it was August. It had made her feel safe somehow, maybe because she knew going in that everything was going to turn out well for the reindeer and the toys and the elf who wanted to be a dentist. Or maybe because her mother had been there to hold her hand every time the abominable snowman attacked.

Shay added a raggedy stuffed leopard to her basket. She didn't need it. Obviously, she didn't need it. But it was a dollar. And it needed a home. So did all the other sad toys in big bin at the end of the aisle, but she couldn't rescue everybody.

She picked up a few magazines and some candy that looked

really unhealthy in a fun way—all Day-Glo colors. "Babysitting?" the cashier asked Shay as she checked out.

"Yeah," Shay answered. In a weird way it was the truth. She was babysitting a vampire who was hundreds of years older than she was. The thought made her smile, although it was nothing to smile about. Really, there was nothing at all to smile about. Jesus. Her mother and Martin—how could they have done this?

She picked up her pace a little, anxiety giving her the jitters, as she left the store and continued toward the IHOP. Shay hadn't wanted to worry Gabriel by mentioning that she'd called home before she went back to him. She didn't want him thinking that Martin might still come after them. But he might. Mom and Martin would know by now that she wasn't coming home. What would they do?

There was a newspaper box outside the pancake place. Shay dug some change out of her jeans pocket and bought a copy of the local paper. She was only about two hours from home. If Martin and her mom had gone public, there'd be some kind of article. A terminally ill girl who went missing would be big news. And if the terminally ill girl had a well-known stepfather, that would make it even bigger.

The hostess waved at her when she stepped inside. "Just one," Shay said.

"Follow me." The hostess grabbed a menu and showed Shay to a booth. As she slid into her seat, Shay was hit by the realization that this was the first time she'd eaten in a restaurant by herself. Another first, thanks to Gabriel's blood.

"Your server will be right over," the hostess told her. Shay nodded, thinking of the way Gabriel had just nicked open a vein for her.

She'd needed blood, and there it was, with no hesitation from him.

Feeding from him, taking the blood directly from his body into hers, had been almost overwhelmingly intimate. And the vision, at the farm with Sam and Ernst, it had felt sharper than the other ones. More . . . textured. The whole time she had experienced his fear and revulsion and anger, the taste of his blood, warm and salty-sweet, had been on her tongue.

"Coffee?" Shay glanced up at her server. The guy's attitude suggested he'd already asked her the question more than once.

"Yes, please." She grabbed the menu. "And chocolate chip pancakes."

"Whipped cream?" the guy asked.

"Definitely." Shay had never had coffee before or chocolate chips. Nothing with caffeine, just in case. But she was basically dead already, just living on vampire blood until she'd erased her debt to Gabriel. And if she was dead, nothing could kill her.

So bring on the junk food, she thought. *Gabriel's blood can take it.* She smiled. Her body felt like it was glowing from within. It had felt that way ever since she'd fed from him last night. It was even better than the strength she'd had at Kaz's party and on the island.

She flashed on Gabriel chained to the exam table, and her smile faded. That's where he'd been while she was at Kaz's party. And while she'd been running on the track. Swimming in the river. Guilt spurted through her. She'd rescued Gabriel as soon as she had discovered the truth. And he'd repaid her by taking her hostage for a while. So maybe they were even already.

Two hours of sitting in a car against my will versus two weeks of being held captive and drained of blood, she thought. *I'm not sure we'll ever be even.*

Shay spread the newspaper out in front of her and began flipping through it, making sure to look at every article. By the time her food came, she'd made it all the way to the last page, and there had been nothing about her running away or being kidnapped, nothing about her at all.

Good. But she needed more info. As soon as she paid the bill and walked back outside, she pulled out her cell to call Olivia. She should be able to catch her friend between first and second period.

"I told your mom about Miami," Olivia said, not bothering with a hello. "She bought it." *Why wouldn't she—from you, devoted friend of her poor sick daughter?* Shay thought. Olivia was like an angel to her mom. Someone who gave her daughter the gift of seminormalcy just by hanging out with her.

"That's great," Shay exclaimed. "Thank you so much. Thank you, thank you." Olivia liked gratitude. And Shay was sincerely grateful. She'd turned to Olivia at a time when Olivia had every reason to reject her, and Olivia had come through. "What did she say?"

"That she was buying a ticket on the next plane. She's going to rent a car there and drive around Miami until she finds you," Olivia answered.

"And Martin?" Shay was a lot more worried about him. Her stepfather was used to getting his way. Anyone who had Martin's money and fame usually did get their way.

"He's staying home, in case you come back or call," Olivia said.

"Good. Good. That's good." Thinking about Martin gave Shay

the jitters. She could imagine how much he wanted Gabriel back. Gabriel's blood was probably the best shot Martin would ever get at his historic medical breakthrough.

Of course, he mostly wanted Gabriel back so he could keep Shay alive. Which meant he would be just as intent on finding her. He knew how easy it would be for her to die out here alone.

"Your mom gave me a message for you, in case you're interested," Olivia told her.

"Of course I'm interested." Although maybe she shouldn't be. How could her mother have kept such a huge secret from her? How could her mother have allowed Gabriel to suffer so much?

"She said that everything she's done your whole life is because she loves you," Olivia said.

Shay felt tears spring to her eyes. She could feel her mother's pain as sharply as if it were her own. But she couldn't worry about Mom right now. She had to protect Gabriel. She had to take care of him. In a way, she was responsible for what her mother and Martin had done to him.

"My turn to ask questions now," Olivia announced. "Are you okay? Don't lie."

"I'm fine," Shay answered.

"*Fine* fine?" Olivia pressed. "You're not feeling sick at all? Or weak? Or feverish?"

"Really, Olivia, I'm fine. Good, even." *Thanks to Gabriel.* He'd given her his blood so freely, even after what Martin and her mother had done to him.

"Call me tomorrow," Olivia said.

"I will," Shay promised, hanging up. She'd reached the motel room again, and she felt a flutter of butterflies in her stomach as she opened the door and went in.

Gabriel lay sleeping. Shay sat back down to stare at him again.

How could she not? He was such a mix of contradictions. He'd treated her so harshly, then so generously. Who was he really?

ELEVEN

○ ○ ○ ○ ○ ○ ○ ○ ○ ○ ○ ○ ○ ○ ○ ○

"Is it weird to drink it cold?" Shay asked, handing Gabriel a bag of blood. He was better tonight. He took the bag, tore it open, and took a long drink, all without her help.

"Refreshing," he said as Shay sat on the bed next to him. "I prefer it Frappuccino-style, but . . ." He shrugged, and Shay found herself fascinated by the way the motion made his back muscles rise and fall under his T-shirt.

She looked away. Were vampires psychic? Hadn't she read something like that once? If Gabriel could tell what she was thinking, it would be beyond humiliating.

"I guess we could get a blender," she babbled, trying to pull her thoughts away from Gabriel's body. His really very nice body.

Gabriel laughed. "I was kidding," he told her.

"So vampires have a sense of humor. Interesting," Shay joked. "What about mind reading? Do they—you— Can you do that?"

"Why?" Gabriel raised an eyebrow. "Have you been thinking things you don't want me to know?"

"Everybody thinks things they don't want other people to know," Shay said, warmth flooding her neck and face. Damn it. She was blushing. You didn't have to be a mind reader to know what that meant.

Gabriel turned away from her and took another long drink. *He's definitely stronger,* Shay thought as she watched him. *He'll be able to take care of himself soon, and I can go home.*

Home. God. She didn't have a home anymore, not really. Yeah, Mom would be overjoyed to see her. Martin—well, who knew what Martin would feel? He obviously didn't think there was anything wrong with imprisoning and torturing a living being in order to find the cure for Shay's disease. He probably thought Shay's horror was a big overreaction, and he definitely thought she was being stupid. He'd all but said that when he told her she'd die without the blood. In Martin's world, the only sane thing to do would be to go home and start stealing Gabriel's blood again.

Shay sighed. She couldn't go back to her old life with them, not now. Maybe she'd actually go through with the lie she'd asked Olivia to tell. Not take off for Miami, but go somewhere, as far as her gas tank would take her, and then live—live, live, live—until she couldn't anymore.

The thought made her feel better. She'd promised herself that she would embrace life, and she could still do that.

Gabriel noticed the Dollar Tree bag on the floor by the bed. "You went out?" he asked, and there was an edge to his voice.

"I made sure the sun wouldn't hit you," Shay told him. "But don't worry, I won't leave you until you're strong enough to manage on your own. You seem like you're feeling better. Are you?"

Gabriel didn't reply. Instead he picked up the bag. Shay playfully snatched it away. "Nuh-uh. No looking until you answer my question."

"Remind me."

"Can you read minds?" Shay asked.

"No. Although, when I feed, I get a rush of emotions from the Giver. They aren't connected to thoughts, just pure emotion," Gabriel said.

"Yes. I remember that from one of the visions. It was like being immersed in an ocean of feeling. And, by the way, I wouldn't know what being in the ocean was like if not for you. I've never done that in my own body, but you went swimming in Greece, and I was there. Buoyed up by the salty water. Swimming on a path of light from the setting sun."

"So long ago," Gabriel said. "I've swum in the ocean many times—many, many times—since then. But never with the colors of the sunset stretched out in front of me, dazzling me." He frowned.

"You miss it, don't you? The sun?" Shay asked.

"Not most of the time. There are compensations," Gabriel replied, but he didn't seem convinced. That streak of sadness she'd often felt in him seemed close to the surface right now.

"Compensations like what? You can't even read minds," Shay

teased him. "And don't tell me that doglike nose of yours makes up for not seeing the sun."

"My nose isn't cold and wet." Gabriel touched it, as if to check.

"Not that way. I mean your sense of smell. I saw on some Discovery channel show that dogs can smell a single drop of blood in five quarts of water. They have more scent receptors than humans," Shay said.

"You watch a lot of TV," he commented.

"I spend a lot of time in bed," she said. Then she clapped her hand over her mouth. "Sleeping, I mean! 'Cause I'm sick. It's a Sick Girl thing."

Gabriel turned away, trying to hide his smile, but she saw it anyway. She dropped her head into her hands, hiding her face and her blushing cheeks. "So you have a Super Nose, and you can see in the dark, and you can hear like crazy," she said through her fingers. "I was in your cave once, and I actually heard the bats' heartbeats."

"I guess," Gabriel said with a shrug. "I can't say it's made that much of an impression on me."

"Everything makes an impression on you," Shay insisted. "I know. I've been you." But that vision in the caverns, it had been different. Gabriel had still been smelling, and hearing, and seeing everything. But it felt blocked somehow, she now realized. He was experiencing things, but he hadn't really been letting them in. *What happened?* she wondered. *Why aren't you appreciating life as much as you used to?*

"Sam used to say I had a thirst for life," Gabriel said. "Ironic, huh?"

"Well, you do literally thirst for it." Shay nodded toward the bag of blood in his hand. Gabriel looked at it, then lifted it to his lips and drained it.

"It's not mind reading, but I do have a link to the other members of my family. I know how each of them is feeling. I know if they're in pain or need help. And I can sense where they are," Gabriel said as he tossed the plastic bag. "That link is broken now. As soon as the hawthorn hit my system, it went away. I don't know if that's permanent or not. I'm assuming my family can't feel me either, or they'd have come for me."

"I'm sorry," Shay said. She didn't know what else to say. Gabriel loved his family, she knew. And to be cut off from them, especially at a time when he'd been treated so badly, well, it had to be awful. He must feel unbearably lonely without that connection. "Do you—do you want to talk about it?"

"No, I want that bag." He reached over and easily plucked the Dollar Tree bag from her fingers. "I've earned my look." Gabriel's lips quirked into a smile as he pulled the stuffed leopard free. "I can't read minds, as you know," he told her. "So I'm going to need an explanation."

"I don't have one. I just— Really, no explanation," Shay said.

"It simply appeared in the bag?"

"It wanted to come with me. What could I say?" she asked, feeling a little silly, especially when Gabriel studied her face for a long moment. "What?" she finally asked.

"Nothing." Gabriel took out the toothbrushes and toothpaste.

"I wasn't sure. Do you even brush?" Shay asked.

He laughed. "Yeah. Thanks."

He added the playing cards to the pile. "I thought we might want something to do," Shay explained.

Gabriel upended the bag, and a rainbow of candy fell out.

"You're planning to eat this?" Gabriel held up a plastic ring with a huge translucent blue gem made out of hard candy.

Shay took the ring, unwrapped it, stuck it on her finger, and took a lick. "I've never been allowed to eat anything like this," she admitted.

"Why would you want to?" Gabriel looked faintly repulsed.

"Because I've never been allowed. It's a Sick Girl thing. Only healthy food. Bland, tasteless, healthy food." Shay took another lick.

"You keep saying that—it's a Sick Girl thing. Is that really how you see yourself, as nothing but a sick girl?" Gabriel asked.

The question was like a smack to the back of her head. "Uh, yeah, sometimes, I guess," Shay replied. She was always mentally accusing Olivia and everybody else in her life of seeing her only as the Sick Girl. She'd never realized that she did it to herself just as much.

"Well, take it from me, there's more to you than sickness. You're one-of-a-kind," Gabriel said. "For starters, you're sitting in a motel with a vampire and you're acting like it's no biggie."

Shay snorted. "You said biggie."

"Don't harsh my buzz," Gabriel shot back. "Seriously, you're not just 'the Sick Girl.' You're Shay. You're unique."

"*Special*," Shay mumbled, embarrassed by the way he was looking at her. "That's the code word for 'sick,' or 'damaged,' or 'weird.'"

"It also means 'important.' 'Uncommon,'" Gabriel leaned closer to her. "'Rare.'"

If he kept looking at her the way he was—like she was *special*, not special—she didn't think she could take it. She reached over and picked up a package of cotton candy off the bed. "Do you eat? I mean, *can* you? Or is it all blood all the time?"

"Blood is all I can digest now," Gabriel replied.

Shay ripped open the bag of cotton candy and put one of the fluffy pink pieces on her tongue. It instantly dissolved. "You could eat this, I bet. There's really no digesting involved. It just kind of evaporates into sweetness."

"I'll pass," Gabriel said.

"Why? Where's my life-embracing Gabriel?" Had she actually just called him *her* Gabriel?

"You realize you've known me at a lot of different ages. I've changed over time. The me you're thinking of, that's an old version," Gabriel answered.

"So now you're the guy in the cave. With all those amazing senses you have on mute. Is that it?" Shay demanded.

"After you're alive for hundreds of years, you tell me if you still take the time to appreciate every minute experience," Gabriel snapped.

"I feel like—I don't even know how to describe it." Shay slid her fingers into her hair, at a loss.

"Why does it matter to you?" Gabriel asked.

"Because you changed my life, okay?" Shay burst out. "Your blood gave me strength and health, but *you*, the way you lived, it inspired me. I wanted to be like you. I wanted to feel everything, do everything the way you did. Back when you were young," she added, disgust roughening her voice. "The transfusions changed me in this profound way. Physically, they made me feel normal. Which to a sick girl—I mean, to me—was the same as feeling superhuman. And seeing your life made me think about the world and my own life in a different way."

Shay reached out and touched his arm lightly. "Now I know that there was a cost for those transfusions. I wouldn't have taken them if I'd known you were real and what you were suffering. But I still want to say thank you. Is that wrong? To thank you for something that it almost destroyed you to give?"

Gabriel didn't answer the question. Instead he asked one of his own. "What did you do after the first one?"

"The first transfusion?" Shay smiled at the memory. "I drank a beer."

They looked at each other for a long moment, and then Shay burst out laughing. It didn't sound so profound and life-changing when she described that part of it.

Gabriel snorted. "Excellent," he teased. "What else did you use my blood for?"

"Running. I went to P.E. and I ran. And dancing. And swimming. And I made out with my best friend's boyfriend," she confessed. "Want to play cards?"

"Back it up. You made out with your best friend's boyfriend?"

"Complete scum move, right?" Shay asked. Gabriel didn't say anything, just waited for her to go on. "I'd never kissed anyone, besides, you know, my mom. Didn't have any grandparents or—" She shook her head. "I'm off-tracking. I'd never kissed a guy. And I didn't think I ever would. I didn't think I'd have . . . time. But then after a transfusion I went to a party, and Kaz—that's my friend's boyfriend—and I were dancing. And I wanted to know, I really wanted to know how it would feel. I didn't think about Olivia. I didn't think about anything. I wanted to feel, and I let myself. Maybe I wouldn't have if I hadn't been drinking, but I just let myself."

Gabriel still didn't say anything.

"The transfusion before the party, it showed me a vision of you on your last day with the sun," Shay explained. "What Sam said to you—it really struck me. Do you remember? He told you you'd always felt things deeply, that you wanted to experience everything about your humanity before becoming a vampire. I wanted to be like you, that human guy who wanted to take in everything the world had to offer."

"It was a long time ago. I was nineteen," Gabriel said.

"Don't you miss it? Don't you want it back?" Shay asked. "Now that I've had the chance to be out in the world and try to suck the marrow out of life—I can't remember who said that—"

"Thoreau," Gabriel said softly.

"Right. Now that I've had that, I don't want to give it up. Even if I lived a thousand years, I wouldn't. That's what I've realized. Before I was just surviving, being careful so my body would keep going for one more day. But being truly *alive* . . . that's different. It's the whole point of everything. Without that feeling, why even bother living?"

"I don't know," Gabriel said. He wasn't answering her, he was talking about himself. Shay didn't know what had happened to steal his joy in life, but she wanted to help him find it again. The way he'd helped her.

"Open your mouth," she told him. To her surprise, Gabriel did. Shay popped a piece of cotton candy inside. "Now savor!" she ordered.

Gabriel closed his eyes and his brow furrowed.

"Don't try quite so hard," Shay coached him. "Tell me what you taste and smell and everything."

"It has an amazing surface area. So many contact points with all those strands. It goes from fluffy to sticky to small bits that are almost crunchy. There's a bitter mineral taste, not at all strong, maybe from the food coloring. Mostly just sweetness, overwhelming sweetness. Not a lot of ingredients."

Gabriel opened his eyes. "It's gone."

"So did you enjoy that?" Shay asked.

"Uh . . . I don't want to disappoint you. I appreciate the effort."

"No, you don't. You were annoyed by the effort," Shay said.

Gabriel laughed. "Well, being ordered to have a pleasurable experience is not exactly—"

Shay was already so close to him. All she had to do was lean a little more. So she did, interrupting him with a kiss, light and fast. So light and fast, Shay couldn't believe that her body responded as strongly as it did. She felt as if an arrow of heat had shot straight down her spine. *That* didn't happen with Chris Briglia. Or with Kaz.

She quickly pulled back.

"What was that?" Gabriel sounded gobsmacked. Shay had picked up that word from a British blood specialist she'd seen once—and it fit Gabriel's reaction perfectly.

"A kiss," Shay said, going for casual, even though her heart was pounding. "Something maybe I wouldn't have to order you to find pleasurable."

Gabriel shook his head, running one finger over his lips. "You really are one of a kind."

"Was it pleasurable?" Shay asked.

"I'm not sure I felt anything but surprise," Gabriel admitted.

"Does that mean we should try again?" Shay asked. This time she went for a teasing tone, but she was absolutely serious. She wanted this. She really wanted this. She hadn't realized how much until that quick, impulsive kiss. She wanted a real one now—long, and slow, and hot.

"I don't think that's a—"

Shay didn't let him finish. She caught his mouth with hers again and twisted her hands into his curly hair. She wasn't an expert in kissing. She'd had two—count 'em, two—kisses in her life. But kissing Gabriel felt so natural. Her tongue found his and slid across it. He put his hands on her waist and pulled her closer. Warm, soft, a brush of slick, hard teeth. Shay gave up trying to categorize the sensations and just turned herself and her body over to the hot rush.

Gabriel gave a groan low in his throat, then jerked away. He stared at her, his beautiful brown eyes wide. "That wasn't— We shouldn't have done that."

"Why not?"

Gabriel moved to the other side of the bed, putting distance between them. He didn't answer.

"Okay, but you were savoring the moment, right?" Shay pressed. "You felt that."

"On all cylinders," he said. But his tone was clipped, hard to read. "Let's play cards." He grabbed the deck and pulled off the plastic wrapping.

Shay watched him, a little stunned. How could he be talking about cards after that kiss? Hadn't he felt it too? There was no way that rush of feeling was one-sided. Shay's breath was still coming fast, her heart still slamming against her ribs. She didn't want to play some stupid game. She wanted to keep kissing him, wanted his arms around her, wanted more.

More Gabriel. There would never be enough.

Oh crap. I'm falling for him, Shay thought. *When did that happen?*

"Two-handed poker?" Gabriel asked.

"What?" Shay's mind was reeling. How could this be? It wasn't the kiss. The kiss wouldn't have been The Kiss if she hadn't already been into him. Was she crazy? She'd known that she had feelings for him, back when he was only a dream. But that was different. Falling for a fantasy guy was fine; it didn't mean anything. But Gabriel wasn't a dream anymore. He was a real live extremely complicated vampire. Falling for *that* was not fine.

"Do you know how to play?" Gabriel asked, his tone annoyed.

"Yeah. Sick Girls know all the card games," Shay answered, distracted. Which part of being . . . what? In love? In like? . . . with Gabriel was worse—the fact that she was dying or the fact that he was a vampire?

"Would you stop saying that?" Gabriel snapped. "I don't want to hear the words *Sick Girl* out of you again."

"Okay," she whispered. Because she wasn't just a Sick Girl. She was rare. Gabriel had said so. Did that mean he felt the same way she did? He certainly wasn't acting like it.

Gabriel began to deal. His fingers were long and strong. Elegant and competent. Shay wished she didn't notice every detail about him.

"What should we play for?" she asked, trying to get this night back to normal.

"Your stepfather took my wallet," Gabriel said.

"I have an idea." Shay stood up and headed into the bathroom. She was glad to have an excuse to get away from him for a minute. With trembling hands, she got herself a drink of water, willing her mind to stop all the drama. She'd wanted to immerse herself in an experience, and she'd wanted to get Gabriel to do the same.

And they had. End of story.

She grabbed the spare roll of toilet paper, then returned and sat back down on the bed across from him.

"We can use this for chips." Shay tore a long, long section of toilet paper off the roll, then tore off a second section of equal length. She handed one to Gabriel and kept one for herself, tearing it into individual squares.

She put a square in the middle and waited for him to tear up his own paper.

"Humans must seem like babies to you. All of us," she said. There was no way he would ever want to be with someone like her. He'd been all over the world, seen so much, lived so long. She probably seemed barely formed to him.

"Why do you say that?" Gabriel asked, adding a TP square of his own to the pot.

"Because you know everything. You've been alive longer than this country has even existed. It must be infuriating to watch all us humans acting so stupid, over and over. How can we not seem like infants?" Shay picked up her hand and studied it. Lousy. But she tossed a second TP square onto the pile. He didn't know her tells.

Gabriel studied his hand, threw down two TP squares. "I see your one, and raise you one," he said. "Age doesn't matter as much as you think. I'm old, but I haven't gotten wiser every year. There are saturation points, I guess you could call them. And some things, no matter how many times you experience them, are as powerful, as overwhelming, as the first time."

Shay raised a square. "Like what?"

"Like grief." Gabriel stared at his cards, but Shay didn't think he was really seeing them. "No matter how many times you've felt it, it's still like a punch to the stomach. That immediate. That hard to deal with, even though you've had to deal with it before. Many times before." He again raised her two. "Maybe love is like that too."

"Don't you know?" Shay asked. It wasn't exactly comfortable talking with him about love. But she wanted to know. She matched him, then raised a square. She'd already used more than half of her bankroll.

"I love my family. I can't imagine anything ever changing that. I think if I fell in love, it would be as powerful as grief, at least I hope so," Gabriel said. He raised. Shay had the feeling neither of them was paying any attention to the game.

"I could really feel how much you love Ernst and Sam and all your family when I was with you," Shay told him. That was a kind of love she could actually talk to him about. "Can I ask you another question?"

"Can I stop you?"

"What happened with you and Sam? Is he okay? Did something happen to him? I got a sad feeling, when you thought about him. You were in the cave with the bats, and Sam didn't seem to be around. Like you'd lost him somehow."

Gabriel tossed his cards down on the bed between them. "You should get some sleep. You were awake all day, shopping and whatever else you did. Do you need food? Have you eaten anything except candy?" He got off the bed and slumped down in the chair in front of the wobbly desk.

Shay pulled the candy ring off her finger. It didn't seem that fun anymore. "I'm good," she said. Actually, she could use a hamburger. But she wasn't going to tell him that. He obviously wanted her to go to sleep and leave him alone. "We didn't even finish the hand."

"You win." He didn't even glance at the cards strewn all over the bed.

Shay swept them into a pile, silently. Then she crawled under the covers and turned on her side, her back to Gabriel. She didn't want him to see her hurt. "Good night, I guess," she told him.

His only reply was flipping off the light.

When Shay woke up, it was after nine. Gabriel must've moved from the chair to the floor sometime while she slept. He lay on the ugly carpet, far from the window, in his daytime sleep. The death sleep, he called it.

Shay gathered the sheets around her and sat up in bed, staring down at him. It was either him or that bad painting of the wildflowers. *I'd want to look at Gabriel even if I were in the Louvre,* she admitted to herself.

As she gazed at him, she did a self-test, but not the usual kind. She focused on her feelings instead of her body, then let out a sigh. She was still attracted to him. Still wanted him. It hadn't all been a hormone storm last night.

"I'm kind of crazy about you," she said to his sleeping form, just to try out the words. "And that sucks, by the way."

It was no Romeo and Juliet situation. For starters, he obviously didn't feel the same—the way he'd turned off after their kiss proved that. And besides, the Capulets hadn't taken Romeo prisoner and drained him of blood. *I wanted to experience everything,* Shay thought ruefully. If this broke her heart a little, well, maybe that was something every girl felt at some point.

Did he know how she felt? Maybe that was why he'd suddenly gotten annoyed last night—so much so that he couldn't even finish one stupid game of poker. *What happened? Did I bring up something really bad when I asked about Sam? Is that what set him off?* she wondered for about the two hundred and fiftieth time. She'd wondered that as she had tried to fall asleep last night. It had taken forever. She'd been so hyper-aware of Gabriel being in the room with her. . . .

Maybe she'd never know the answer. No more transfusions, no more drinking from Gabriel—so no more visions of his life. Soon he'd be back to his own life and she'd be on her own.

Get over it, Shay told herself. She checked her watch. Second period would be over soon. She should be able to catch Olivia in between classes. Shay grabbed the car keys. The cell needed charging if she was going to keep calling Olivia every day. And that was a must do. If she didn't keep Olivia calm, she—and Gabriel—were going to have more problems than a little pissiness.

Just as the sun set that night, Gabriel awoke. He knew instantly he was being watched. He was on his feet before he realized it was Shay. Why did he have to sleep so deeply? He hated being vulnerable in front of a human. If he'd been at full strength, perhaps he would have been able to force himself to stay awake; but weak as he was, he hadn't a chance of stopping the death sleep from overtaking him.

"Nightmare?" Shay asked.

Gabriel raked his fingers through his hair. "No," he said. He wasn't ready to talk to her. Last night had been . . . unsettling. With that kiss. Kisses, actually, except he hadn't exactly participated in the first one. The second one, though . . . What had he been thinking?

He knew the answer. He hadn't been thinking anything. He'd just gone with the sensations, the way he used to before he learned to keep them in check. Before he learned the consequences of following your heart.

Shay had broken a big hole in the wall he'd built up so carefully. With that damn cotton candy and those damn kisses. And then she had to start asking about Sam. When his guard was down. The guilt and self-loathing had smashed into him full force.

Put her back in her proper place, he told himself. *Get back to when she was nothing more than the human girl. She's just a part of my plan. Once I'm done with her, I'll let her go, and it'll be like I never met her.*

He strode into the bathroom and grabbed a blood bag from the ice bucket. At least her question about Sam proved that she didn't know what had happened to him, what Gabriel had done. If she'd known, she wouldn't still be here. If she'd known, she'd have let him die that night he'd been poisoned. Gabriel tore open the top of the thick plastic bag with his teeth, then poured a stream of the cold blood down his throat. He suppressed a shudder. He'd lied to her. Cold blood tasted more than weird. It tasted wrong. Dead. But it did the job—bagged blood had kept his family alive for years now. Maybe that was why his enjoyment of life had dimmed, as Shay had pointed out. That, and Sam.

But the blood was enough. As he drank it down, he felt his body finish its recovery.

"When you're in the death sleep, do you dream?" Shay asked when he returned—reluctantly—to the main room.

She really did see him as something completely *other*, and that wouldn't change, not because they'd talked a lot, not because they'd kissed. Humans could never be trusted to understand his kind, to accept how similar they truly were. It helped to think that. It reminded him of his anger, his need for vengeance.

"Yes, I dream. I'm not so different than you," Gabriel snapped. "You want to think of me as some unnatural creature, so—" He forced himself to stop. He sighed. "I dream the same way I always have, the same as when I was a little boy."

"Oh," Shay said in a small voice. Gabriel felt as if he'd just kicked a puppy. *She's a piece of the plan. Soon I can let her go,* he reminded himself.

"I've had enough blood," he announced. "I'm strong enough to leave."

Shay immediately stood up, twisting her hands in front of her. "Okay. That's great." She began gathering up all her strange little purchases, shoving them into the plastic bag in a nervous haste. "Well, I hope you make it back to your family safely. I have to take Martin's car. I'm sorry."

Gabriel's heart sank. She thought he was going to let her go.

Not a possibility. He needed her to bring his captors to him—him and his family. He needed her to achieve the revenge he burned for, the revenge he deserved. "Shay."

She looked up at him, hope in her eyes. "Yes?"

"You're coming with me." There was no better way to say it.

"What?" Shay paled. At least that was better than her blushing. Last night when the blood had flooded her face, he'd wanted her so badly, even knowing that a taste would destroy him.

"I'm taking the car, and I'm taking you," he said. "So you can either walk out there on your own. Or I'll put you in myself."

TWELVE

· ○ ○ ○ ○ ○ ○ ○ ○ ○ ○ ○ ○ ○ ○ ○ ○

SHAY STARED OUT INTO THE DARKNESS flying by. Her head rested on the cool glass of the Range Rover's window, her body curled as close to the passenger-side door as she could get it, within the restraints of her seat belt. She wanted to be as far away from Gabriel as possible.

She'd thought she cared about him. She'd thought she'd actually known him in some deep way. She'd been so, so wrong.

A cluster of lights—gas stations, fast food places, probably a mini-mart—flashed past. The buildings looked the same as the ones she'd seen soon after they'd gotten on the highway, and a few more exits down, she'd see another set that was almost identical.

Hours had passed since Shay had walked herself over to the Range Rover. There'd been no way she was going to let him, Gabriel, put her inside. If he'd touched her, Shay thought her body probably would have ignited, that's how furious she'd been.

How furious she still was. Why was she huddled up in the corner like some sad little girl? Shay straightened up and whipped her head toward Gabriel. He didn't react.

"I just want to remind you of a few things," she burst out. "I broke you out. I set you free. And you, you used me as a human shield! You hid behind me like a coward."

Gabriel opened his mouth.

"No. Still talking," she snapped. "You took me prisoner. And I went out and got blood to save your life. I didn't have to. I could have driven away, just left you there. You would have died. We both know it. But I came back. God, I nursed you. I fed you when you couldn't feed yourself. Doesn't that mean anything to you?"

"You left a few things out," Gabriel shot back, without looking at her. "You let me free—after your parents took me prisoner. They turned me into a cow, a blood-producing cow. I was only kept alive because *you* needed something from me. That was the beginning. I didn't start this."

Shay gave a harsh bark of laughter. "What are you, five years old? If we're using that logic, I didn't start it either. I haven't done anything but try to help you!"

"You're human; that's all that matters," Gabriel spat. "My family has to live in hiding. All my kind does. Because of you. If humans believed, truly believed, we existed, we'd be slaughtered. All of us.

Don't think there would be any trials. We aren't human. We have no rights. Not even the right to live."

"All humans aren't identical. I'm not Martin. And Martin isn't all humanity," she told him. She couldn't bear to bring her mother into the conversation. Not that she expected him to listen. She was human, and he had his mind made up about her, no matter how much evidence she could lay out that she and Martin had treated him in exactly opposite ways.

"You sound like Sam!" He gave his head a vicious shake. "I'm not letting another human walk away unpunished." Gabriel finally looked at her then, his eyes glittering with emotion. "They'll come for you. We both know that. And when they do, I'll be ready."

"They?" Shay repeated. "You mean . . ."

"Your mother. Your famous doctor. They'll come."

It was as if he'd reached out and slapped her. "I'm bait?" Shay gasped.

"What did you think?" Gabriel said.

Shay knotted her hands in the hem of her sweater, trying to hold in the terror that had suddenly speared her. "What are you going to do to them? What are you going to do to my mother?"

Gabriel didn't answer. It was the worst response he could have given.

"What are you going to do to her?" Shay screamed.

"You know what she did," Gabriel replied. "What do you think should happen?"

Shay felt most of her anger drain away. It was replaced by slimy, cold despair. "Doesn't it matter why?" she asked. "My mother did what she did to keep me alive. Because she loves me. She loves me more than anything else in her life, and she didn't want me to die. And Martin loves her, so he wanted to save me. Obviously the way he did it was wrong, but—"

"Don't flatter yourself. He couldn't care less whether you live or die. He wants to figure out what makes me work, and then he wants to synthesize it and sell it for a billion dollars and win a Nobel Prize for *his* scientific breakthrough." Gabriel's voice was as cold as ice. "I spent a lot of time with Martin, you may recall."

"You don't know him. It's not like you could read his mind," Shay snapped. "You assume all humans are evil."

"I didn't have to read his mind," Gabriel said. "You're just so used to being *special* that it never occurred to you that he was using you for his own purposes."

Shay gasped. Nobody had ever been so nasty to her before. Or maybe nobody had ever been so honest? She knew Martin wanted his breakthrough. But he also wanted to cure her. Definitely he had some kind of freakish God complex, but the fact was that he had tried to cure Shay on the way to getting his Nobel Prize. Whatever other bad things drove Martin didn't change that basic truth. Gabriel was wrong. His view of the whole world was skewed by hatred.

"God, you really are that far gone, aren't you?" she said. "You hate humanity so much that you can't even believe in love—"

"Love wouldn't justify them taking my freedom and harvesting my lifeblood," Gabriel cut her off. "Love is the excuse people use for doing stupid, dangerous things. Selfish things."

He was angry now, as angry as she was. He probably thought she should be terrified, locked in a car with a furious vampire. But Shay didn't care.

"You never had time to be human—you were taken when you were so young. You clearly can't understand what human love is," Shay said. An image flashed through her mind, as if in response. Gabriel hiding that little girl, giving up his human life to save hers. "What happened to the boy who saved Elena? He knew what it was to love someone more than he loved himself."

"Keep talking, and I'll gag you," Gabriel said, his voice ragged.

He'd do it. Shay knew he would. He was going to use her as bait. He was going to kill her mother. Gagging her was nothing compared to that. Talking wouldn't do any good anyway. Nothing she could say would change his hatred.

Escape. That was her only hope. Hers and her mother's. Shay turned and stared out the window again. Escape. To save herself. To save her family. But how? Gabriel had regained most, if not all, of his strength. She'd been *in* him. She knew how powerful he was.

She had to try something anyway. Anything. So what if it killed her? She'd rather die than be the cause of Mom's death. Not that that was especially noble of her. She was a walking dead girl. What did it matter if she died a little sooner? At least it would be for a reason, for love, rather than because her body finally just gave up.

First things first. And first was getting out of the Rover, which meant getting Gabriel to stop. She couldn't hurl herself out of the speeding car even if she'd wanted to. Gabriel had control of the door locks.

He was determined for vengeance. But he wouldn't kill innocents to get it. In her gut, in her soul, she knew that. She might end up dead, but Gabriel would not kill someone who hadn't harmed him.

Yeah, and my gut and soul have really been on target so far, she thought sarcastically.

Shay stared out the window for almost an hour. She didn't want to try anything too soon after the fight, after the threat. She was sure Gabriel would be suspicious anytime she asked to stop, but he would have been on high alert right after that.

Eventually she twisted around in her seat. "I need a restroom," she mumbled. He didn't answer. God, she hated that. She was right here in the car with him. He could at least acknowledge that she existed.

"I said, I need to go to the bathroom," Shay said, much more loudly.

"When I see a place," Gabriel answered. The next exit had signs for a couple of gas stations, a Wendy's, a Taco Bell, and a Subway. He blew right past it.

"Didn't you see—" Shay began.

"When I see a safe place," Gabriel told her.

"You could have guarded the door," Shay said. *While I screamed, and screamed, and screamed,* she silently added. Gabriel didn't comment. Surprise.

They passed three more exits. All of them with signs announcing at least one place that would have a bathroom. Shay pulled a Gabriel. She didn't comment. She wasn't going to shout. Or beg. She was going to wait and see what he did. Although, now she did kind of have to pee.

He breezed by another likely exit. Shay clenched her teeth together. She wasn't going to let him win the no-speaking game.

Finally, two more exits down, Gabriel pulled off the highway—and into an almost deserted rest stop. Men's room. Women's room. A couple of beat-up vending machines. And lots of scrubby grass. Crap. Now what?

Gabriel pulled into a parking stop directly in front of the women's bathroom. "I will be guarding the door," he said as he flipped the master door lock. *At least he's not going to come in with me*, she thought. She walked into the bathroom, hoping he couldn't tell her knees were a little wobbly. He'd scared her, but that didn't mean he had to know it.

Except he could smell fear. And he noticed everything. At least he used to.

Shay entered the stall farthest from the door. She might as well pee, since she was there. When she'd finished, she reached for the toilet paper. There was a scrap about as big as a hangnail—perfect. In the scheme of things, not such a biggie. She made do with one of the paper toilet seat covers, then washed her hands and did a quick survey of the room. There was a small window in the back wall.

She walked over to it. What was the point of trying to bolt? There was no one around to help her, and she'd need help. She stood up on her toes to get a better view, and her heart began fluttering with a happy dance. Or a scared-shitless dance. Or some combo of the two. Across the scrubby grass, behind some scrubby trees, Shay glimpsed what she was almost positive was a truck. There was another parking lot back there. Probably more trucks. At least a couple of guys should be napping in the backs of their rigs.

Good thing Sick Girls are skinny, she thought as she slowly started sliding the small window up. Gabriel would tell her to stop thinking of herself as a Sick Girl. It had actually seemed like he cared last night—

Shay pushed the thought away, as the window gave a soft creak of protest. All Shay could do was pray that Gabriel hadn't heard it. Which was stupid. Of course he'd heard it. She just had to pray that he didn't know what had made the sound.

Got to at least try. Shay hauled herself through the window, arms shaking. She fell to the ground, then shoved herself to her knees and scrambled to her feet. She locked her eyes on the faint shine of the side of the truck and ran.

Shay's hair whipped out behind her as she lengthened her stride as far as she could. This wasn't anything like that day on the track. There was no feeling of freedom and power and joy. She was running like a prey animal would, heart skittering, taken over by instinct and adrenaline.

She hadn't even reached the midpoint of the wide stretch of grass before she heard Gabriel behind her, coming up fast, fast, fast. It was hopeless. But Shay wasn't going to give up. She was used to pain. Every day for years she'd had to fight the pain and weariness of her body. She leaned forward and forced her legs to pump harder, ignoring the jolts of fire in her calves.

Close. He was so close. She could hear him breathing, panting. He was right behind her. Shay dropped to the ground and rolled. Gabriel charged past her, but only a few steps. Then he spun, and a second later, he was on top of her, using his body to pin hers to the damp ground.

Gabriel pressed one hand over her mouth as he glared down at her. Shay met his gaze. He'd caught her, but that didn't mean she was his. She still had her own will. "You're going to stand up now," he told her, voice tight. "You're going to walk back to the car with me. Aren't you?" When Shay didn't respond, Gabriel grimaced. "Aren't you?"

Shay had her own will. But she didn't have a choice. He was bigger, faster, stronger. Shay felt as if she had no strength left. When Gabriel moved away from her, pulling her up with one hand, she didn't resist.

He turned her around so she was in front of him. He had one arm wrapped around her waist, the other still across her mouth. Together they walked back toward the parking lot. When they were almost there, Shay's knees buckled. Only Gabriel's arm kept her from falling to the ground.

It's not just fear, she realized. The exertion of her escape attempt had used up all the power Gabriel's blood had given her. She needed another transfusion. She wasn't sure she'd be able to take a single step without it, not even with Gabriel supporting most of her weight.

"Stop faking," Gabriel ordered. "I'm not letting you get away again."

She laughed, a bitter sound. Figures that he would be the only one in the history of her life to accuse her of faking. No one else would dream of saying such a thing to the Sick Girl.

The Sick Girl. The dead girl.

Gabriel turned her in his arms, staring at her face. The set of his jaw relaxed, his expression growing gentle as he seemed to get it, to really see her, Shay, for a moment. He lowered her to the ground, then he raised his wrist to his lips and slashed through his skin, opening a vein for her. He knelt beside Shay and held his bleeding wrist out to her.

No. She wasn't going to take his blood. She didn't want him inside her. The only reason he wanted her to feed was because dead bait was useless. *Let me die here,* she thought, turning her face away from Gabriel, even while the scent of his blood drew her. It was as if she could almost feel the warmth of it in her body, nurturing her, reviving her.

"You have to drink. You're about to pass out," Gabriel said.

"No."

Gabriel didn't bother arguing. He used one hand to imprison her head, then he brought his wrist to her lips until her mouth was wet with his blood. The taste of it, the little rush of *life*, was too much for her. Her body wanted it. And her body took it.

An electric shock went through her, then Shay was with Gabriel. *Was* Gabriel.

His eyes were closed. He was deep under, his legs and arms heavy. *Not restrained. Asleep.* Shay's own thoughts felt distant, the way they always did when she was receiving his blood.

She became aware that someone was shaking Gabriel. Maybe had been for a while. He tried to open his eyes, but his lids felt weighed down. "Gabriel, get up!" The voice was low and urgent. Familiar. Shay wanted to obey it—Gabriel wanted to. But the death sleep had already claimed him.

"Gabriel," the same voice growled. Then he felt—and heard—a sharp slap to his cheek. He fought to open his eyes, and his eyelids cracked enough to see Ernst crouched over him. He hauled Gabriel up to his feet, keeping an arm wrapped around him to support him.

Not weak, Shay's own thought whispered. *Tired. So tired.*

A scream rang out in the family's main sleeping cave, and the smell of blood overwhelmed him as he came more fully awake. Ernst was crying.

"Don't look. There's nothing we can do. Come, my son." Ernst urged Gabriel toward one of the tunnels leading deeper into the warren of caverns. *The caves in Greece*, Shay managed to think. *Not the ones where they study the bats.*

"Some back there have awoken," a man yelled. "They're escaping!"

"Let them go," another man answered him. "Finish the others."

Ernst gave Gabriel a rough push. He saw Sam partway down the tunnel, waving him on. But the blood. The smell. It was the blood of his family. Lysander, Philo, Lizette, Alejandra. He could smell each of their scents. He could smell their terror. And he could smell death.

Gabriel turned his head, his eyes fully opened, his mind finally clear. Blood soaked the floor of the sleeping cave. It was still warm, giving off steam in the cold air of the caverns. Reluctantly, Gabriel moved his gaze a little higher, and a guttural moan split the air. It took him a moment to realize it had come from his own mouth.

Lizette's throat had been sliced open, more than once. Blood streamed over the phoenix tattoo that marked her as one of them. Her beautiful lips were twisted in a silent scream.

And Lysander. Sander was—

"Gabriel!" Sam shouted. "Run. Don't look. Run!"

Ernst gave him another push, then Gabriel was running. Running away from his family, the bodies of his slaughtered family.

CHAPTER

THIRTEEN

○ ○ ○ ○ ○ ○ ○ ○ ○ ○ ○ ○ ○ ○ ○ ○

GABRIEL LEANED HIS HEAD BACK as Shay fed on him. He felt a hot line moving from his wrist, up his arm, across his chest, and into his heart. It was the path his blood was taking from his body into hers. Sweet pain.

Dizziness swept through him. His head felt like it was a balloon hovering over his body. *Taking too much. I'm letting her take too much.* Gabriel pulled his wrist away. Shay gave a little moan of protest and used both hands to pull his wrist back to her. "No," he told her. He twisted his free hand in her hair and gently urged her lips away, breaking the connection between them again. His skin felt cold in the spot where her mouth had been.

He ran his fingers over the wound on his wrist. It was already healing, but his skin was wet, not with spilled blood, but with tears. Shay was crying. How long had she been crying? Her shoulders were heaving with sobs.

"What?" he asked. *What?* As if he hadn't chased her across the field, tackled her, and dragged her back here. As if he hadn't made her his prisoner. "Are you hurt? Did I hurt you?"

Shay raised her eyes to his. "I saw— In the sleeping cave—" She couldn't continue, not until she'd pulled in a deep, shuddering breath. "I saw what happened to your family, back in Greece. I saw them slaughtered."

Gabriel stared at her. That night had near destroyed him. Thinking about it, he felt tears burn his own eyes and bile rise in his throat.

"Did anyone else get out?" she whispered. "Anyone?"

He shook his head. "Ernst and Sam were old enough already that they could fight the death sleep. I couldn't resist it on my own, but I could be roused. The others—" he fought back a sob. "Sander and our sisters . . . and those in the chamber next to them . . . they were all asleep. Nothing could wake them, only death."

Shay retched, tears running down her cheeks as if she'd known them, any of them.

"Now you see. You know what humans are capable of. The same thing would happen if anyone discovered our existence now. The only reason I was spared was to keep you alive." Gabriel spat.

The fury felt good. It felt righteous. It reminded him of the truth. After what humans had done to his family, they were his enemy, all of them, for all eternity. Their capacity for cruelty was staggering.

"Get up," he told Shay. He would take her back to his family, then when the other humans came for her, they would be destroyed for what they had done to him, for what they'd been doing to him ever since that night in Greece.

Gabriel stood. The look he gave Shay was an order. She slowly got to her feet. He saw that she had a rivulet of blood running from her mouth and down her chin. "Clean yourself up," he told her.

She raised her fingers to the corner of her mouth, then brought them up in front of her eyes and gazed at the blood. Her mouth twisted into a grimace.

Hypocritical bitch. Gabriel wanted to hold on to his anger. He needed it to do what had to be done. "You couldn't get enough of it a few seconds ago. You would have drained me if I hadn't pulled you off me."

Shay wiped off her face with her sleeve, removing most of the blood and the tears she'd shed as she watched the mass murder of his family. "You're the one who made me feed. Dead bait wouldn't be nearly as effective."

She was right. He'd had to force her to take the blood, and once she'd begun, it had overpowered her. He understood that. It had happened to him many times when he was young. If Ernst hadn't been with him each time Gabriel had fed until he'd learned to control the blood rush, Gabriel might have— He pushed the thought away.

"Do you want to try to escape again? Or are you going to get in the car?" Gabriel asked.

Wordlessly, Shay got back in the Range Rover. Gabriel slid behind the wheel, hit the master lock, not that he was really worried about her making another escape attempt tonight. She looked beaten down. Maybe she'd accepted that he was stronger than she was and that it was hopeless to fight.

"You're no better than they were," Shay said as he started the car. She was gripping the dashboard with both hands, kneading it with her fingers. "I love my mother as much as you loved anyone in your family."

"You don't know that." Gabriel pulled out of the parking lot, going too fast, the tires spitting gravel.

"When I have the visions, I don't just see what you see. I am you. I feel your emotions. Why do you think I was crying like that?" Her voice was edged with hysteria. She swallowed hard. "I know exactly how much you loved them. And when you kill my mother, I'm going to feel it the way you did. I'm going to feel like someone reached inside me with a cold, cold hand and scooped out everything."

That was how it had felt. After the pure horror of the massacre, Gabriel had been left dead and empty. It had been years before he truly felt anything, even grief. Finally, it came, and after yet more time, he'd begun to feel happiness again. When they'd come to America, when he and Sam had—

Gabriel wasn't going to think about Sam now. If he could, he'd wipe every memory of his friend from his mind. What had happened to Sam had proved that emotions were a burden. Emotions made you weak. And yet, he suspected that even if he were able to scrape every bit of emotion out of himself, he'd still feel the ache of guilt.

I did the right thing, he told himself, *the right thing for my family. I will never lose another family, no matter what it costs me to keep them.*

"You've got nothing to say to that?" Shay asked. "It doesn't bother you that you're going to hurt me the way you were hurt?"

"My family was innocent." Gabriel re-entered the highway. "You can't say the same. Can you?"

Shay didn't answer for several moments. "You drink from us," she finally said.

"Not enough to kill. Not enough to even cause much pain. I know. You've drunk from me," Gabriel told her.

She turned away from him then, pressing her forehead against the window, staring out into the darkness, the way she had begun this ride.

Which was the best thing she could do. He didn't want to hear her voice. He wanted to pretend she didn't exist. But he couldn't block out the soft sound of her breathing or the intoxicating perfume of her blood. She got to him. He'd managed to keep his sensations mostly dull. It was part of keeping his emotions in check. But she got to him.

Gabriel focused on the road as much as he could. About an hour before dawn, he began looking for what he needed. Another small, no-name motel, where the employees weren't paid enough to give a shit.

Along I-81, a motel like that wasn't hard to find. He parked on the all-but-deserted street, just in case the night desk clerk was ambitious enough to wonder why there was a new vehicle in the lot when no one had checked in. "Do I have to gag you, or are you going to act like you have some sense this time?" Gabriel asked.

"I'm not going to do anything. I know I can't get away," Shay answered.

"You start to scream, you aren't going to be happy," he warned her, although he doubted there was anyone who'd hear her if she did cry out for help. Gabriel got out of the Range Rover and walked around to Shay's side. He had about forty minutes of darkness left. He believed she wouldn't try anything right now. But when the daylight sapped his energy, and he fell into the death sleep, she could do anything she wanted to. Gabriel had never acquired Sam's and Ernst's ability to fight the pull of that sleep at will, and after so long without fresh blood, after being chained to a table so long, he was too weak to even try.

He opened the door for Shay, the courtly gesture getting a mocking smile from her. She might be beaten down, but she hadn't given up. Gabriel took her by the arm, circled around, and opened the SUV's trunk.

It was well equipped. No surprise, since it was the car of someone like Martin. A first-aid kit. Thermal blanket. Jumper cables. Jack. Some basic tools. And, yes, what Gabriel needed—a length of rope. He picked it up.

He saw Shay's eyes widen, and her pulse began to beat faster. He was hyper-aware of the blood now rushing through her at a higher speed. She was scared, but she didn't say anything. He understood that. Admitting her fear, even asking a question, made her more vulnerable to him. During his weeks in that room, he'd never spoken to his captors, not even when Martin had tried to force him to. Gabriel had worked hard not to let even the twitch of an eyelid show his emotions.

Gabriel led Shay across the motel parking lot and over to the room farthest from the office. He broke open the door with one sharp jerk of the handle and guided Shay inside. "If you have to use the bathroom or anything like that, do it now," he told her. "I'm going to tie you up while I sleep."

Shay nodded. She crossed the short distance to the bathroom, stepped inside, and shut the door behind her.

Gabriel ran his hands through his hair as he paced back and forth in the small room. He couldn't wait to be home. And tomorrow, he would be. Ernst would be elated to see him. By now, he must have come to believe that Gabriel was dead. Would the effects of the hawthorn ever fade? The idea of living without his psychic bond to his family made Gabriel feel cold.

Soon I'll be with them in person, he reminded himself. And after the elation faded, Ernst would be incensed over what had been done to Gabriel. All that would calm him down was the realization that Gabriel had already begun a plan for vengeance. Ernst and Gabriel would come up with the details together. Shay was the important element. They would figure out the best way to use her to make his captors pay.

Gabriel crossed to the window. The curtains were shut, but he pulled them tighter together. "Door," he muttered. He moved back across the room and fastened the chain. He left the DO NOT DISTURB sign where it was, hooked over the inside doorknob. It would just advertise their presence. No one should be trying to come in to clean. The room was already prepped. In this place, a cigarette burn in the bedspread and a water stain on the ceiling with a matching stain on the carpet below still counted as ready for guests.

Shay came out of the bathroom. "Lie down," Gabriel ordered her. He nodded to the double bed in the center of the room.

"There?" Shay asked.

"Or we can both lie on the floor," he told her. "I'm tying you to me. You're not going to escape again."

Shay hesitated, then lay on her back on the bed, as close to the edge of the mattress as she could get. Gabriel measured out a length of rope, then he released his eye teeth and sliced through it. Shay's head jerked back a little. She shouldn't be surprised. She'd seen how easily he could tear open his skin.

It wasn't because she was surprised; it was because she was scared. The thought was unwelcome. She was a hostage, nothing more.

"Don't do anything stupid, and you won't get hurt." He ran his eyes over her, thinking. "Shoes on or off?" he asked.

"I guess off." Shay sat up to take off her boots. Gabriel was faster. He quickly slid them off. He started to bind her feet together, then hesitated. The rope was rough, and her socks were more like stockings. He didn't want her skin to get rubbed raw.

He strode into the bathroom, grabbed one of the pathetically thin towels, then returned to her. He ripped the towel into three strips, and used two of them to wrap her ankles before he tied them together with the rope.

Then he sat down on the bed next to her. He used the last strip of towel to wrap the wrist closest to him, then tied his wrist to Shay's. She kept her eyes squeezed shut the whole time. It was as if she were a little kid who thought if you didn't see something, that meant it wasn't happening.

Gabriel stretched out, keeping to his side of the mattress. He reached out his free hand and flicked off the light switch. It wasn't much longer till daybreak. Sleep would overtake him soon. He welcomed it. He didn't want to be aware of Shay lying so close to him, so warm, her smell so intoxicating. His hand was tied so tightly to hers that he could feel her pulse fluttering. He knew drinking her blood would poison him, but his body craved it anyway.

"Don't bother trying to untie the ropes while I'm asleep," Gabriel told her. "The knots will hold. And even if you did escape, as soon as darkness fell, I would come after you. Your scent would lead me straight to you."

That same scent that was driving him near to madness right now. He closed his eyes and waited for relief.

Shay's back hurt. She couldn't get into a comfortable position. She felt hyper-aware of each tiny sensation as she lay next to Gabriel. And that included the heat coming off his body. His warmth was soaking into her skin, and it was almost as if he were touching her.

He had talked about tracking her by her scent. If she had his powers, she knew she would be able to track him, too. The smell of him—salty and musky, with a hint of motel soap—was imprinted on her memory. No, more than that. It was coded in her blood. Maybe it was more than his scent. Maybe drinking from him had somehow made him part of her, forever and always.

She wished she could drink from him now, feel the power flooding her, escape into the life of the visions. Shay was repulsed by the thought. True, the blood had saved her life, but she didn't want anything of him in her. He hated her. And, now, she hated him. The little boy in her visions, the teenager who had been such good friends with Sam, the man who had appreciated every streak of color in his last sunset—that wasn't Gabriel. Not anymore. It couldn't be. Shay didn't believe that person, the person she had *been* so many times, could use her the way this Gabriel was. He could never kill for vengeance the way this Gabriel was planning to do.

She wanted to check her watch, but it was on the wrist tied to Gabriel's. It had to be eight or nine. Shay wished she could fall asleep as deeply as Gabriel had. Even a light, half-awake and half-asleep nap would be a relief, but she didn't bother to close her eyes. Sleep wasn't going to come.

Shay rolled onto her side, which brought her right up next to Gabriel. She immediately returned to lying on her back. She tossed her head back and forth on the pillow. She needed to move. The thought took her over. She started to feel panicked, frantic. Her heart was racing, and the skin around her mouth was starting to feel numb.

She bit her upper lip lightly, then a little harder. Numb. That was bad. She'd never felt numbness like this during any of her million and two self-checks. Was this it? Was she dying right now? Sweat popped out between her fingers.

Stress mask. The phrase just popped into her head. One time her mother had been seriously freaking out because Shay's white blood-cell count was extremely low. Martin had sat her mom down, taken her pulse, and asked her if she was feeling any facial numbness. When she said she was, he said she had what was called a stress mask.

Okay, see, you're just stressed, Shay told herself. Not dying. At least not yet. Just stressed.

She pulled in a deep breath, then another. It was taking a while for her body to get the message that there was no need for a meltdown. She took another breath, as deeply as she could, then held it for a five count, and released it slowly. It was a relaxation technique she'd learned on one of her hospital stays.

Better, she thought. *That's better.* Although she still had hours to get through before Gabriel awoke and untied her. If she could drink, the blood would bring her to another place where she could run and—

No. God, it was like she was addicted. Her brain kept saying, *No, I don't want to drink his blood. He's evil.* But her body—her body didn't care about good and evil, right and wrong. It just kept chanting, *Give me, give me, give me.* She could roll over, sink her teeth into his neck—

She needed a distraction. She was completely losing it. Why hadn't Gabriel turned on the TV or the radio? Her cell rang, pulling her attention away from her thoughts. It was way over on the dresser across the room. No way could she get it. Gabriel would have to be pretty stupid to tie her up and then leave her cell in reach. And stupid, he wasn't.

The cell rang and rang. *It has to be Olivia,* Shay thought. *Okay, Liv. Do what you do best—worry about me. Call the police. Call my parents. Call the cavalry. Please, please, please, just get me some help.*

Martin and her mother had captured Gabriel once. They knew his weaknesses. If Olivia could get them here, they'd have a chance against Gabriel. Much, much more of chance than if they were lured into a trap at Gabriel's compound with all his family to back him up.

The cell started to ring again. Shay gave a low groan of frustration. Olivia wouldn't be able to send help. She had no idea where Shay was. If Shay could talk to her for just one second— But her cell might as well be across the country as across the room.

Distraction. She needed distraction. If she was at home, she would write in her journal after a transfusion. After a vision.

She could do that now. She could do a head journal. Shay closed her eyes and tried not to feel stupid as she imagined she was back in her room, sitting at her desk, her journal open in front of her, her favorite green pen in her hand.

Okay, here goes. I've drunk from Gabriel two more times since the last time I wrote. I don't know if it's because I need the blood more to function, or if I just want it. Once I read this article about some celeb's addiction to pain pills, and he said after a while his body kept telling him he was in pain, because he needed to think he was so he could have a justification for taking the pills. The pain was mostly in his mind by that point. When he got off the pills, and stayed off for a while, he real-ized it.

Am I really getting weaker faster? Do I need the blood so often? Or am I just jonesing and so I convince myself that I'm weaker so I can get a hit? God, even knowing what Gabriel has planned, I still want his blood.

The blood is a complete rush. It's like I can feel every vein glowing inside me as Gabriel's blood is pumped through my body. Maybe that doesn't sound good—but it feels amazing. Sometimes I can even feel individual blood cells bouncing off the walls of the veins. I guess not just veins. Arteries and capillaries, too. It's kind of like that song. The "it tickles my nose" one.

But the visions . . . They weren't all happy and feel-good. The one where Gabriel saw Ernst kill a human was horrific. Even

Gabriel thought so. And then, the vision of the cave that night—I don't even know if I can describe it in words. Annihilation. Genocide. Extermination. Obliteration. They all apply, but they don't give the emotion I felt when I—I mean, Gabriel—witnessed almost his whole family wiped out.

How can he not understand that I will feel everything he did if he kills my mother and Martin? Maybe not everything. Gabriel saw so many slaughtered. But not one of his parents. The thought of losing Mom—I can hardly take it in. It's like my brain jerks away from it.

I guess you can't compare one kind of grief with another. Or at least it's pointless if you do. But I expected Gabriel to realize what he'd be doing to me. I'm sure there are people he'd do anything to keep alive. Sam, and Ernst. Can't he understand that it's why my mother and Martin did what they did?

Or maybe not Martin. Gabriel says Martin was using me. But how can I trust anything Gabriel says? He pretended everything was all right between us. He even kissed me back, and all the time he was planning to use me as bait.

What I do know is that Martin was always kind to me. No matter what he did to Gabriel, he treated me well.

And my mother . . . I know with absolute certainty that whatever she did, she did to keep me alive. Her entire life has been about me for seventeen years. And now her death will be about me too.

Mom told me Gabriel was a killer. Maybe I should have taken her more seriously.

Shay's cell rang again. Sixteenth time. But this time was different. This time Gabriel heard the phone. He didn't say anything, but she could feel his body tense as he lay next to her.

He rolled onto his side, so he was facing her, and quickly untied the knot that held their wrists together. He had her feet free a moment later.

"I have to return that call," Shay told him, her voice rough because her throat was so dry after the endless day.

Gabriel raised one eyebrow. Shay translated the eyebrow move as—who are you to demand anything?

Shay changed her approach. "Gabriel, I asked my best friend to give my mom some fake information. She told my mother that I was going to Miami to have some fun before I die."

"When?"

"When what? When did I talk to her?" Shay asked. Gabriel gave a brief nod. "That would be during the days when you were dead asleep and I could've taken off any time I wanted to. But I didn't."

"Why did you come back?" He sounded almost as if he wished she hadn't.

"I told you already. I wanted to make sure you were safe," Shay told him. "I thought I owed you something, because all of this was about getting blood for me."

She felt anger swell up inside her again.

"Listen, I don't care if you want to throw my phone in the trash. I just thought you should know that the only way Olivia would help me was if I promised to check in every day. I'm the Sick Girl, remember? My friends want to know that I'm okay. I'm not sure what she'll do if I don't call her back. Maybe she'll alert the police; I don't know."

Gabriel picked up her cell and handed it to her. "Put it on speaker and play the messages."

The first three calls were from Olivia, like Shay had thought they would be. They were all variations of "Call me."

What can I say if Gabriel lets me call her back? He'll definitely have the whole call on speaker, but maybe I can find some way to sneak in a coded message, Shay thought. Olivia knew so much about her. At the very least, Shay should be able to signal that everything was *not* okay, even if she couldn't tell her she was at the Skyview Motel in Shawsville, Virginia, being held captive by a vampire.

The next message yanked Shay away from her thoughts. Tears sprang up in Shay's eyes as soon as she heard the familiar voice.

"Shay? It's Mommy," the message said. "I'm staying at the Royal Palm. I'm not leaving Miami without you. Call me, sweetheart. We have to talk. I have to make you understand. I'm here, Shay. I'm here for you. Call my cell or call me here." Her mother rattled off the phone number at the hotel. "I love you, baby," she added before the voice mail cut off.

"I guess your friend followed through with your plan," Gabriel commented. He was rubbing his finger around a white water ring on the dresser, as if the thing fascinated him.

"Of course she did," Shay answered, not mentioning that she'd had her own doubts about whether Olivia would be too worried about Shay to do what Shay had asked.

Gabriel gestured for her to continue playing the messages, still not quite looking at her. Message after message was from Olivia. Still basically "Call me" messages, some angry, some worried, some threatening, some pleading.

Then came something different. It was another message from Olivia, but her voice was urgent and she spoke so quickly that it was a little hard to understand her.

"Shay, oh my God. Martin just came over. He pretty much interrogated me. He thinks I know something, and he kept telling me you would die without medical care," Olivia said in a burst. "What's going on, Shay? Are you okay? I'm picturing you passed out somewhere without me to pick you up. The cops found Martin's car in Virginia someplace. He reported it stolen. I should have said that first, sorry. He said you took his car, but he reported it yesterday because he's getting desperate. He says if you die, it'll be my fault because I won't tell him where you are. Shay, call me. Are you in Virginia? I think Martin might come for you."

Virginia! Martin knew they were in Virginia. *Please let him be on the way*, Shay thought, *with the hawthorn that will knock Gabriel out*. She didn't want Gabriel chained up back in Martin's lab, but she needed him disabled for a while, long enough for her to explain to her mom and Martin that Gabriel wanted to kill them. She had to save her mother's life.

Gabriel strode to the window. Shay followed, listening to the end of Olivia's message. "I hope that you're safe. Call me. You have to call me."

"Range Rover's gone," Gabriel announced. "We're leaving. Now."

Had Martin taken the car? Or had the police just towed it? *Stay calm*, Shay told herself. *Stay focused. This is going to be the time to escape*. If Gabriel had to choose between getting captured again and letting her go, he'd have to let her go.

Gabriel grabbed her by the hand, jerked open the door, and ran out into the dark parking lot. In the same moment, the door of the motel office swung open. And Martin walked out.

"Martin!" Shay screamed. She wanted Martin's attention and she wanted an audience. She wanted Gabriel to run. And she wanted to get into Martin's car and go home. Home!

The clerk stepped out of the office behind Martin. Good. Shay tried to twist her hand out of Gabriel's iron grasp. "Let me go!" she shrieked. "It's over! You go back to your family and let me go back to mine."

"You need me to call the cops?" the clerk asked Martin.

"I've got it covered. Go back inside," Martin ordered. He started toward them, and Shay saw the flash of a syringe in his hand.

"He's got hawthorn. Just go," Shay begged Gabriel. "Please."

Gabriel abruptly released her hand, and for one miraculous second, Shay thought he was going to do what she'd said and walk away. That this could end without Martin dying or Gabriel being recaptured.

Then, with a hiss, Gabriel's fangs extended, and he began moving toward Martin.

No. Shay wasn't going to let this happen. She hurled herself at her stepfather, slamming both hands into his chest. He staggered back a step. "He's going to kill you. We have to get out of here. Now! That's your rental car, right?" She started toward the sleek sedan parked in front of the office.

Martin didn't follow her. He kept striding toward Gabriel as if he hadn't even seen or heard her. Shay didn't think. She just reacted, putting herself between Gabriel and Martin right before they reached each other. Again, she planted her hands on Martin's chest.

"Martin, I know everything. I'm sorry if it ruins your chance to make a big breakthrough, but I don't want this. Even if you get Gabriel back in the lab, I'm not taking his blood. I know you want to save me, and that's the only way to do it, but I won't. Let's leave. More people are watching." It was true, she'd seen a curtain flick open in one of the rooms. "There's no way for this to end well."

"Get out of the way," Martin told her.

"Get out of the way, Shay," Gabriel echoed.

"No." Shay tightened her fingers on Martin's lapels and tried to push him toward the car. It was like pushing on a brick wall. Martin was the size of a linebacker, and Shay was small and thin. "Martin," she begged.

He looked down at her for one brief second, his eyes meeting hers. Then he backhanded her across the face.

Shay fell to her knees, her head slamming against a beat-up car parked next to her. She blinked, stunned. How could Martin have done that, Martin who had always been so gentle with every procedure she'd needed?

"Stay there. This isn't about you," Martin ordered. He raised the syringe, and he and Gabriel began to circle each other.

Shay climbed to her feet and stumbled between Martin and Gabriel again, the world spinning wildly around her. "Stop it. This is insane."

"Move!" Martin shouted. "I won't tell you again."

Shay's knees buckled, and she fought to stay on her feet. She didn't know if it was from the pain in her head—she could feel blood coursing from her forehead down her cheek and chin—or from shock. Gabriel had said that Martin didn't care about her. He'd said Martin was obsessed with his scientific prize. With his vampire. Shay hadn't wanted to believe it, even though her own brain and instincts had begun whispering the same thing.

She was a part of Martin's research too. That's what she was to him, another lab rat. Maybe that's why he'd even married her mom— so he could have Shay at his disposal. But she was expendable. There were other people with other blood disorders he could use in his experiments. It would be a lot harder to get another vampire.

Martin darted around her, hypodermic held high. Shay threw herself at him and grabbed his wrist with both hands, trying to keep the needle immobilized. "Gabriel, go! Go to your family. Please!"

Like begging him would do anything. He was as obsessed as Martin. All Gabriel wanted was vengeance. All Martin wanted was glory.

"Goddamn you, Shay. Let go!" Martin pried one of her hands away, bending back the fingers until Shay screamed from the pain. She heard Gabriel hiss with fury. Martin kept his grip on her hand and used it to fling her away from him. Shay braced herself to slam into the cement again, but it didn't happen.

Instead, she was rising up. Gabriel had caught her in his arms. He turned and ran to the opposite end of the parking lot. Martin was behind them, but he wasn't nearly as fast.

Gabriel used his fist to smash in the window of an old Plymouth Barracuda. He put Shay inside, the gash on his hand already healing as he climbed into the driver's seat beside her. Martin was almost to them as Gabriel yanked a panel under the steering wheel free and pulled out two red wires.

Martin reached through the smashed window with the

hypodermic. Gabriel twisted away, shoving an elbow into Martin's arm. The syringe went flying, and Martin scrambled after it. Gabriel stripped the ends of the wires, twisted them together, then touched them with the end of a brown wire. The engine started. Gabriel slammed down on the gas. Martin stumbled out of the way as the car sped out of the parking lot.

"Are you all right, Shay? Are you okay?" Gabriel demanded. Shay lightly touched her forehead. It was still bleeding, but that was supposed to happen a lot with scalp wounds, wasn't it?

"I think so." Shay was still trying to process what had happened with Martin. He was supposed to come and save her.

But instead it had been Gabriel who saved her.

FOURTEEN

° ° ° ° ° ° ° ° ° ° ° ° ° ° ° ° °

"SEE IF THERE'S A MAP in the glove compartment," Gabriel instructed as they traveled down the highway at exactly 65 miles per hour. He'd slowed to regulation speed almost as soon as they'd gotten out of Martin's line of sight. Shay figured it was because he didn't want any chance of getting pulled over, what with the car being stolen and her being kidnapped.

Shay was glad to have a nice simple task. "Yeah, there's one," Shay answered. Whoever owned this car was on the anal side. The glove compartment didn't have a stray piece of lint or a stick of gum. It was empty except for the map, the car's registration, a little notebook that had CAR MAINTENANCE written on the front, and a small package of tissues. Shay pressed a wad of tissues against her forehead and took out the map.

"We need to get on a back road. Fast," Gabriel said.

We. For a while they'd been a *we*, back when she was nursing him. But now? She felt so confused. Gabriel had been planning to use her for bait. Maybe that was still his strategy. He'd wanted to get Martin and her mother to his family compound.

But she knew the abilities of his body. She knew how strong he was, how fast. Without the element of surprise, Martin would never have been able to subdue Gabriel. Gabriel could have taken his vengeance right there. Shay knew how deep his fury ran. She was sure he was aching to rip Martin apart. But instead, Gabriel had chosen to protect Shay.

She'd been wrong. She'd thought Gabriel and Martin were equally obsessed, but Gabriel had at least momentarily put aside his obsession—for her.

"Shay! Map!" Gabriel said.

"On it," Shay answered. She flicked on the overhead light and studied the map. "Take Exit 72. It's about ten miles up. Then make a right."

"Good."

Shay noticed that Gabriel's eyes kept flicking to the rearview mirror. She looked over her shoulder. She didn't spot Martin in his rental car.

"See anything?" Gabriel asked.

"No. No Martin. No cops," Shay told him.

∘ ∘ 243 ∘ ∘

"He's not going to call the cops," Gabriel said.

"Yeah, you're right," Shay agreed. "If the cops took you in, at some point the truth would get out."

"And Martin wouldn't get his blood supply," Gabriel replied.

"Somebody else might have called, though. The desk clerk." She took another look behind them. Still good.

"You were right about Martin," Shay said, still shocked. "I've never seen him like that. So cold. He was like a monster."

"That's who he always was, with me," Gabriel replied. "He didn't bother putting a nice face on it for my benefit."

"So it was never about me," Shay said slowly. "He was studying both of us—your blood and its effect on my blood. It was never about making me better. Well, except for the part where making me better would mean success for him."

Gabriel didn't answer.

"But my mother wouldn't have gone along with that," Shay said. "My mother would never let me be used as a lab rat."

"She let *me*—" Gabriel started.

"Because she doesn't love you," Shay cut him off. "She didn't even think of you as human."

"No kidding. She hated me," Gabriel said.

"What?" Shay cried.

"Every time she looked at me, it was with hatred," Gabriel said. "With Martin, it wasn't personal like that. He treated me like I was an element in an experiment. A thing, not a person."

"Maybe she was afraid," Shay said. "Fear could look like anger or hate."

"It was hate. I could smell it. It's a completely different scent from fear." Gabriel's voice was icy, but Shay knew he was telling the truth. He'd told her the truth about Martin, too, she just hadn't wanted to believe it.

"Did you . . . did you see her a lot?" Shay asked, wrapping her arms around herself. She didn't really want to know, but she had to. How much had her mother done to Gabriel? And why?

Love was the one reason Shay could understand. She would never have a daughter of her own. But she still knew, if she did, she would never put the life of a stranger, a stranger who was something out of a horror movie, above the life of her child.

But hatred didn't make sense. It would be more in character for Mom to try to make friends with him, to get to know him and ask him for his blood.

"Gabriel, please just tell me," she said. She needed reassurance that her mother was still her mother. That although Mom had lied to her and done a horrible thing, that she wasn't like Martin, that she wasn't evil.

Gabriel sighed. "Your mother was there when I was captured. She was the one who pretended to meet me, to talk in person. Martin came up from behind. Other than that, she was in the room with me maybe a few times."

Mom was bait, sort of, Shay thought as Gabriel took the exit off the highway. *Just like I am now.*

Is that what she still was? Had Gabriel simply put off his moment of revenge? She'd thought they were a team once before and had been so wrong. Was she helping him use her right now, by giving him instructions on how to get away?

At least they were going in a direction away from Martin.

Shay checked the map. "Go down to Highland Street." She did a quick count. "It's seven streets down. Once we're on it for a couple of miles, it looks like we can get on a back road that basically parallels the highway."

"I don't care where it goes," Gabriel told her. "We need to get off the road entirely for a while. Martin saw the car we took off in. He wouldn't call the cops, but that doesn't mean he isn't using other resources. He has a lot of money, right?"

"Yeah. You're thinking of, like, private investigators?" Shay asked.

"For the right amount of cash, you can get quite a search team mounted," Gabriel said. "We've got to dump this car and find a place to hide out at least until people will think we're long gone from here."

Shay nodded. She had this crazy impulse to reach over and click on the radio, find one of her favorite songs, and just check out. Not think. *No, no radio,* she told herself. She wasn't going to let herself fall into passivity. She had to stay sharp and figure out what Gabriel's plan was now and make a plan of her own.

"Highland should be the street after this one," she told Gabriel. "You take a right." Shay made sure to lock every move they made into her head. She might need to find her way back to an area with lots of people or give Olivia directions on how to find her. Shay would trust Olivia with that info now. She thought she'd trust Olivia with anything. Olivia had completely come through for her, lying to Mom, giving Shay the heads-up that Martin was on the way.

There weren't many landmarks on this road, not that Shay could see. There was a little grocery and bait shop coming up on the left. Shay felt a hysterical laugh welling up. Bait. Maybe she should just tell Gabriel to stop in there and get something else to use besides her.

About a half mile down, the car's headlights brushed across a closed-down gas station. There was something about abandoned gas pumps. They were the loneliest-looking things. As they drove on, the road grew bumpier and began to wind. "I think there's something up ahead," Gabriel said.

Shay leaned forward. "I don't see anything."

"I don't either. Not yet," Gabriel answered. "But there's a smell of cows, and people, apples, grain. Farm smells. But old, nothing alive there now. Maybe there'll be some kind of shelter left." He slowed down, and about five hundred feet later, there was a dirt road off to the left. Gabriel turned onto it, still driving slowly.

"There," he said a few minutes later, and in the darkness, Shay could see the shapes of a couple of buildings. She was guessing house and barn, although there were no lights on anywhere to show them for sure.

Gabriel made a tight three-point turn, and then started back the way they'd come. "Didn't like the way it smelled?"

"I want to get rid of the car, then we'll go back," he answered. When they got to the main road—which wasn't very main—he took the direction leading farther away from the town. After they'd gone about two miles, Gabriel guided the Barracuda onto the soft shoulder, then eased it between two trees, parked, and turned the car off, leaving the keys in the ignition. He climbed out and circled around to open Shay's door before she had the chance to do it herself.

As soon as she stepped out, Gabriel swept her up in his arms again. "This will be faster. I want us away from the car as quickly as possible." He used his foot to slam the car door shut, then he ran. Although *running* didn't seem like the right word. There was no right word. A word would have to be invented for the way Gabriel darted between the trees, so fast. And smooth, even though the ground was rocky and bumpy. And silent. Shay couldn't hear even a hint of a footfall.

She'd barely had time to register these thoughts before Gabriel was setting her back on her feet in front of the deserted old barn. She shivered.

"Let me look at that head." Gabriel leaned close, so close she could feel his breath on her cheek, and studied the spot where her head had gotten slammed into the car.

"You're already growing a goose egg, and it's turning black and blue, but I don't think you need stitches." He tucked her hair behind her ear, taking a last look. "Shouldn't even have a scar."

"I feel like my whole head will be one big scar." Shay winced, touching her wound.

"You won't. Trust me, I'm a doctor." Gabriel smiled. "About ten times over."

"Yeah, a *bat* doctor," Shay said sarcastically, proving she wasn't too seriously injured.

He turned toward the barn. There was a rusty lock holding the big double doors together. He snapped it easily and ushered Shay inside.

"How come you couldn't break out of your chains in the lab and escape?" Shay asked.

"Martin pretty much starved me," Gabriel answered as he shoved open one of the doors. "He gave me enough blood to keep me alive, but that's it. You saw how weak I was the night you found me."

He climbed up to the hayloft and tossed down a couple of the bales of hay that remained up there. They hit the floor with solid thumps, sending up clouds of dust. Gabriel leaped down to the ground beside them.

This is the real him, Shay thought. *The running, the leaping. The way he snapped that lock like it was Styrofoam. This is usual for him.* She'd known him first when he was weak. He was back to full strength now, and his power was staggering. She'd gotten little tastes of that power in her visions, but what was it like to have that strength available all the time? It had to be so much more thrilling than when she'd finally gotten to run on the track or when she'd made her epic swim.

Gabriel picked up a ragged horse blanket that was hanging over one of the stall doors. He walked over to Shay, studied her, then wrapped the blanket around her shoulders, still holding on to both sides of the cloth. "You're cold," he told her. "If you need something, you have to tell me."

"I need my mother—alive," Shay answered.

"What else?" He pulled the blanket more tightly around her, still not letting go. Why didn't he let go? And step back? She was acutely conscious of a vein running down the side of his neck, just below the skin, through the center of his phoenix tattoo. She knew it was impossible, but she felt as if she could hear the blood, warm and full of life, pumping through it.

Shay swayed toward the vein, toward Gabriel; then, mortified, jerked herself away. She backed up a few steps, pulling the blanket out of his grasp. "I need to know what's going on," she burst out. "Am I still your hostage? Are you still planning to use me to kill Martin and my mother? I just—what exactly am I to you?"

Gabriel sat down heavily on one of the hay bales. He pressed his head into his hands. "I don't know," he admitted.

Shay sat on the bale across from him. "You saved me. You probably could have killed Martin right there, even though he had that syringe. But you didn't. You saved me. Why?"

"I don't know," Gabriel said, head still in his hands. "You're right. I could have killed him. When he and your mother captured me, they had surprise on their side." He raised his head and stared at her. He looked as overwhelmed and confused as she felt. "I didn't think about reasons. I didn't think at all. He threw you—and I couldn't let you fall again."

"It's ironic. Martin's the one who has spent years trying to keep me well—although I guess that wasn't about me, not really. But he's the one who hurt me. Not you," Shay said. A shudder rippled through her.

"Do you need another blanket?" Gabriel asked.

"No. It's not that. I think it's all just hitting me. I thought it had hit me before, but I guess not," Shay answered. "I feel shaky."

"Maybe you need to feed," Gabriel suggested.

That was all that Shay wanted. She ached for his blood. But she couldn't take it, not until she knew where they stood. "Gabriel, when I was nursing you back to health, I thought things were okay between us. I thought things had changed. I had no idea you considered me your hostage. But then as soon as you were strong again. . . ."

"Yeah."

"That's it? Yeah?"

"I couldn't have done it if I hadn't turned you back into the human girl," Gabriel admitted.

"I was always a human girl," Shay said.

"No, for a while you were Shay. Who stupidly kept thinking of herself as 'the Sick Girl.' Who was getting started on a nasty candy addiction. Who felt sorry for a stuffed animal. Who . . . kissed me. I couldn't have Shay as a hostage."

Shay spread her hands open in front of her. They trembled a little. She really was getting hit full force by what had happened. "And yet . . ."

"And yet—you saw what happened to my family. They were slaughtered by humans. On that day, we began to live in fear. Our lives changed completely." Gabriel explained. "In this age, most don't believe in us. That makes us safer. Martin and your mother—they are a danger because they know the truth. If they aren't dealt with, they are a danger not just to me, but to my family. I won't let anyone put my family in danger, not ever again." Gabriel hesitated, then went on. "I thought that having you would bring Martin and your mother to me. You were vital to keeping my family safe—"

"And to getting revenge."

Gabriel nodded. "Fine. Yes, they made me suffer, and I want them to feel the same way." He reached out and took her hand. "So I had to pull back from you. Stop thinking of you as Shay. But I couldn't. And I guess that's why I saved you back there, because, as hard as I tried, I couldn't unknow you. You saved my life. Twice. I couldn't unrealize that not all humans are the same, even though I wanted to."

Shay swept her hair away from her face. "Maybe we're catching up to each other. I knew you so well, before I ever saw you that day in Martin's office. I'd actually been you. I'd experienced your thoughts and feelings." She shook her head. "If the first and only thing I knew about you was that you were a vampire, I probably never would have set you free."

"I wish I could talk to Ernst," Gabriel said.

"I wish I could talk to my mom."

Gabriel stood up and paced back and forth in front of her. "I don't know what I'm going to do about Martin. Or your mother. But I'm sure of this—you aren't going to be involved in any way. I can't use you like a pawn. Not anymore. Tomorrow, I'll get you to a bus or a train. And we'll need to make a plan to get you blood."

"You're going to keep giving me your blood?"

"I'm not going to let you die." Gabriel stopped pacing and faced her. "You need some now. I can see it. You've got those little drops of sweat above your lip."

"How attractive," Shay said, trying to sound casual. But inside she was going crazy. He was going to save her—again. He was going to let her go! He was wonderful, and now she was right back to falling for him again. Which was hopeless and pointless and probably a bunch of other *less*'s. She had to get over it. Now.

But Gabriel hadn't been able to unrealize that she was an actual person. Shay was afraid that unrealizing that she wanted him was going to be just as impossible.

Gabriel used one of his fingernails to open a vein in his neck. *I do need it,* Shay thought. *Whether it's my body or my mind making the call, I have to have it.* She stood up, walked over to him, wrapped her arms around his neck, lowered her mouth to his throat, and drank.

The darkness became bright. She looked up. It was one of those nights when the moon was full and spilling silvery light over everything. The surface of the river glinted like diamonds. Despite the beauty, she—Gabriel—was tense. Shoulders knotted, stomach queasy.

She picked up a stone with Gabriel's hand and threw it into the river. "I hope you weren't trying to skip that, because if you were, it was a pathetic attempt." Gabriel turned toward the voice and saw Sam coming toward him, the grin on his face so wide it almost looked painful.

Sam's arrival didn't lessen Gabriel's anxiety. It raised it.

What's going on? Shay's thought whispered somewhere at the back of her consciousness. Gabriel was upset, but Sam looked way too happy for anything to be wrong.

"Did you decide what to do?" Gabriel asked.

"I'm going to marry her!" Sam exclaimed. "She's having my baby, and all I want is to be with them. I even want to change diapers. I swear I do. It doesn't hurt that they have those throw-away ones now." He laughed, the sound full of joy.

Gabriel felt ill. How could Sam act like a child with a human was anything but a tragedy? "Stop this. You know a baby won't live—"

"No," Sam cut him off. "Modern medicine has changed everything. You're a scientist, you know I'm right."

Gabriel sighed. Clearly Sam wanted to deny the truth. He changed tactics, taking his brother by the shoulders and squeezing them, willing him to listen. "It isn't the child. Being with a human is forbidden."

"I don't care. Since I first saw her, I was gone. She's everything I want," Sam replied.

"What about the family?" Gabriel demanded. Shay felt his hot anger rise inside her, but underneath that was an ocean of cold fear.

"The family has been my whole world since the day I was taken. And I'm thankful for what Ernst gave me that day—a place to belong. But Emma gives me all that too."

Emma, Shay managed to think. *My mother's name.*

Sam put his hands on Gabriel's shoulders now. "I love her. Love shouldn't be forbidden. It's the purest, most all-consuming thing I've ever felt."

Gabriel dropped his hands and stepped away. "Love isn't forbidden. You can love—"

"Anyone of our kind," Sam interrupted. "I know. But love isn't like that. You don't pick and choose it that way."

"You know what happens to those who break the laws of the family," Gabriel warned. He felt as if a hand had punched through his ribcage and was squeezing his heart.

"But I'll be leaving the family," Sam said. "And you need to be happy for me, little brother. I'll put you in a headlock until you are, I swear it."

"I want you to be happy, Sam," Gabriel said. "But—"

"Good! Because I am," Sam said quickly, before Gabriel could continue. "And so is Emma. And the baby will be happy too. Now look at what I'm giving Em. It was a gift from Gret, Ernst's own love, before she sought the sun. She was a mother to me. She believed in love." He pulled a small, handkerchief-wrapped bundle from his pocket, then carefully unfolded it. A locket lay inside—a locket with two birds flying across a sky that held a sun and a moon both.

Shay gasped and pulled away, Gabriel's blood still upon her lips. Her mind reeled. She felt almost drunk from the effect of the vampire blood, from her deep submersion in the vision. Her body ached for more. But the shock of seeing the locket was even greater than the pull of Gabriel's blood.

"What?" he asked, frowning. "Did you—what did you see?"

In reply, Shay pulled her locket free from her shirt and held it up to him. It was the same locket Sam had shown Gabriel in the vision.

It's what he'd been planning to give Emma, the mother of his child.

"Where did you get that?" Gabriel's voice was sharp.

"My mother," Shay answered, her voice shaking. "She said my father gave it to her." She swallowed hard. "When was it? When did Sam show you this locket?"

Gabriel didn't have to think about it. "The spring of 1993."

"I was born October 17, 1993," Shay told him. "My mother's name is Emma. I have this locket that she said belonged to my father—and it's not like there's one in every store." Shay clenched the locket in her fist. "Sam . . . do you think . . . is Sam my father?"

Gabriel lowered himself onto one of the bales of hay, looking old for the first time since she'd known him. "Remember how I told you Martin and your mother knew about someone in my family? That person was Sam. I couldn't figure out how they could know anything about him—or about something like the effect of hawthorn on our kind—but of course Emma would know. I'm sure Sam told her everything. He was completely in love."

Shay's mind was whirling. The images she'd seen of Sam rushed through her. Sam letting the little girl at the orphanage stay hidden. Sam comforting Gabriel on the night of his last sunset. Sam alive with joy, so in love with her mother. Sam ecstatic at the thought of their baby. He'd wanted her.

"You know what this means, don't you?" Gabriel raised his head and looked at Shay.

"My father loved me," she said. "He wanted me." She was dizzy with the realization.

"Yes. He did. You can be certain of that," Gabriel answered. "But that's not all. Shay, you're half-vampire."

FIFTEEN

○ ○ ○ ○ ○ ○ ○ ○ ○ ○ ○ ○ ○ ○ ○

GABRIEL SHOT A QUICK GLANCE over at Shay. She hadn't spoken since he'd told her she was half-vampire. What was she thinking? He'd had years to prepare himself for the idea that one day he would be a vampire. He'd chosen the moment it would happen. How would it feel to discover that kind of truth about yourself at her age?

It's not the same for Shay, though, he reminded himself. *She didn't have to give up the sun. She didn't have to live on blood.*

Christ. That wasn't true. She did have to live on blood. His blood. Or at least vampire blood.

"It's why I'm sick, isn't it? Why I've always been sick," Shay said suddenly. "And why your blood is the only thing that's really helped me." Her thoughts had followed a track similar to his.

"I think so. It has to be, doesn't it?" Gabriel asked.

"Don't you know?" She used both hands to push her long dark hair away from her face. The movement caused the blanket to slip down her shoulders. Gabriel wanted to reach over and pull it up, but he was half-afraid if he touched her, he might not be able to stop. Letting her feed from his throat—an impulse that had overtaken him—had been the most intimate experience of his life. He'd never wanted her to stop. He'd never wanted her to take her arms from around his neck.

"How can you not know?" Shay asked again.

Gabriel shook his head. "It's forbidden for us to have contact with humans, at least in my family, and it has to be that way in most others, or our existence wouldn't have remained a secret. I've heard rumors that a child was born from the union of one of us and one of you. But it was hundreds of years ago, and supposedly the child died after only a few days."

Shay winced.

"How has it been for you? Have you always been sick?" He couldn't believe he hadn't asked her that before.

"Yeah. I was an incubator baby. My mother couldn't actually hold me until I was almost three months old," Shay answered. "From then on, it was good days, bad days, good days, bad days. Although the good days were more like normal days for other people. Days I could go to school. Days I could have a little time to myself, without doctors, without my mother hovering. She's a big hoverer."

Shay choked back a sob. "This isn't for me. This isn't the Sick Girl feeling sorry for herself. It's just thinking about my mom. . . . She has to be insane with worry. She's—is *crazy* a level below *insane*? If it is, then she's crazy with worry on an almost daily basis. But her not knowing where I am . . . She could even think I'm dead by now."

Gabriel reached over and took one of Shay's hands in his, unable to resist. "You'll make sure she knows the truth. Tomorrow, you can go home."

"She's in Miami. At least I think so," Shay said.

"Then you can go there. That would be better. I don't want you anywhere near Martin," Gabriel replied.

"Martin. I don't think my mom ever loved him, not really. I mean, I think she just loved him because he would do anything to keep me alive. He acted like he really cared. And he seemed like a steady kind of guy, a guy who would always be there. Unlike my—"

Shay stopped mid-sentence. "Gabriel, what happened? Sam was so excited and happy in my vision. He clearly gave the locket to my mom. And he wasn't freaked by the idea of a baby. He was talking about diapers and everything. Why did he abandon her?"

Gabriel froze. That question felt like a knife to his heart. He couldn't answer it; he would never answer it for her. He could imagine the hatred that would appear on her face, her beautiful face.

"I don't know," Gabriel said. "Sam left the family. All he wanted was to be with her. I never saw him again, but I didn't expect to. He couldn't be with a human and be a part of the family," Gabriel explained. His heart felt like it had turned to granite; it was that heavy.

"You didn't want him to be with her," Shay said, sliding her hand out of his. "I felt how badly you wanted to stop him. You would have done almost anything."

"True." There was no point in denying it. She had looked so deeply inside him. Gabriel thought if she kept drinking his blood, she'd know him better than anyone, even Sam, even Ernst. "I didn't want him to leave the family. I didn't want to lose him. And I would have done anything to change his mind." If only he'd been able to.

"But he loved her so much. I know you saw that. I was there with you when he showed you this." Shay lifted the locket's chain, so the locket swung from her fingertips. Gabriel wished he had never seen it. If Sam hadn't shown it to him, everything might be different. Shay might have been able to grow up with her father. And if Sam had figured out that his blood was her cure, she would have had her life, not the half-life she'd had to live because of her illness. *There is no illness,* he reminded himself. *All her symptoms came from being half-vampire.*

Gabriel realized Shay was waiting for a better explanation. "For us it is taboo," he said. "It's almost unthinkable, like cannibalism, like sleeping with the dead."

"That's how you feel about loving a human? Wanting to be with one?" Shay sounded appalled.

He struggled with what to say. "I didn't mean—I wasn't trying to say that it's repulsive or abhorrent."

"Cannibalism? Necrophilia? Repulsive and abhorrent." Shay's voice was like a whip. He'd hurt her. Again.

"I was just trying to express how deeply the law is ingrained. *Law* isn't a strong enough word. What Sam did was *verboten.*" He studied her face. Had he made her understand?

"I'm sure my grandparents wouldn't have been too happy about their daughter doing it with an undead bloodsucker," Shay shot back.

Gabriel knew she'd wanted to hurt him, and she had. But he'd hurt her, too, with his own careless words. He didn't comment.

"Just her having me was bad enough," Shay continued. "They disowned her. I've never even met them."

So much pain. It would have been a million times better if Sam and Emma had found each other repellent. But Sam had always had an open heart. It seemed the same was true for Shay's mother. With parents like those, no wonder Shay had broken him out of Martin's prison. No wonder she had returned to nurse him through the poisoning, even after he had taken her hostage. No wonder she had been able to look at him and see a person, not a monster.

"Sam would be proud of you," Gabriel said. The words just slipped out. And they were true. She was so like him. Rescuing that beat-up toy from the dollar store, that was a Sam thing. Except that Sam rescued people. He loved that part of being in the family, being able to make a home for unloved children.

"And he'd never have left your mother of his own free will," Gabriel continued. "He would never have abandoned you. Believe it, Shay. Remember what you saw. That was true. Sam couldn't wait to begin a life with your mother."

"My mom. What are you going to do about my mom?" Shay asked. "I know you said it won't have anything to do with me, but everything to do with her has to do with me."

"I could never hurt anyone Sam loved, I promise you that," Gabriel said. "I'm not even sure anymore what she saw when she looked at me. There was such intense hatred in her, but maybe it was less about her seeing me as an evil creature. Maybe she was looking at me and being reminded of the man she believed abandoned her."

"She does hate him," Shay admitted. "She can hardly talk about him, it makes her so crazy. I'm still reeling. All my life I've thought my dad had no interest in even taking a look at me. You're sure he didn't just go to another family or something?"

"I knew Sam for hundreds of years. If he was alive, he would have returned to you and your mother," Gabriel swore. He knew it was true.

Shay slid down to the floor, her back against the hay bale. "He loved her even though he wasn't supposed to," she murmured. "Even after the massacre of your family, Sam was able to fall in love with a human."

"Sam was a rare person. Your mother must be too," Gabriel said.

"Didn't it make you think that maybe things could change between us, between vampires and humans?" Shay asked.

Gabriel tried to think of what Ernst would say. Ernst would know how to explain it to her. Right now, Gabriel wasn't sure he could.

Shay sighed, then changed the subject. "Is there any way I can cure myself—now that I know what I am? All that's keeping me alive is your blood."

"And you'll have it as long as you need it. Until we figure something out," Gabriel promised.

"Which means as far as you know, there's no cure," Shay said.

"No. But there are scientists in my family. We're all scientists," he said.

"Bat scientists," Shay pointed out.

"I want to bring you home with me." Something loosened inside Gabriel, knowing that he wouldn't have to let her go too soon. "We'll work on it. There's never been a reason to search for a cure before, but—"

Shay cut him off. "Because I'm not supposed to exist. I'm the product of the unthinkable. And you're probably right about humans. Not all, but a lot. I'm sure there are millions who'd like to keep me in a lab and examine me. Martin would. Martin *did*, I guess. Our whole house, our whole life as a so-called family, was just one big lab experiment to him." Shay shook her head. "Although if he had to choose between the two of us, you'd win."

"That's why Martin is a danger, to both of us."

"Not only him. I'll never be able to let *anyone* know the truth about me." Shay looked at him steadily. "You said you wouldn't hurt my mom. You didn't say anything about Martin."

Gabriel let his silence answer her. She nodded.

"Are you sure about bringing me home? Your family might not—"

Gabriel pushed down his doubts. "You're Sam's daughter. That makes you one of us."

Shay smiled, one of her smiles that covered up years of hurt. "I've always been a freak girl. Now at least I'll be a more interesting type of freak. Step right up! Come see the half-human, half-vampire!"

"Would you stop that? You're not the Sick Girl. You're not a freak," Gabriel said sharply. "You're not like anyone else, but you're not a freak. You're amazing. You're . . . rare."

"I'm not one thing or the other, though. It's like I suddenly have no place. Not even my old Sick Girl–mascot place. Or my new messed-up, kissed-her-best-friend's-boyfriend place," Shay said. "You say all humans hate vampires. And that vampires believe any contact with humans is taboo. Where does that leave me?" She immediately answered her own question. "All alone."

"You won't be alone. I won't let you be alone."

"Right, you'll be keeping me alive with your blood. I saved your life; you save mine," Shay answered.

"Yes. No. Your saving my life is part of it. It showed me something about you. It—"

It showed me that you're incredible, Gabriel thought, the realization striking like a bolt of lightning, bright and frightening. *It showed me that you care about me as much as I care about you.*

Gabriel shook his head. "It showed me your compassion. It showed me your heart." He had to get out of there. He couldn't be so close to her. Not right now, when a terrifying truth was worming its way into his mind. "I . . . I'm going to go look for some firewood." He rushed out of the barn before she could offer to go with him. He needed at least a little time alone to get control of himself, of his emotions. Of his desire for Shay. A human.

He should be back by now, Shay thought. Not that she needed to worry about Gabriel anymore. He had his strength and energy back, and there was nothing out there in the night that could hurt him.

But it was a lot simpler to worry about Gabriel than to think about the rest of her life. She was half-vampire. And her mother knew that. Her mother had been in love with a vampire. Her mother had had an entire secret life that Shay had known nothing about.

Shay was on information overload. She felt dizzy with it. She pulled her cell out of her pocket. The desire to hear her mother's voice was suddenly overwhelming. She hit the speed-dial number.

Her mother picked up, sounding breathless. "Shay! Oh God, Shay, are you all right?"

"I'm fine," Shay answered. "I'm really, truly fine, Mom." Her eyes pricked with tears. "And I'm sorry. I said some horrible things to you."

"What you saw in the lab—I know how shocking it looked. I'm sure you couldn't understand," her mother said.

"Yeah." Shay tried to come up with a way to express it, but failed. "Yeah, it was."

"It really isn't what you think," Mom began.

Shay didn't want to hear the rationalizations. What her mom had done to Gabriel was still unfathomable to her. "I can't talk about it right now." Shay understood so much better than she had, and her heart ached for her mother. But she wasn't ready to go into all the secrets, all the lies her mother had told her.

"Where are you, baby? We don't have to talk. Tell me where you are, and I'll come get you, and I promise I won't say a word until you want me to—about anything."

Shay closed her eyes, tears spilling down her cheeks. No matter how much she missed Mom, Shay couldn't give her the slightest idea of where she was or where she was going. If she did, her mother would come for her. Gabriel wouldn't hurt her mom now that he knew the truth, but what about his family? They all hated humans so much—with good reason.

"I can't tell you, Mom," she said. Her mother gave a little cry, and Shay felt her heart shredding. "But I promise I'm okay. And I love you. I love you so much. I know that everything you did, you did for me."

Shay hung up before her mother could reply. She knew if she stayed on the phone much longer, it would all come spilling out, even her plan to go with Gabriel to his family.

Her cell rang, and Shay was sure her mother would call, and call, and call. She wouldn't stop calling until Shay answered. Shay turned the phone off. "Love you, Mom," she whispered.

Why wasn't Gabriel back? How long did it take a superfast, superstrong vampire to get some wood?

Everything's going to be different between us tomorrow, she found herself thinking. *It won't ever be like this with Gabriel again. Just him and me, in our own world—not the human one, not the vampire one.*

What would happen if she told him the truth? If she came out and told him she had feelings for him? Shay felt her heart skitter as she tried to imagine it.

No, she wasn't going there. She'd been needing Gabriel's blood more and more often. It wasn't going to keep working forever. She was still dying, and not all the scientists in the world could save her in time. Maybe half-human, half-vampire people weren't supposed to live. So why tell him how she felt when they had no future? Telling him could only hurt them both.

But maybe she could have something. A night. A night when they were between worlds. If he would only come back already.

Gabriel took a deep breath and walked back into the barn. He'd gathered up some firewood and found an old metal oil drum to burn it in. Then he'd just wandered around, not ready to come back. As if he could stop wanting Shay, if he only walked long enough.

"Hi," she said. He loved her voice. Her loved her blue eyes. He loved the way she was looking at him right now. The walking hadn't changed anything.

"Hi," he said back. He set the empty oil drum near the hay bales they were using as seats and dumped the firewood inside. He tossed in some dry hay as kindling.

"Did you find any matches out there?" Shay asked. There was a slight tremor in her voice. Why wouldn't there be? She'd had a lot of shocks in the past several days. And she was probably nervous about going to his family tomorrow.

"I don't need them," Gabriel answered. He pulled two small sticks back out of the oil drum and rubbed them together. With his strength and speed, it was easy to quickly get them smoldering. The hay went up in flames as soon as he returned the smoking sticks to the drum.

"Nice," Shay said.

Gabriel sat down on one of the bales. He didn't know what to do with himself. How could he make small talk with her, when all he wanted to do was grab her and never let her go? But that could never happen. That would be madness. It was *verboten*.

Shay walked over to the hay bale where he sat and stood in front of him.

"What?" Gabriel asked. Did she have to stand so close? Her scent was making him weak with hunger and desire.

"This." In response, she tunneled her hands into his hair and tilted his head back. She leaned down and brought her lips close to his, until they were a breath away.

"This," Gabriel repeated. He didn't pull back, but he didn't close the slight distance between them. If he kissed her, he'd be done for. He had to get control of his feelings, and if he kissed her, he didn't think he'd ever be able to.

"You inspired me, remember? You made me want to feel everything. I want to feel this—with you," Shay said.

Get up. Go back outside. Or tell her you don't want her, Gabriel ordered himself. But his body—his emotions—weren't taking instructions from his brain.

"While we're not with the humans. While we're not with the vampires. While for a little while longer, we're just Shay and Gabriel," she continued.

Gabriel closed the slight distance between their lips. It might be the stupidest thing he'd ever done, but he couldn't stop himself. The rest of the wall he'd built up to keep his feelings at bay crashed down. He wanted to feel all of this, every detail—the smell of her, the soft sweetness of her mouth, the feel of her hands as they moved to cup his face.

He wanted more, more closeness, more of her. He brushed his tongue across her lips, and they parted. He groaned low in his throat as her tongue met his. The taste of her was intoxicating. The more he had, the more he wanted. Shay lowered herself to his lap, straddling him.

Gabriel slid his hands from her waist up under her shirt. His fingers were hungry for her skin. God, she was perfect, her skin like silk, but warm. Shay gasped as his hands moved higher, sliding over the lacy cups of her bra. *Slow, slow, take it slow, he told himself.* This was an experience to savor, not gulp down.

But Shay was impatient. She slid her hands under her own shirt, nudged his away, and unfastened the front clasp of her bra. She shoved the cloth aside, giving him complete access. As he learned the shape of her, Shay began unbuttoning his shirt. She ran her hands across his bare chest, as though her fingers were just as hungry as his were. When she lightly bit his nipple, he felt his self-control snap. Next time could be slow. He needed her now.

Gabriel stood, swinging Shay off his lap, and setting her on her feet. He ripped open the bale of hay he'd been sitting on, spreading it out in a thick pile. He found another horse blanket and spread it out on top, then he turned back to Shay, and held out his hand.

She smiled at him as she put her hand in his. She lowered herself to the blanket, gently pulling him down with her.

Feel everything. Remember everything, Gabriel told himself. This night had to last him forever.

Shay wasn't tied to Gabriel while he slept. She didn't have to be. This is where she wanted to be, her head resting on his chest.

I need to call Olivia, she thought. *It has to be after ten. She'll be worried.*

Shay allowed herself one more moment curled up next to Gabriel, then got up and walked over to the bale of hay where she'd left her jeans. She fished out her cell and checked the time. Almost 10:20. Perfect. In a few minutes, she should be able to catch Olivia between classes.

At 10:31, Shay hit Olivia's speed-dial number. Olivia answered on the first ring. "What's happened? Did Martin find you? I went by your house before school and he wasn't home. I called over there last night and got no answer," she said in a rush.

"He didn't find us," Shay said.

"Us. Wait. Who's us?" Olivia demanded.

The word had just come out. Shay had been feeling so close to Gabriel.

"So you're still lying to me." Olivia's voice was flat and angry.

"Why am I even talking to you? We're not friends. Obviously."

"Don't hang up!" Shay cried. "I'm sorry. I'm so sorry. You've been an amazing friend to me. Most of that stuff I said to you—about you not knowing me? That was my fault. I didn't let you know me, not really."

Olivia was silent.

"Liv?" Shay asked.

"Last chance. What's going on? No lying," Olivia told her.

No lying. That was a big order, when there was no way Olivia would ever believe the truth.

"Start talking," Olivia said.

"I'm with a guy. His name is Gabriel. I've been with him from the beginning, from when I left town," Shay began to explain. "I know this is going to sound completely crazy, like something out of a bad movie—but, Liv, Martin was keeping Gabriel captive. He was experimenting on him. Gabriel—"

"Captive? Like locked-up captive."

"Yeah, he'd outfitted one of the rooms in his office. He kept Gabriel in chains."

"You're right; this does sound like a bad movie," Olivia said. "Are you going to tell me Martin's a serial killer?"

"No." Shay bit her lip. If the captivity part was too hard to believe, there was no point in even going on.

"Weirdly, I buy it," Olivia said thoughtfully. "I can tell when you're lying, and you're not. I guess you could be crazy. You've been acting crazy enough lately."

"It is the truth."

Olivia chuckled, and Shay joined in. It felt good. It felt normal, in spite of the bizarre circumstances.

"Okay. Why did Martin do that?" Olivia asked.

But Shay couldn't tell her the rest. She just couldn't. "He has this genetic mutation, and Martin's obsessed with it. He thinks it can unlock the cure to leukemia and maybe even what's wrong with me."

"Martin couldn't just throw a bunch of money at him?" Olivia asked.

"Gabriel wasn't interested. And Martin wouldn't take no for an answer. He'd never seen anyone with a mutation like Gabriel's. I guess he didn't know if he ever would again," Shay said.

"Hang on, I'm heading into the bathroom. I need a place to hide out for a few," Olivia told her. "I'm not waiting until after Calc to hear the rest, and the bell's about to ring."

Shay waited, listening to the sounds of her school day through the phone. Her regular life, going on without her. Shay felt a strange sense of disconnect. She had never fit in at Black River High anyway. Would she ever go back? It seemed impossible.

"Okay, I'm back," Olivia said breathlessly. "So here's my big question. How old is this Gabriel? And what does he look like?"

Shay laughed. She realized that Olivia had always been pretty good about making her laugh—when she wasn't in complete nanny mode. If Shay had let her in more, she might have been good at a lot of other best friend stuff. "He's about nineteen." *Close enough,* Shay thought. He looked about nineteen. "And he's beautiful."

"Oh my God!" Olivia exclaimed. "Shay, you slept with him."

"I hope the bathroom's empty," Shay said.

"It is. So, I'm right, right? You slept with him."

"Yes." There was nothing else to say. Words couldn't describe what she'd felt with Gabriel.

"If you're going to go crazy, I guess doing it with a beautiful guy is the way to go," Olivia replied. "And I'm going to need details. First, back up. How'd you meet him? I mean, how'd you know about the Martin situation? You didn't know, did you?"

"I went to Martin's office. I was pissed off, and I wanted to get away from the house, and I didn't have anywhere to go, so I went there," Shay explained.

"You could have come to my place," Olivia said pointedly.

"We were kind of fighting, remember? Anyway, when I got there, I found him. He was chained up. I couldn't believe what I was seeing. I unlocked him, and we took off together." There were lots and lots of gaps in that version, but it was mostly true.

"So that's what you found out about Martin?"

"Yeah. I'm sure he'd try to convince you that the only reason he was keeping Gabriel was because of me, because he wanted to save my life so badly, but that's not why. He's a glory hound. He wants to find a cure so everyone will think he's the most brilliant man in the world. He wants everyone to remember him a hundred years from now. I honestly don't think he'd care if I lived or died, once he'd proved he had a cure."

Olivia didn't say anything for a moment. "So what are you going to do, you and Gabriel?"

"We're basically hiding out right now. Martin almost caught us, but we got away," Shay answered. "In a while, we're going to go to some of Gabriel's friends. They're off the radar. We'll be safe there."

Shay heard a voice in the background. "I'm being ordered to

class," Olivia said. "And probably detention-bound. Be safe, okay? And keep calling me."

"I will," Shay promised. "You're my best friend, right?"

"Right. And I've got to tell you—a lot of the time it's a pain in my ass," Olivia said.

"Deal with it." Shay hung up, laughing again.

There were still hours before nightfall when Gabriel would awaken. Shay returned to the bed of straw and slid up against him. She didn't care whether she fell asleep or not. This was where she wanted to be.

Anticipation grew in Gabriel as he and Shay drove across the state line into Tennessee. Home. They were almost home. He fought to keep the Escalade under the speed limit. He'd liberated the vehicle from a Costco parking lot a short run—for him—from the barn.

"Okay, so give me the Millie scoop," Shay said.

Gabriel kept telling her she didn't have to memorize every member of his family before she met them, but she was insanely curious.

"Millie. She loves the animals, but she really wasn't cut out to be a scientist. She hates having to live such an isolated life. She's always looking for fun. It drives Richard nuts, he's so serious."

"I like fun," Shay said. "Oh wait. I can't believe we skipped Ernst. Other than my father—it still feels so weird to say that. Good weird. Other than my dad, Ernst is the one you're closest to. It was easy to feel that when I was connected to you."

Shay's anticipation about getting to the compound was in overdrive too, he could tell by her rapid speech. But she was nervous. He could smell it.

"Ernst. How to describe him? He's my father. The only father I've ever known."

"Do you remember your real parents—I mean your human parents—at all?" Shay asked.

"I think I might have one memory of my mother. She was cutting bread into the shape of a duck. Maybe I liked ducks back then."

"That's sweet."

Sweet, and Gabriel hardly ever thought about it. The memory always came with a slash of pain. "I have no memory of my father. I don't know if he was with us. So when I think of my father, I think of Ernst. I've been with him since I was five. The whole family raised me, raised all of us who were taken that day at the orphanage. But I lived with Ernst."

"What kind of father was he?" Shay asked.

"Strict. There were many rules. Not just for me, for everyone in the family. Mostly rules to keep us all safe," Gabriel answered. "But he was also an amazing teacher. Incredibly patient. And funny. He has a sense of humor that is so dry you don't even know that he's kidding unless you know him well."

"I'll keep that in mind," Shay said. "Are you sure he's going to be okay with me coming? I'm human."

"You're Sam's daughter. Sam was one of us. That makes you one of us."

Regardless of what had happened to Sam, Gabriel knew that the whole family had loved him. Ernst had loved him. He was as much a father to Sam as he'd been to Gabriel. Ernst would welcome Sam's daughter. He had to. And even if Shay hadn't been related to a family member, she had saved Gabriel's life. As far as he knew, she was the only human who had ever chosen one of his kind over one of their own. Ernst would be amazed at Shay's courage, her compassion.

"How much farther?" Shay asked.

"About a mile less than last time you asked."

"I didn't expect Tennessee to be so steep," Shay joked. They'd been driving up a mountain road for half an hour now.

"Only the part with the caves, and the bats, and the vampires." Gabriel let himself exceed the speed limit for the first time since they'd left the barn. Just by ten miles. Not much risk of getting stopped. They were almost home.

Shay flipped down the vanity mirror and ran her fingers through her dark, thick hair. "Don't be nervous," he told her. Which was crazy. She was about to walk into a compound full of vampires, and until a few days ago she'd never even known they existed.

"When are you going to tell them about Martin? Right away, or . . ." Shay let her words trail off.

"I think I'll open with the fact that you're half-vampire, that you're Sam's daughter," Gabriel told her. "The rest can wait until tomorrow night. We'll all make a plan together."

"And my mother?" Shay's voice shook. Some of the sparkle had disappeared from her eyes.

"I promise you, she'll be safe," Gabriel said. "My family knows Sam was in love with a human woman. I think that's all they need to know."

Shay nodded. She grabbed the dashboard. Gabriel put one hand over both of hers, before she could start that anxious kneading she did.

His heart thumped hard as they turned up the private road that led to the compound. Soon he saw the lights of the lab and lodge in the distance. Shay probably couldn't, but it wouldn't be long. Gabriel grinned. He was really here. He'd started thinking he would never see this place again, never see his family. He'd actually begun wishing he would die in his prison. It was better that than being chained up. But he was free. And it felt like the world had been washed clean, or even reinvented with only the best parts left in.

He even had Sam back, in a way.

His only worry was that Martin was still out there, looking for him. Or for any vampire. He was a danger to every one of Gabriel's kind. But not for long. The family would figure out how to handle it.

"Is that it?" Shay leaned forward and peered through the windshield. "I think I see lights."

"That's it." He rolled down the window, so he could breathe in the familiar smells. His family would be able to catch his scent too. By now they'd know he was on his way.

He was right. When he pulled to a stop in front of the research center, his family was already rushing out. Gabriel had barely opened the door when Ernst pulled him out and into a rib-crushing hug. Gabriel felt his father's tears on his neck.

"I'm back," he said into Ernst's ear. "I'm back and I'm fine."

"What happened? Where were you?" Ernst asked, not letting him go.

"I'll explain everything," Gabriel told him, gently pulling away. "First, I want you to meet someone." He went around to the passenger side of the Escalade and opened Shay's door. He held out his hand and helped her out. "This is Shay."

Millie's eyes went wide. Richard moved closer, muscles tensed in preparation to attack.

"You brought a human here?" Luis demanded.

Gabriel tightened his grip on Shay's hand. "Listen to me." He looked around at his family, meeting their eyes. "I know you're all going to find it hard to believe. But she's a member of this family. She's part of our family by blood."

"You turned a human?" Horror coated Richard's voice. Gabriel understood. It was taboo to transform an adult human. Only children raised with the family were allowed to become one of them.

"No," Gabriel said quickly. "She's Sam's daughter."

"His daughter with the human?" Ernst asked, his voice shaking with emotion.

"Yes. I know it's hard to believe, but this is Sam's daughter." Gabriel smiled at Shay, trying to reassure her. It would take a little while for Ernst to get used to the idea of her. Right now, his family was in shock. But soon enough, they'd see how incredible Shay was. They'd realize they had a tiny piece of Sam back in their lives. They'd come to feel as attached to her as he did.

Well, maybe not *quite* as attached.

Gabriel turned back to Ernst, putting the thought of Shay's body—of her lips on his—out of his mind.

Ernst stared at him, aghast. "She's human. That's all I need to know."

"Only half," Gabriel said, gazing around at the furious, terrified faces. His eyes came back to Ernst, and his father's face had become that of a stranger. Gabriel's breath caught. He should have expected the feelings rushing through Ernst. He should have seen the signs, smelled them. But he'd been so focused on Shay.

"You have risked all our lives by bringing her here!" Ernst

bellowed. Fast as a snake strike, he grabbed Shay's wrist and yanked her away from Gabriel. "Take her to the cellar," he ordered Richard and Luis. "And lock her there. Make sure there's no possibility she can escape."

"No!" Gabriel shouted as his friends—his brothers—obeyed, each taking one of Shay's arms. He lunged for her. Ernst blocked him.

"Ernst, she saved me!" Gabriel cried. "Twice, she saved my life. I know how you feel about humans, but she's Sam's daughter—"

Shay was struggling, yelling his name as they dragged her inside. Gabriel shoved Ernst to the side, running for Shay. Ernst leaped in his path with one graceful bound. Millie followed, locking her hand on to Gabriel's arm.

"Gabriel!" Shay's voice cut off as the heavy doors closed between them. Anger flooded through Gabriel. He'd been so stupid. He'd been deluding himself that Shay being half-vampire—half-Sam— would be enough for the family. She was still half-human. And humans were deeply despised and feared.

Gabriel forced himself to speak calmly. This wasn't time for a confrontation. "She's not like the rest of them. Ernst—" he locked eyes with his father, "—she saved my life. I'd still be chained up in a—"

"Who did it to you?" Ernst asked.

"We're talking about Shay," Gabriel said, his voice rising despite his efforts to keep his emotions in check. "She went against everything she knew and loved to rescue me. And even after I took her hostage, she saved my life a second time."

"What do you mean?" Ernst asked. "Why would you take the human?"

"I thought we would use her as bait. I didn't know she was Sam's," Gabriel said. "That changed everything—"

"Bait?" Millie cut in. "Bait for what?"

"Her stepfather was the one who captured me," Gabriel admitted. "I thought if I took her, he would come for her."

Ernst nodded. "It is a good plan. We'll keep her until he comes. We'll make him watch her die—he deserves that. Then we'll kill him. You will be avenged, Gabriel."

"I promised her safety," Gabriel cried.

"Have you forgotten seeing your family die? Have you forgotten their death screams?" Ernst demanded, eyes blazing with fury.

"No. But Shay's different. I swear it to you." Gabriel's throat felt like it was made of sandpaper. His heart felt as if it was about to explode.

Ernst turned his head and spit on the ground. "She is an abomination."

"Then I'll take her away. I'll make sure she never comes back," Gabriel said desperately. Never seeing Shay again would tear his heart in half. But he'd do it. He'd do anything it took.

"She's unnatural. She should have died the day she was born." Ernst turned to Millie. "I promise you the abomination will be slaughtered as soon as she draws our enemies to us."

Gabriel squeezed his eyes shut. In the distance he heard Shay screaming his name. What had he done?

The answer slammed into his mind. He had fallen in love with her. It had clouded his judgment.

He loved her, heart, soul, and body. And he had sentenced her to death.